IN$URANCE BLUES

IN$URANCE BLUES

A JOHN SMITH MYSTERY

CHARLOTTE STUART

LEVEL
BEST BOOKS

First edition

ISBN: 978-1-68512-950-7

Cover art by Level Best Designs

This book was professionally typeset on Reedsy.
Find out more at reedsy.com

*To my cousin Dianne who suggested that Laney play a larger part in John's life.
And to my cousin Debbie for her ongoing support.*

"Any fool can solve the most difficult of cases if everyone told the truth."

—Nero Wolfe in Three Doors to Death
by Rex Stout

"Even a blind squirrel finds a nut now and then."

—proverb

Chapter One: My Name Is Delia

"Please call me Delia."

"Like in the flower?"

"What flower?"

"A dahlia. My mother grows them."

"It's not *DAY lee-uh*. It's *DEAL ee-uh*."

"Oh. *DEEL-ya*."

"No—*DEAL ee-uh*."

With each exchange, the gravelly voice of the elderly woman seated in the client chair on the other side of my desk sounded more and more like someone was squeezing her throat. I didn't want her to choke—I had failed my Red Cross first aid class. Nor had I done that great in my high school Spanish class. I apparently don't have a "good ear" for languages. I was in college before I learned that the holy infant referred to in Silent Night didn't sleep in "heavenly *peas*." The advice often attributed to W.C. Fields flickered through my mind: *If at first you don't succeed, try, try again. Then quit. There's no point in being a damn fool about it.* I wasn't sure if I'd gone beyond the "try, try" stage when mispronouncing the woman's name, but I was ready to quit.

"Well, ah, Mrs. Flowers," I began.

She quickly interrupted me.

"Mr. Flowers has been gone for over twenty years. And he was a pain in the...well, you know what I mean. So please don't call me by that name."

Her "please" was clearly not a request. It was more like Katherine Hepburn putting Spencer Tracy in his place in one of the classic movies in which the two of them spar back and forth with clever jibes. Not that I would compare

1

my nondescript persona to Spencer Tracy. But she, on the other hand, did a pretty good Katherine Hepburn impersonation. With her haughty attitude, powdered face, and bright red lips, she reminded me of an aging actress who still considered herself a star to be reckoned with. To complete the look, she was dressed in a retro pantsuit with padded shoulders. A fur stole hung from her neck, ending in two tiny heads in front. I found the vintage stole unnerving. I could almost hear their thin voices mocking me with the correct pronunciation of her name.

With several strikes against me, I decided to take the easy way out and simply avoid referring to her by name. Plowing ahead, I said, "I understand you are here to find out about term life insurance."

"Yes, my niece and nephew want me to obtain some. I need to know what it is and why, from your perspective, they think I should have it."

"I can tell you *what* it is, but not *why* they think you should have it."

Delia and the two rodent heads glared at me. "Aren't the 'what' and the 'why' the same thing?" To my ears, she sounded like a woman who was used to being told what she wanted to hear. I may not be that assertive as a rule, but as an insurance professional, I had an obligation to be honest and accurate.

"Not necessarily. First, can you tell me your age?"

She gave me what was either a grimace or a coy smile that misfired. "A woman never tells her age."

"Well, for term life insurance, it makes a difference. You see, it's a contract between an individual and the insurance company; the company only pays out if the policyholder dies within a certain number of years—usually 10-30."

"My niece and nephew suggested a five-year policy."

"Are you unwell?" I was starting to get a bad feeling about the link between the *what* and the *why*.

"Why on earth would you ask that? Do I look unwell?" Some powder dust slid off her chin as she shook her head in disapproval. It left a sprinkle of sheen on the fur of the two dead animals around her neck.

"The term life insurance people will consider your age, health, the death benefit amount, as well as term length to calculate the cost of your policy.

But that wasn't why I asked."

"Then why did you ask?"

"Well, I'm wondering why your niece and nephew want you to have a five-year policy. I mean, it would be cheaper than a longer policy, but that shouldn't be the only consideration." Hint, hint. Perhaps they thought she was unwell and didn't want her to waste money on a longer policy. Or, perhaps—a cynical thought flashed through my mind. Perhaps they had plans to shorten her life expectancy.

"I thought you said you couldn't tell me the 'why.'"

"I…did." She had me there and apparently wanted the hint spelled out. But I wasn't going to draw a picture for her. It seemed to me that if her niece and nephew were encouraging her to purchase an unusually short-term policy, they were hoping for a big payout sooner rather than later. If that was the case, it was a family matter—or a criminal matter—only indirectly a business decision. I was neither a family counselor nor an officer of the law. I wasn't even an insurance agent. I was simply a lowly claims adjuster doing a favor for a friend of a friend of my mother's.

"In any case, I was under the impression that I wouldn't need a health exam to get this type of insurance." Maybe she knew more about term life insurance than she was letting on. If so, what did she want from me?

"Whether you do or don't will affect the amount of your premiums. I mean, on the one hand, signing up for term life insurance is a fairly simple proposition, but the cost of the premium depends on the factors I mentioned, including your life expectancy."

"I definitely expect to continue living for some time."

"Well, term life insurance is a gamble on just *how long* you expect to keep living. It only pays out to your beneficiaries if you die before the end of the set term."

"So, why do you think they would suggest I look into a five-year policy?"

Why indeed. "That's why I asked about your health." I was repeating myself, but I wanted to make absolutely certain she understood what I was saying as well as what I was implying, a feeble attempt to warn her of the fine print that no one bothers to read until it's too late.

"I see."

"May I ask if they are in your will?"

"No, you may not." She sat up even straighter, the tiny heads on her stole shifting so their beady, dark eyes were looking right at me.

Trying to be honest but diplomatic, I said, "If you want to make sure your beneficiaries are taken care of and you don't have a lot of other money or property to leave them, then it makes sense to get term life insurance. That's why the typical client for term life insurance is a young couple with children." HINT. "It's a trade-off between paying up front in the present to ward off disaster for your beneficiaries in the future. And if you guess wrong, your premiums are simply gone."

"You're saying that unless I anticipate dying soon or would leave my beneficiaries destitute if I died, then term life insurance is a waste of money."

"Well, keep in mind that we can all die unexpectedly." I wasn't about to accuse her relatives directly of anything underhanded, but they either knew something she wasn't telling me about her health, they thought she was too naïve to suspect them of not having her best interests at heart, or they were not as clever as they thought they were. Of course, they could also simply not understand how term life insurance worked. My bet was on a combination of two and three—they thought she was naïve, and they were on the dim side.

"Well..." She paused and looked around at my tiny office. "A bit cramped in here, isn't it?" Before I could respond, she said, "Thank your mother for me. She said you would be thorough and forthright. This was...ah... enlightening."

Before I could say "you're welcome"—although she had asked me to thank my mother rather than thanking *me*—she stood up and departed faster than I would have thought possible at her age. Although even an aging lioness can probably sprint a short distance.

As I sat there pondering our conversation, I wasn't sure what I was going to tell my mother when she asked me whether I was able to help her friend's friend. One thing I was sure of, if I asked my mother to take out a five-year term life insurance policy, she'd not only refuse but write me out of her

4

will. After regaling me with a few choice words that were not necessarily motherly.

Chapter Two: Clueless

I was in my office at Universal Heartland Liability and Casualty Assurance Company of America, Incorporated: "The Company with a Heart." It's on the second floor in what everyone refers to as the "old section" of the building. My tiny space is squeezed between a broom closet and an alcove housing closed files that have not been digitized. The only window faces a brick wall covered with splotches of white bird droppings, like a ghostly Jackson Pollock painting. But I'm not complaining. I have a window. And I have a door. Most of the other Universal employees occupy cubicles ringed with colorful half-wall partitions. They can't snack, nap or scratch without being seen.

Because we're an insurance company, our office atmosphere is subdued, conservative, like a men's club without the comfortable chairs and waiters asking if you would like something to drink. There is tea, coffee, and packets of cocoa mix available, but if you want any, you have to trek to the break room and make it yourself. There's no service on a silver tray.

Given the open office concept, it's actually amazing that the area is as quiet as it is. You may hear the rustle of paper, the clacking of computer keys, whispered conversations, or the occasional one-sided conversation of a voice on the telephone. But for the most part, the entire floor is hushed library quiet. So, when I heard voices yelling at each other from out in the main room, I was surprised. Especially when I realized that Emma our office manager was doing most of the yelling. She never yells. She doesn't need to; just a look from her could wilt a flower. But in this instance, not even a full-throated *"stop, stop, I say"* from Emma kept two people from apparently running past her desk and shortly thereafter bursting into my office uninvited.

The man was panting, as if Emma had either chased or frightened him, or both. He was shortish and lean with a wrestler's grimace tugging at the corners of his wide mouth. The woman was taller and full-figured. She too was breathing hard. Both looked to be in their mid-fifties. And both appeared angry, really angry. It was too late to hide under my desk; I was visible, unarmed, and unable to do anything but stare at them. My fight-or-flight survival response wasn't kicking in. Besides, they were blocking the only exit from my tiny office space.

"You're John Smith?" It sounded more like an accusation than a question. Because of her threatening tone and demeanor, I wanted to deny it, but there was an aluminum nameplate next to the door, and my office was the only one in this part of the old section.

"Yes," I said hesitantly. "What can I do for you?" I wasn't sure I wanted to hear the answer.

"Who do you think you are?" the man bellowed, his voice loud enough to carry easily to the 2nd floor cubicles beyond Emma's desk, maybe even traveling all the way to the executive office area.

"What gives you the right…?" the woman shouted, her voice as loud as his but higher-pitched.

The man interrupted before she could complete her question, screaming: "Why did you have to butt in?"

Before I could try to answer any of their questions or ask about what I had butted into, they continued hurling strident insults at me, two slinger ball machines spewing out words instead of tennis balls. Even if they had the wrong John Smith, it didn't pay to make waves in an environment where customer service was the cornerstone of our mission. I needed to stop them, but I had no idea how.

All at once, Emma appeared in the doorway, put two fingers in her mouth and came out with a piercing whistle that got the attention of our two intruders. They stopped screaming and twirled around to glare at her. "I've called security," she said calmly. "You can either leave now or be hauled out of here by armed guards. It's up to you."

Emma's face was ripe tomato red and lined with irritation. The two uninvited guests were lucky she had called security instead of taking care of them herself. The rumor was that she had a taser in the bottom drawer of her desk. It was allegedly for protection when walking from the office to the bus stop at night, but who knew what other uses she might put it to.

Before the two intruders could continue with their barrage of angry accusations, two men in gray uniforms appeared behind Emma. They didn't look particularly tough, more like ex-military or former boxers who had long since let themselves go and were now moonlighting as security guards. Nor did they have holstered guns on their ample hips or mean-looking batons in their hands. Still, they were in uniforms with badges on their shirt pockets. That made them official. Emma stepped aside, making space for my two "visitors" to leave peacefully. They gave me one last look mean enough to frighten fellow prisoners at Rikers before reluctantly retreating, delivering a few parting shots as they exited, but with less volume:

"You won't get away with this."

"You'd better have a good lawyer."

"You're scum, you know that, don't you?"

As they disappeared from sight, the man shouted one last epithet: "Scum!" The word echoed throughout the 2nd floor with its open space office configuration and high ceilings. Loud as yodeling in an alpine village.

As soon as they were gone, flanked by the two security guards, Emma stepped into my office. "What was that about?" A few strands of hair had come loose from the hump captured in a tightly-wound bun at the back of her head. For an instant, I imagined her taking off her brown-rimmed glasses, shaking out her hair, and being instantly transformed into a sexy babe. But the image quickly yielded to reality, and I found myself facing her usual daunting watchdog persona.

"I have no idea. Did you catch their names?"

"No. I saw them get off the elevators. When they reached my desk, I asked if I could help them, but they didn't even slow down. It was clear that they were headed straight for your office. Someone must have told them where it was. I yelled for them to stop, and they yelled something obscene back." She paused. "What did you do to get them all riled up like that?"

"What did *I* do? I don't even know who they were. I've never seen them before."

She looked skeptical, eyebrows raised, head tilted to one side. "Perhaps it's related to some case you're working on."

"All I have pending are fender benders. Maybe they have the wrong John Smith. It's happened before." Other people complained about hard-to-pronounce surnames, but my cross to bear was having the most common last name in the United States combined with one of the most popular first names for men.

"Hmmm. I suppose that's possible." It was clear from the way she hummed "hmmm" that she suspected I was withholding information.

"Seriously, I haven't a clue." Maybe that wasn't the right thing to have said. Being clueless is never a good defense for anything.

Suddenly, a large figure filled the doorway directly behind Emma. Sensing his presence, she leapt to one side, emitting a tiny "yelp."

"Bruno," I said. "What are you doing here?"

"Is that an invitation?" he asked, stepping inside.

"You startled me." Emma's tone made it clear that was not something he should have done. Although she obviously recognized my friend Sergeant Bruno McGinty from other visits he's made to our office, she wasn't about to let him off the hook for sneaking up on her like that.

"Sorry. I just need a few minutes with John." He sounded somewhat contrite as he looked down at her and added, "In private."

She hesitated a moment before deciding there was no option but to leave. He closed the door as soon as she was gone and sat down on the old wooden chair on the other side of my desk. The chair hadn't aged well in spite of how seldom visitors came by. When I first moved into my office, there was only one chair, the one behind my desk. I'd confiscated the visitor chair from the storeroom one night after hours. It wobbled on uneven legs and looked like it belonged at a 1950s kitchen table rather than in an office. One time, I tried to even the legs out with sandpaper, but I'd only made it worse. Still, although I had been granted "permanent" status with the company at the end of my probationary period, I hesitated to requisition a better chair. After all, it was "at will" employment.

"You were way out of line," Bruno said.

"Out of line? What are you talking about?"

"What you did was not only unprofessional but not at all like you. I never imagined you were that greedy."

"Greedy?"

"And it puts you high up on the suspect list. At the top, in fact."

"Suspect list?" I seemed to be echoing random words. And I was getting more and more confused. "Maybe you could tell me what this is about."

"As if you don't know."

"Bruno, I swear I don't have a clue what you are talking about." There it was again; an admission that I was clueless.

"Does five million dollars ring any bells?"

"Noooo." But it did have a sweet ring to it.

"Come on, John. You can't bullshit me. I've known you too long." We'd been friends since we were young kids living in the same neighborhood, thrown together by age and proximity. That bond had lasted into adulthood, even though we have little except poker and drinking in common.

"Why don't you just tell me what this is about?"

"I suppose you don't know that Delia Flowers is dead."

"*Deel-ya* Flowers?"

"No, *Deal-ya* Flowers."

"She's dead?"

Bruno locked eyes with me and didn't blink. "The truth, John. I want the truth."

"No, I didn't know she was dead. Why would I? Was it in the papers?"

"She did come to you about term life insurance, didn't she?"

"Yes. She's a friend of a friend of Mother's."

"And what did you discuss with her about term life insurance?"

"I just explained how it works. That's what she asked me to do."

"Nothing else?"

"Well, we did talk a bit about why her niece and nephew wanted her to get a five-year policy. They are usually for ten to thirty years."

"Did you write up a policy for her?"

"That's not something I do. I'm not an agent. Nor did I direct her to anyone in Universal. She already had a company in mind."

"So, how did you become her beneficiary?"

It felt like he had poured a gallon of cold water over my head, something he had actually done once when we were in middle school. But that time it was a joke. This time I was fairly certain he wasn't joking...or was he? "Her beneficiary? Me? Don't be ridiculous. I don't even know the woman."

"Past tense—didn't know the woman."

"Okay, I didn't know the woman."

"Tell that to her niece and nephew."

"Her niece and nephew?" I was doing that echo thing again. "Is the nephew a short guy with dark hair, fiftyish? The niece, about the same age, a bit taller, full-figured with dishwater blonde hair?"

"So, you *do* know them." The statement was more accusation than deduction.

"Two people forced themselves into my office just before you got here. They were mad about something, but it wasn't clear about what. All they did was yell at me and call me names. Emma had security escort them out."

"They had a right to be mad. You're getting a five-million-dollar windfall from *their* aunt."

"Term life only pays if someone dies within a certain timeframe. I, ah, cautioned Deel-ya about purchasing a short-term policy."

"You cautioned *Deal-ya* against it?"

"She wouldn't tell me her age, but she said she was healthy, so I didn't see why anyone would be suggesting a five-year policy for her. I wasn't even sure that she needed *any* term life insurance, but she was unwilling to share enough information about her assets with me to determine her insurance

11

needs. All she told me was that her niece and nephew were encouraging her to take out a policy. I assume it was the same man and woman who paid me a visit earlier."

"And you definitely told her it was a bad idea."

"I didn't want to insult her family members by implying they wanted her dead, but I explained why that type of insurance might not be appropriate for her situation."

"So, why do you think she went ahead with a five-year term life insurance policy?"

"I have no idea."

"Did you talk to her after your initial meeting?"

"No. I never heard from her again. I thought she might be angry because I implied her niece and nephew were expecting her to die in the near future. How *did* she die, by the way?"

"I can't discuss that with you. You're a suspect."

"Why would I be a suspect?"

"I can give you five million reasons."

"You don't honestly think I had anything to do with her death?"

Bruno stood up. "As soon as I get the coroner's report, I'll let you know what I think. Meanwhile, stick around."

"Like 'don't leave town?' You know I wouldn't desert Mother."

"Maybe the two of you are planning a trip to the Maldives."

"Don't be ridiculous. Mother doesn't like hot weather."

"Look, John. You may be innocent. But you've got a lot of explaining to do." With that, he made a show of slamming the door behind him.

I was still in a state of shock when Emma came in without knocking. "What's going on, John? First two wild-eyed people come barging in followed by a visit from your detective friend. Don't tell me you don't know anything about any of this."

"Remember *Deel-ya* Flowers?" I really was trying to get her name right, but it sounded the same to me, no matter who said it or how I tried to change the shape of my mouth.

"*Deal ee-uh* Flowers. Yes, I remember her—the one with the mink stole."

12

I hadn't realized they were minks; I'd had them tagged as ferrets. "Right. Well, she died. And not necessarily of natural causes. They don't know yet for sure."

"And...what does that have to do with you?"

"Bruno says she named me as the beneficiary in her term life insurance policy."

"Why would she do that?"

"I haven't a clue."

Chapter Three: Five Million Dollars

ll afternoon, I kept expecting my mother to call. After all, it was her friend of a friend who got me into this mess. But for once, she was complying with my request not to interrupt me at work. Or, it was also possible that she hadn't heard about Delia's death and the rumor about her term life insurance policy yet. Knowing my mother, to me that seemed the more likely explanation.

Instead of focusing on the auto accident claims that the company was paying me to deal with, I called every insurance agent I knew or had ever had a conversation with to see if they were handling Delia's term life insurance or if they had any suggestions as to how I could track down who she had signed with. The insurance business is highly competitive, and insurance information is confidential, but it seemed to me that there should have been some reciprocal camaraderie. I was disappointed to come up against what felt like a blue wall of silence. Or, given the insurance business, maybe a gray, pinstriped one.

I thought about calling Bruno and asking him if he had the name of Delia's lawyer, but he'd been pretty upset with me, so I decided to wait. If what he'd said was true, sooner or later I'd get a call from either the insurance company involved or the lawyer handling her estate. However, I was convinced it was all a mistake. I couldn't think of a single reason for a woman I had talked to for less than a half hour to leave me five million dollars. No screenwriter would consider a plot pitch like that for even a low-budget, made-for-TV movie, on a second-rate network: *Elderly woman leaves five million dollars to a nondescript claims adjuster that she talked to for thirty minutes and who couldn't even pronounce her name correctly.*

Although I never get many calls at work, I do occasionally get one. But today, when I was anxious for someone, *anyone*, to call to get my mind off of the five-million-dollar problem, my telephone seemed unusually quiet. Disgustingly quiet. I checked several times to make sure it was in working order, willing it to ring. I would have been happy with a sales call, a complaint, even someone trying to scam me. I was that desperate for a distraction.

When my phone finally went briinggg, I cut off the second briinnggg by grabbing the receiver and delivering my usual call answering message: "This is John Smith with Universal Heartland Liability and Casualty Assurance Company of America, Incorporated." Because that was all I can say in one breath, I leave out the part about "the company with a heart."

"Do you really need to provide the entire company name every time you answer your phone at work?"

It was Laney, Laney Drew. I've only known her a short time, but I already considered her my best friend. It was too bad that she looked like the girl next door, lacked big bosoms, and was a lesbian. Otherwise, we might have ended up in a romantic relationship. I'd met her through a dating app that my poker buddies signed me up for as a joke. She'd been hoping for a cat lover and a friend to fly drones with. I was neither, but we hit it off anyway. She's the yin to my yang, so to speak. She's bold, logical, organized, and colors outside the lines. Whereas I was raised as a "follow-the-rules" type of guy and would probably not be labeled as "adventurous."

"How did you hear?" I asked.

"Hear what?"

"Oh." I was disappointed. Her "hear what?" response meant she didn't know about Delia's death and therefore hadn't called to add any new information. But at least I could count on her to be supportive when I explained what had happened. She would never suspect me of bilking an old woman out of five million dollars. FIVE MILLION DOLLARS. For the first time, it crossed my mind that if the claim *was* legit, I would be a whole lot wealthier soon. It would be a giant leap from middle class to the one percent.

"So, what didn't I hear?"

"Why did you call?"

"You're not supposed to answer a question with a question. But since you asked, I called because I thought we might catch a bite to eat after work. Maybe you can explain what I didn't hear then?"

"That sounds great. Thank you."

"Huh? Why so formal?"

"Sorry. It's just that there's something I want to run past you. Over dinner would probably be better than over the phone."

"Something interesting?"

"Interesting, appalling, and amazing—all at the same time."

"You got me with *appalling*. Any hints?"

"It's complicated."

"Okay then. See you at the usual place, usual time? I look forward to being appalled and amazed."

* * *

I arrived early at the ThaiLicious restaurant, a small eatery near my office where Laney and I are regulars. I ordered a Singha to pass the time until Laney arrived. When we first started going there, I only drank the pale lager Singha because the waiter said it represented *the joyful Thai spirit with sparkling magic in every sip*. I didn't exactly get the promised joy with every sip, but over time, I've acquired a taste for its slightly sweet, floral flavor. I'd never serve it at any of my poker parties, though.

The food at ThaiLicious is consistently good, the cost moderate, and the booths comfortable. Laney is a paralegal in a law office not too far from Universal, so the location is convenient for both of us, and we've fallen into the habit of frequently having either a drink or dinner after work. She's certified as a PI, but she gave that a try and quit when she was bored by most of the jobs that came her way—too many employment checks and spousal surveillance assignments. However, because of her PI background, her law firm uses her for investigative work. There's lots of variety and it's steady employment.

The only drawback from Laney's perspective is the expectation that she stay within strict legal boundaries to gather information. Her PI mentor introduced her to a number of useful tools and tricks that were either flat-out illegal or borderline unlawful. Like using lockpicking skills to let yourself into someone's office or house to look for evidence, lying about who you are or who you represent to get someone to open up, trespassing to spy on an individual, or tapping someone's phone. Law firms frown on that sort of thing. Although Laney is as honest as they come in all the ways that count, she isn't above bending the law a little to help someone she believes is innocent or who is being treated unfairly. I like that about her; it encourages me to be a bit bolder in my approach to things.

As usual, Laney was dressed like a cross between Nancy Drew and Buffy the Vampire Slayer, slightly trendy, but with an edge. "I like your leather jacket," I said. "Is it new?"

"No, I just pulled it out from the back of my closet. The color is called cognac brown. Here. Feel how soft it is." She held out her arm and I petted the sleeve.

"Nice. Like one of those Sphynx cats."

She swatted my hand away just as the waiter came to take our order. After he left, she said: "Okay, I'm listening."

That was all it took, one sympathetic offer to unload my woes, and the dam instantly broke. I started with Delia's visit and how I'd explained the ins and outs of term life insurance to her and hinted at concerns for the five-year policy her niece and nephew were advocating. I went on to tell her what I knew about Delia's recent demise and about the dramatic visitation from the niece and nephew and the doubt in Emma's eyes when I told her I was clueless about why they were so angry with me, ending with: "Even Bruno seemed to believe that I might have manipulated Delia to get her to leave me the five million dollars."

"That's a lot of money."

"I thought I'd steered her away from getting a policy, especially a short-term one."

"Obviously, you didn't. And you have no idea why she might have named you as beneficiary."

"I only talked to her that one time. And we didn't exactly bond."

"You didn't throw her across your desk…"

"Noooo." I shuddered. "She is, er was, older than my mother. And not my type at any age."

"Your taste in women has always been, well, a bit tasteless."

"Did you hear me say she was wearing a mink stole with tiny rodent heads dangling down the front?"

Laney laughed. "That's right, you're a big-boobs man, not a two-headed stole kind of guy."

"This isn't funny."

Laney reached across the table and put a hand on mine. "Sorry, John." Then she gave me a mischievous Laney grin, the dimples on either cheek deepening with mirth. "But if you do inherit five mil, I expect you to take me on one helleva nice vacay. You might even consider gifting me a mink stole."

"Laney, be serious. Bruno says I'm a suspect."

"You told me he said that he doesn't have the autopsy report yet. Maybe they'll find she died of natural causes after all. Or that it was an accident—"

"But what if someone murdered her?"

"Look at it this way—it's highly unlikely that the term life insurance is a set-up to get you to take the rap for her death. I mean, unless you have someone named in *your* will who would benefit…" Laney was switching to analysis mode. I've seen her do that on numerous occasions. She loves solving problems and puzzles, and an unsolved murder is the ultimate conundrum. "That would actually be a nice way to get away with murder," she concluded.

"I don't anticipate dying any time soon."

"You told me that's what Delia said."

"Oh." I hadn't thought of that. "Well, since I don't have a will, that doesn't make any sense anyway."

"You don't have a will?" Her tone was definitely disapproving, but that wasn't the point she was trying to make. "So, with no brothers or sisters, your mother would inherit, right?"

"You think my mother got Delia's niece and nephew to approach Delia about term life insurance, tricked her into naming me as her beneficiary, then murdered Delia and framed *me?*"

Laney smiled. "No, I'm saying it's doubtful that it's a set-up. There has to be another explanation."

"My best guess is that the niece and nephew thought they were going to get the money for themselves. They were, after all, the ones who approached her about taking out the policy in the first place. Although, I don't know if they made any suggestions about other possible beneficiaries. Maybe they were hoping she would name their kids."

"That still wouldn't explain why they thought it should be a five-year policy." Laney tapped her spoon against the table. "You need to verify that you're the beneficiary. And if you are, you need to figure out why she left you the money rather than naming her niece and nephew or some other family members. Until you know that, we are blind to other possibilities."

We set aside my problem and finished our dinner, talking about this and that, a movie we wanted to see, a new recipe she'd tried—nothing special. By the end, I was feeling calmer. Laney was right, until I verified whether I really was a multi-millionaire, I shouldn't count my chickens. Besides, if I counted anything tonight, it would be sheep. Chickens tended to meander around rather than jumping over fences one at a time. Whatever I counted to help me sleep tonight, tomorrow I would sort everything out.

I had a pleasant drive home in my yolk-yellow Saturn that I call Bee. It was once my mother's car, but she sold it to me when she quit driving. She was also responsible for naming Bee. I've kept the name. It's not that I think you *should* name your car or believe that the car won't like it if you do away with its name or rename it something else. "Bee" suits my Saturn, so why not?

It was a mild evening for March. I was listening to an oldies music station, and when *"I Heard it Through the Grapevine"* came on, I started singing along. I couldn't remember all of the words, but I came on strong on the chorus, belting out *"honey, yeah"* and *"baby yeah."* Although not quite in synch with

Marvin Gaye's classic vocalization, it felt good. *Yeah, yeah*, good.

I live at The Haven, a houseboat community on Lake Union in Seattle. My landlord's house is the only structure on land, nestled against an embankment on a narrow strip that runs along the waterfront between the stairs from the off-street parking to the wood-planked dock the houseboats share. He and I have an uneasy relationship, so when I saw him sitting in a chair on his front porch, I was hoping I could sneak by without being seen—which would only have been possible if he had his eyes closed or I suddenly turned invisible. Unfortunately, neither was the case. As soon as he saw me, he leapt out of his chair and raced down his steps as if he'd been waiting for me to show up. He was wearing his usual overalls and T-shirt, one of his bib shoulder straps loose and flapping as he hurried toward me. My paranoia was verified when he started shouting: "I've warned you! You keep that crazy cat of yours inside, or I'm going to call Animal Control." Although my first impulse was to make a run for it, his reference to my cat made me stop and turn toward him.

"Is Wild Thing okay?" I asked. My cat was kept locked up 24/7 due to past incidents when he ran free, so I wasn't sure what the man was talking about.

"I mean it," he continued without answering my question. "He dug up my daffodils and terrorized your neighbor's dog."

Oh no. The neighbor's dog is a large German Shepherd. Although at their last encounter, Wild Thing played David to the dog's Goliath. Still, you never knew what might have happened in a rematch. The Shepherd could easily rip Wild Thing to shreds with a couple of well-positioned swipes of one clawed paw. "Is Wild Thing okay?" I repeated, feeling panic rise from my stomach to my throat, like acid reflux.

"He won't be if I catch him outside one more time." My landlord twirled around like someone wearing a cape rather than bib overalls. The metal buckle on his shoulder strap swung at a different rate than his twirl. It bounced off his ear with a barely audible thwacking sound. He swore and rubbed the side of his head as he raced up his steps and went inside.

On several other occasions when Wild Thing managed to escape, he'd done the same thing, going after my landlord's garden and the neighbor's dog. He's obsessed with both. Maybe I needed to send him to a pet therapist. Or did they have rehab programs for cats?

I started to call, "Here Wild Thing, here Wild Thing" as I scanned the area for him. Wild Thing is black all over and manages to blend into the shadows when he doesn't want to be found. Even inside my houseboat, he can fade into a corner at will. "Wild Thing, here Wild Thing."

It was at times like this that I wished my cat had a single-word name. Like Inky, or Luna, or Pepper. But my neighbor's daughter Valerie had aptly named him Wild Thing when my mother forced me to adopt him as a kitten. Mother wasn't able to keep him at her condo, and no one else wanted him. She convinced me that if I didn't take him, he would be put to sleep. Sometimes I think that might have been the better option. He's a disagreeable, anti-social, petulant pet. But he loves Valerie, and she loves him. Her father won't let Wild Thing live with them because of their German Shepherd, so I let Valerie visit Wild Thing in my houseboat. Not only do her visits keep my rambunctious cat somewhat under control, but in return for letting her have visitation rights, she no longer torments me by putting smelly and slimy things in my mailbox. Some kids have a strange sense of humor.

I headed toward my houseboat, calling all the way for Wild Thing, hoping he had already returned home, not sure what I would do if he hadn't. There were so many places on the lake to hide. The most likely scenario was that he would enjoy his freedom for a while, doing whatever mischievous thing he felt like doing, and return when he got hungry. He's a fussy eater with dainty habits. He probably wasn't going to dine on meals from garbage cans.

My houseboat is at the end of a string of houseboats clustered along both sides of an aging wood-planked dock. It's small, a one-story floating home with a terrific waterfront view of the city at one end of the lake and marinas, houseboats, restaurants, parks, residences, shipyards, and various other businesses filling up the rest of the surrounding land. The lake is connected to saltwater through the Lake Washington Ship Canal. I'm told you can walk the 6.4-mile loop around the lake in a couple of hours, but I've never tried. I'd rather sit on my deck and enjoy the view with a cold beer.

As I drew near, I noticed a dark figure sitting on the bench on my porch. He was obscured by flickering shadows; I couldn't see his face clearly until I was about six feet away. By then, it was too late to run.

"You took you time getting here," he said.

"I didn't realize anyone was waiting for me." I noticed that my door was open a few inches. "Did you go inside?" I asked.

"Your door was open."

I knew he was lying. "And you let Wild Thing out." That explained the *what*, but not the *why*.

"You mean that black cat with the bad temper?" He sounded unconcerned. "Look, we need to talk."

"Not until I find my cat." And not when it was just the two of us.

I'm not sure how the situation would have played out if my neighbor's daughter Valerie hadn't appeared carrying Wild Thing in her arms like he was a large baby. She was swinging her long straight brown hair over him, and he was batting at it with one paw. It was a gentle, friendly game that, if pictured on YouTube, would have gone viral.

For Wild Thing and Valerie, it had been love at first sight, whereas for him and me, there had been *no* love in sight. However, I admit that since he came to live with me, Wild Thing and I have developed a relationship of sorts, but it would not be labeled as companionable by any stretch of the imagination. It's more like a truce, a conditional suspension of hostilities. I provide him with food and lodging, and he doesn't attack me. It's a relationship that could easily snap like a rubber band if stretched too far.

"Wild Thing came to visit me," Valerie explained. She was wearing a frilly yellow dress. One day it was blue jeans and sloppy sweatshirts, the next something fussy and feminine. Wild Thing didn't care what she wore; his love was unconditional.

"Valerie, would you take Wild Thing inside and feed him? I'll be in shortly."

"Everyone is mad at you," she said in her thin, little girl voice.

"Because of Wild Thing?"

She nodded and rubbed her nose against Wild Thing's head. "Don't be long; my dad expects me home." She slipped past us and went into my

22

houseboat.

"So, what do you want?" I asked the man I now recognized as Delia's nephew.

"I just wanted to hear your explanation before..." His voice trailed off. Mentally I finished his thought: "Before I beat the crap out of you." He wasn't big, but he was muscular. It was too bad Wild Thing was an uncontrollable attack cat instead of a guard dog.

"Look, I have no idea why your aunt may have named me as a beneficiary. I say 'may have.' I don't know if that's true or not."

"Oh, it's true. Her lawyer told my mother. You must have manipulated her..."

"No, I simply told her about the pros and cons of term life insurance. That's all."

"She was a stubborn old harpy, but she wouldn't have dumped on the family like that without being pressured to do so."

"Stubborn old harpy? It sounds like you didn't care for her."

"She fancied herself as *lady of the manor.* Living all alone in that big house, wearing the family pearls, acting like she was better than the rest of us."

"So why did you think she would take out term life insurance for five million in your name?" Assuming he'd thought that was the arrangement.

"Because we're family." His logic was both mind-boggling and understandable. Families are often dysfunctional yet bound together by invisible ties that can be incomprehensible to outsiders.

"So why are you here tonight?"

"I've been asked by the other members of the family to tell you about your two options: you can either sign the policy over to the family or be sued."

"If it's true that she made me a beneficiary of her term life insurance—and I still think you're wrong—I will definitely be exploring all options. First, I have to verify what you've been told. But honestly, it makes absolutely no sense for your aunt to have named me as beneficiary. I only talked with her that one time."

"You insurance people are all alike." His lip almost literally curled upward in disdain. I wondered if it was a look he practiced in the mirror.

Ignoring his comment, I said, "What were you looking for in my house-boat?"

"The door was open; I just went inside to see if you were there."

"Sure." Whatever he'd been looking for, I doubted he'd found it. Because I didn't have anything related to his aunt anywhere in writing. Why would I? And it was way too soon to have the five million lying around. There had been a six-pack of Bud Light in the fridge, though.

He glanced at the open door. Like me, he probably thought that Valerie was listening to our conversation. If he assaulted me, she would be a witness. After a short pause, he pushed past me, yelling over his shoulder, "If you think we're going to let you swindle us out of five million dollars, you don't know what we're capable of."

And I sincerely hoped I didn't find out.

Chapter Four: Suspect

"Y ou stole five million dollars?" Valerie sounded more impressed than critical. Her innocent hazel eyes glinted with longing. Maybe she wanted a cut.

"No, the man who was here thinks I persuaded his aunt to name me as a beneficiary in her term life insurance, but I didn't."

"What's a ben-e-fish-e-airy?"

"It basically means she left me money when she died."

"Wow. Five million dollars? She must have been rich."

"But I don't know for sure that she did. I think there's been a mistake."

"Would you buy me a paddleboard if it's true?"

"Ah, sure. But don't count on it."

It would be like winning the lottery; everyone I knew would want a little something, maybe a big something. I reminded myself that it couldn't be real, though. There was some logical explanation for the misunderstanding. "Thank you for bringing Wild Thing back."

"Sure. Gotta go." She gently put Wild Thing on the floor. "See you tomorrow," she told him.

I was glad she was leaving—I needed to kick back and get my mind wrapped around what I should do to get this mess straightened out.

Valerie paused in the doorway and swiveled around like a ballerina, only on her heels instead of her toes. "And a kayak. I'd like a kayak." Then she ran off with an energy I envied.

I put a Stouffer's Meat Lovers Lasagna in the microwave, and as soon as I hit the timer button, my phone started making gorilla grunting noises.

At first, the ringtone sounds were amusing; now they're getting tiresome. Maybe I'd try for cooing doves next. I was hungry and would have ignored the call, but it was my mother. If I didn't answer, she would keep trying. And if I kept on not answering, eventually she would call an Uber and come by. Besides, it was possible she had talked to her friend that knew Delia's friend and had heard something about Delia's estate. She might be able to confirm that I wasn't actually the beneficiary of five million dollars. That was what I wanted to hear...wasn't it?

"I just put my dinner in the microwave," I said. It seemed smart to put her on notice in case she just called to chat.

"Is that a nice way to greet your mother?"

"Hello, Mother. How are you?"

"Concerned about my only son."

"You've heard."

"I've heard that the entire Flowers and Plover families want you strung up, if that's what you mean."

"Plover?"

"Delia's sister Dorothy married a Plover. I believe you've also angered some Dicks."

"I'm surprised to hear you use that kind of language."

"Stay focused—there's a branch of the family with the last name of Dick."

"Oh."

"I talked with my friend who has the friend who knew Delia for years. Her name is Mildred. They were at boarding school together and were apparently besties back then. They remained in touch all this time. Mildred did tell her, however, that Delia had never been an easy person to get along with. A bit domineering and cantankerous at times. Somewhat of a bully, actually."

"Why would she be friends with Delia if that's what she thought of her?"

"I can't say for sure. But sometimes it's nice to have a friend who can stand up to other kids. If the bully likes you, they can protect you. Like Bruno did for you."

"I could have defended myself," I said. Defensively, of course.

"John, you weren't big and athletic like Bruno. I was glad you were friends."

"So, you think Mildred used Delia as a protector?"

"That's not what I'm saying, although that could have been part of it. But I can imagine being friends with someone you know has some bad tendencies. And although Mildred was apparently quite surprised to hear about what happened, she admitted that Delia was perhaps spiteful enough to do what she did."

"I'm not sure I know what happened."

"According to the family, what happened was that you cheated them out of five million dollars."

"I'm still having a hard time getting my mind wrapped around that. I mean, if Delia didn't want to make her niece and nephew or some other family members beneficiaries, then why take out term life insurance in the first place? Assuming she did purchase a policy. How do they know this for sure?"

"Supposedly, the family lawyer told her sister Dorothy about it. And Dorothy told the rest of the family. I'm not sure who told Mildred."

"Has he already gone over her will and assets with them?"

"No, a meeting is being scheduled to do just that. I think that's why Dorothy talked to the lawyer. Apparently, according to my friend's friend, Mildred, the family was also upset to hear that Delia had made some changes to her will recently. They're concerned that YOU may have inherited EVERYTHING."

"That's ridiculous. Why would they think that?"

"That's what I told my friend. Charming an old woman is not what I would consider a core strength of yours. Nor can I picture you keeping something like that a secret from me." It was implicit in her tone that if I had, I would be in big trouble. Worse than opening hidden presents the day before Christmas when I was a kid. Then again, five million dollars might go a long way in soothing over hurt feelings, even between me and my mother, who valued trust and loyalty above most other virtues.

* * *

27

That night, I had trouble sleeping. After changing positions and adjusting my covers for the umpteenth time, I got up and looked in the refrigerator for something to eat while I watched some TV. I settled for what was left of a pint of Chunky Monkey in the freezer. I remembered hearing on some talk show that no monkeys were harmed in the development of the product, although it wasn't clear to me if they'd actually tested it on monkeys. Did monkeys eat ice cream? I bet they would love frozen chocolate-covered bananas.

I fell asleep watching a Seinfeld rerun, the one in which Kramer is in a hospital viewing gallery during a surgery and drops a Junior Mint into the patient being operated on. It's one of my favorites. I love the expression on Kramer's face when he realizes what he's done. I also empathize; I've done my fair share of clumsy things like that.

I was enjoying a dream about volleyball playing women in skimpy swimsuits when licking and slurping sounds shattered the image. I opened my eyes and saw Wild Thing attacking what was left in my ice cream bowl. As I shifted position, he looked up at me with eyes that said, "Let me finish or you'll be sorry." For a tiny creature, he can send monster messages. A miniature Godzilla cat. I had no doubt he could terrorize the citizens of Tokyo if let loose there.

Leaving him with the bowl, I retreated to my bedroom, only to discover I was wide awake again. How did that happen? I flipped from one side of my bed to the other before finally grabbing my phone off my nightstand and googling what to do if you can't sleep. What did people do before cell phones when they needed a quick answer to a question?

It upset me to learn that one of the main recommendations for someone with insomnia was to avoid using any kind of electronics because of the blue light they emit. Too late. Most of the other suggestions either took too much effort or sounded really boring. However, near the bottom of the list, it said that taking a warm shower could help. It was supposed to relax muscles and wash away stress. An added benefit was that it would save me time in the morning.

Fifteen minutes later, I was cleaner but still wide awake.

Feeling desperate, I tried counting backwards from one hundred. It was both tedious and took a lot of concentration. Counting sheep was easier, but still boring. Eventually, I gave up trying to sleep, found a book I'd been meaning to read that was described as a page-turning thriller that would keep you up at night. I was already up, so why not?

* * *

I woke up with a kink in my neck from leaning forward in my lounger with the book in my lap. It was open to page 7. My alarm must have already gone off in my bedroom, but I hadn't heard it. If I wanted to make it to work on time, I would have to hustle. At least I didn't need to shower.

I wasn't at my desk for more than a few minutes when I got a call from Bruno's department admin. Bruno wanted me to come to the station to answer a few questions. No, the admin couldn't be more specific. And no, the meeting was not at my convenience, but right away. When a long-time friend and poker buddy has an admin call to demand an immediate meeting at a police station, that suggests something not-so-good is up. In spite of not wanting to go, I wasted no time in rushing over to the station.

I should have moseyed instead of rushed. In fact, I would have had time to stop for coffee, stroll along the waterfront, and grab a piroshky from my favorite vendor. Instead, I sat in an uncomfortable and unattractive waiting room for an hour and a half before I was finally ushered into an interview room. Bruno wasn't there, although I assumed he was looking and listening from behind the giant mirror that took up the better part of one wall while I was questioned by two officers I'd never met before. That's the way it would have been if we were on Chicago P.D.

The first question had to do with where I was the night Delia died. Oh, oh, that didn't sound good.

"At home, alone." It was too bad I hadn't been with a hot date that night. It would have been fun to toss that little fact out there, both to get me off the hook and to impress Bruno. Instead, I had to admit that I was at home alone with my cat and no alibi.

The second question was why she had made me her beneficiary for her term life insurance.

"As far as I know, that hasn't been verified yet," I said. And I sincerely hoped it wasn't true. The windfall sounded nice in theory, although if I was actually going to receive that much money as the beneficiary of Delia's term life insurance policy, I could be in big trouble on multiple fronts. It wasn't worth it...was it? It *was* a lot of money.

The two officers exchanged looks that I couldn't interpret before moving on. The third question was whether I was mentioned in her will.

"I can't imagine I would be. I only talked with her that one time."

"And how did she end up coming to you when it says here..." He looked down at a piece of paper in a manila folder. "...you don't handle term life insurance."

"Mrs. Flowers was a friend of a friend of my mother's."

"So, your mother doesn't know what you do."

I wanted to ask if their mothers could explain what they did on a day-to-day basis. But I held my tongue. My mother is both nosy and intuitive, but hopefully I have a few secrets from her. That wasn't the question, though. "She simply asked if I would provide an overview of what a term life insurance policy is for Mrs. Flowers. That was something I felt comfortable doing."

"And that's all you did."

"Yes."

"Didn't you also discuss her niece and nephew with her?"

"Not specifically. And not by name. I'd never met them."

"It all comes back to why she left you five million dollars—a tip for good advice?" When I didn't respond to his sarcasm, he pushed harder: "Take a wild guess as to why you are her beneficiary."

"As I said before, I don't even know for sure if what you've told me about being her beneficiary is true. Have you seen the policy?"

The two officers exchanged looks again. I wondered if they were also getting messages from Bruno via some hidden receiver. Like the Wizard of Oz behind the curtain. After a brief pause, one of the officers said, "The sister talked to the lawyer."

"So, you haven't seen it."

"The lawyer has no reason to lie. And the family intends to sue you."

"On what grounds would they sue me?"

"That's up to the lawyers. But the family members are convinced that you murdered Mrs. Flowers for the money. That's what we're looking into."

It sounded like they had determined that she didn't die from either natural causes or from an accident. Someone murdered her. Poor Delia. I wanted to ask how she was murdered, but wasn't sure if I should. On the other hand, maybe it was strange if I didn't. Being a prime suspect isn't something I know much about.

The two officers excused themselves and left me there for what seemed like forever. I wasn't sure if anyone was watching or not, but I resisted the urge to pick my nose. I don't pick my nose that much, but whenever I think someone might be watching, I get the urge. The problem was that I didn't know what an innocent person should do while waiting in an interrogation room in a police station. Nor did I know what a guilty person would do. What if I accidentally did what a guilty person would do instead of what an innocent person would do?

When Bruno came into the room, I wasn't sure whether to be relieved or concerned. He didn't smile, but after he sat down, he said he had some good news. "Your story about being home the night of Delia's murder checks out."

"How? Was Wild Thing wearing a body cam?"

"No need to be flip."

"Seriously, how can you possibly know whether I was home or not?"

"Are you arguing against your innocence?"

Oh, oh. "Just curious."

"You apparently don't know about the cameras at The Haven." He was smiling now.

"There are cameras?"

"Let's just say we know you didn't come down the dock or move your car that night. So, unless you swam ashore, changed into dry clothes you stashed somewhere in advance, and then either took public transportation or hired a taxi or an Uber..." He left the scenario unfinished. "Frankly, that

31

doesn't sound like you."

Too clever or too stupid? I was afraid to ask. But there was one thing I did want to know. "Who put up the cameras? Neighbors? The landlord?" If it was the neighbors, I was okay with it. But if it was our landlord, I wasn't so sure.

"Why does that matter?"

"And where are they? On the dock? In the parking area?" Hanging from a cloud in the night sky?

"Again, why does that matter? You are lucky there were cameras there to prove you were telling the truth."

"It matters because someone is spying on the residents of The Haven without our permission. Isn't that something to be upset about?" I was working myself into a tizzy. Big Brother was watching me. I wasn't sure whether I was angry because I was being watched or because I hadn't noticed that I was being watched.

"John. Calm down. When you go home, look around. My understanding is that the cameras are in plain sight. Although I agree, whoever put them up should have told all the residents."

"Did I mention that my door was open when I got home yesterday? And Delia's nephew was waiting for me? He said he didn't break in, but if there's a camera pointed at my front door, someone could have warned me if they saw him in the act, or, at the very least, told me about it after the fact."

"I get why you're angry. But having cameras around is a good safety measure."

"Apparently not that great if someone can break in without getting caught."

"Count your blessings and move on. That's my advice."

"If you won't tell me who put the cameras up, how do I get access to footage to prove the nephew broke into my home?"

"Was anything missing?"

"He let Wild Thing out."

"Oh, oh. Did your crazy cat go after the neighbor's dog again?"

"Of course. But Valerie found him and brought him back."

"Well, under the circumstances, unless you find something is missing, I'd let it slide. Give the family a chance to calm down. And off the record, I'd asked your landlord about the cameras."

I chewed on that a moment, then decided he was right. About letting it slide with the family. But I was definitely going to check out the cameras and make sure all the other neighbors knew about them. But first, I had one more question for Bruno. "Are you going to tell me how she died?"

"It will be in the papers soon enough, but keep it under your hat until then, okay? At this stage in the investigation, the less information out there, the easier it is for us to do our job."

I made a zipped mouth gesture. Corny but clear.

"For some reason that we don't yet understand, she went out to her greenhouse in the middle of the night and tripped over a pot that had fallen off a bench. She hit her head on some concrete blocks sticking out from under the bench."

"That sounds like an accident."

"At first blush, maybe. There are too many coincidences, though. My gut tells me it was staged to look like an accident, but it was a setup. As soon as we get the autopsy report, we'll know more."

"Who found her?"

"A neighbor. He smelled something that he thought was a decomposing animal and went to check it out. Otherwise, who knows how long she might have been there?"

"She was decomposing?"

"Well, he thought he smelled decaying matter, but it wasn't her. It was a Voodoo Lilly."

"What's that?"

"It's also called a corpse flower because of the smell. It's a tropical plant that she was growing in her greenhouse. According to a horticulturist we consulted, it only blossoms once a year, and the flower only lasts a few days. The bloom apparently has a rank smell. It's the flower that stinks."

"I didn't know there were flowers that smelled bad. Except for skunk cabbage." Was that considered a flower or a vegetable?

"I'd never heard of a Voodoo Lilly until this happened. The officer who answered the call threw up after viewing the body. He thought the foul odor came from her. Said there were flies everywhere. After that, everyone on the scene wore masks."

"You're saying that you strongly suspect someone got her down to the greenhouse in the middle of the night and rigged a situation in which she would trip and fall, hitting her head on a concrete block. That doesn't sound like the surest set-up to me."

"I agree. And it seems incredibly strange that she would go down to her greenhouse in the middle of the night wearing a nightgown and robe. Then there's the pot that just happened to fall a few feet inside the entrance. With a concrete block in just the right place for her to hit her head if she tripped on the pot. And why didn't she turn on the lights when the switch was on a post just inside the door? Suspicious, right?"

"You don't think she could have been meeting someone there?"

"In her night clothes? It seems unlikely, doesn't it?"

"What if she heard something and went down to investigate?"

"On her own, and without a weapon?"

"She was a pretty feisty old lady."

"There's always the possibility that she had insomnia and simply went outside to get some fresh air before returning to bed, decided to check on the greenhouse, and tripped before turning on the light. Possible, but highly unlikely."

"I see what you mean."

"Like I said, we'll know more after the autopsy. But for now, you're free to go."

I stood up. Free to go was good.

"You're not completely off the hook, though—the family intends to go after you big time."

"Well, as nice as it would be to have five million dollars in the bank, I still think there's been a mistake."

"Maybe you could offer to share it with them." He paused, then added, "Although I don't know if I would. Think of the high-stakes poker you could play."

"Given how often I lose at poker, the five million might not last that long." Although, it would be fun while it lasted. I needed to find out if I was a potential high roller or still destined to lose at poker with my beer-drinking buddies.

Chapter Five: Attacked

After grabbing a sandwich and returning to the office, the work day dragged on forever. At one point, I fell asleep in my chair, without even trying. No counting exercises, no deep breaths, just awake one minute and oblivion the next. When the phone rang, my head snapped up, giving me a minor case of whiplash. It was Mother. "I heard that you're off the hook," she said."

"As far as the murder goes, it sounds like it. But not with the family. The nephew still thinks I hypnotized his aunt."

"Really?"

"I'm exaggerating. He doesn't have a theory about how I got her to make me a beneficiary—assuming she did, but the family is certain I committed some kind of criminal act."

"My friend's friend says Delia was fully compos mentis and a very savvy woman, although, as I told you before, she also said that Delia was difficult and could be mean-spirited at times."

"That's how she struck me. Smart, but a bit abrupt and overbearing."

"And she wasn't apparently fond of her family."

"I can't say that I am either."

"Well, I'm just glad you can sleep easy tonight."

* * *

When I returned to The Haven after work, I immediately started looking for cameras. I didn't see any in the parking area, although I was suspicious that the bird nest in the upper branches of the tree whose limbs hung out over my car was not a real nest but a disguised spy cam. I'd have to get a ladder to check. And maybe there was a camera further away that had a view of the entire parking area.

One of the logical places for a camera aimed at the walkway to the docks was on my landlord's porch. I didn't want to confront him until I knew more, so I didn't go up close to check it out.

Now that I knew what to look for, I spotted one camera on a post at the entrance to the dock. Had the post always been there? It looked newish, the wood fresh with clear varnish. I stared at the camera. Although it was tempting to give him the finger, I waved at the landlord's unseen face, the one I imagined peering at me from inside the small box.

I didn't see any other cameras on the dock, although I knew at least one of my neighbors had a wireless mini cam over her door. I wasn't going to make it a crusade, but I definitely wanted to know how many eyes were on me as I walked home in the evening. And I had that urge to pick my nose again.

* * *

Unfortunately, Mother was wrong about me sleeping easy that night. Although I'd barely been able to keep my eyes open at work, dozing off now and then for a few minutes while trying to catch up on some files, as soon as I stepped inside my houseboat, I was fully awake. I couldn't get Delia and the five million dollars out of my mind. I tried every trick I could think of to grab some shuteye. It wasn't until I gave up and went back to reading the thriller that I fell asleep. This time at page ten.

* * *

Friday morning, I fumbled with my rude alarm as I tried to shut it off. It slipped out of my hand and continued its annoying beeping as it skittered across the floor. Half awake, I swore and dragged myself out of bed. Suddenly, Wild Thing was underfoot, chasing my alarm clock, batting at it with his paws. It slid under my bed, its beeping even louder now that it had been attacked.

Once he'd achieved his goal of knocking my clock out of arm's reach, Wild Thing made himself scarce. Still groggy, I lay down on the floor and tried to wedge my shoulder under the bed far enough to get at my clock. I was about to resign myself to leaving it there until it died when I remembered that it wasn't battery-powered but a plug-in. I inched my way out from under the bed, got up, brushed the dust bunnies off of my pajamas, found the cord, reeled in the clock, and switched off the alarm. By then, I was awake, but still somewhat muddle-headed.

Wild Thing was waiting for me by his food dish. If he'd been human, he would have been tapping his foot impatiently. As it was, he was telegraphing his displeasure with the slow food service through not-so-subtle glares and a rigid, hunch-backed posture. A disagreeable but communicative cat.

The one cup of coffee I drank before leaving for work didn't clear the fog from my brain, so I decided to stop for an espresso before planting myself behind my desk at the office. When I found a parking spot right in front of the coffee shop, I began to have some hope for the day. Then two small dogs with short legs sticking out of colorful sweaters reminded me how quickly Lady Luck can turn against you. They came at me, yapping and nipping at my ankles. "Hey," I yelled to the woman holding onto the other end of their retractable leashes, "Call them off." Trying to escape from their tiny spiked teeth, I stepped back and bumped into an elderly woman.

"Watch where you're going," she said as she whapped me across the knee with her walking cane.

One of the two dogs took advantage of the distraction to dart in and clamp his vicious jaws around my ankle. I tried to shake him off, but he doggedly held on.

"Stop, you're hurting Precious," the dog's owner yelled in a high-pitched voice that sounded like an angry bird.

By then, a crowd had gathered to enjoy the show, smiling at the sweater-wearing dogs and apparently either uncaring or oblivious to my distress. I continued to shake my leg, hoping to detach myself from the beast. Then a bystander screamed: "Shame on you. Picking on those cute little dogs." Several others chimed in, repeating the phrase "shame on you." One person yelled, "Go, Precious." The crowd was apparently composed of dog lovers who had no sympathy for me, the true victim of the attack.

As I paused to assess the situation, it looked to me like Precious had caught an incisor on some strands in my wool-blend sock. If so, no amount of shaking my leg was going to dislodge the animal. Meanwhile, the crowd was growing in size and becoming more openly hostile toward me for picking on the small, sweater-wearing pooch. I had to detach the little monster quickly, or I could face a mob of humans joining forces with him.

Unfortunately, each time I reached down to try to back the dog's incisor out of the weave, the owner screamed at me not to touch him. It was a stalemate. If it hadn't been for a passerby who apparently grasped the situation and either took pity on me—or on Precious, I'd still be there. Initially, I feared that his intention was to punch me out as part of a hostage release attempt, but he simply reached down, secured Precious with one hand while using the other to unhook tooth from sock. I thanked his back as he disappeared into the crowd.

Once the surgery was performed and I was separated from the dog, Precious growled at me as her owner tugged on her leash. Her doggy-in-crime chimed in with a combination of barking and growling as the trio thankfully went on their merry way.

Now that the drama was over, the onlookers lost interest. With a few final guffaws and shouted jeers, they dispersed, leaving me with a ripped sock and in a full state of wakefulness. At least Precious had saved me the price of an espresso.

I was hurrying past Emma's desk toward the solace of my office when Emma held up her hand for me to stop. "I have a message for you." She handed me a 4 x 4 square of pink paper with the word MESSAGE printed at the top and a neat hand-written telephone number for Bushmole, Treemont, and Greenleaf next to Benjamin Treemont, Esq. I hadn't seen one of those pink message slips for years. I thought they had gone the way of dial telephones and pet rocks. Emma probably didn't get many excuses to show off her cursive script anymore.

"Thanks."

"He said he needed to talk to you as soon as possible."

"Did he say about what?"

"No." She looked me up and down. "Is something wrong?"

"I was attacked by two dogs," I said, stepping back so she could see my sock when I pulled up my pant leg. "Look what one of them did to my sock." As I stared at it with her, I admit it didn't look like much, just a pulled thread, no blood seeping from a wound.

"Big dogs?" she asked.

"Well, no, not exactly." At that point, one of the cubicle dwellers I knew by sight but not by name came over, a huge grin on his face.

"Cute sweaters on that pair, huh?"

Emma looked at him, waiting for more, and he willingly obliged.

"This fellow here had to defend himself against a pair of wiener dogs wearing sweaters. It was quite a show."

"His teeth were wicked," I complained.

"It was a good show," he repeated as we wandered off, still grinning. Out of the corner of my eye, I could see Emma struggling to suppress a smile.

"Small dog, big pointed teeth," I said as I headed for my office.

"Wearing a sweater?" she called after me. "What color?"

My day was definitely not going well. I just hoped the lawyer who'd left a message wasn't going to make it worse.

Benjamin Treemont's assistant answered my call in a crisp voice and informed me that there would be a reading of Delia Flowers' will at 11:00 and that Mr. Treemont would expect me in his office at 10:30. She made it sound like a command performance. I itched to say that I was busy with an important client at 10:30, but curiosity won out over ego.

Chapter Six: Legalese

At 10:15, I was standing at the entrance to the building that contained the offices for Bushmole, Tremont, and Greenleaf LLP. From the outside, it looked like a tower of reflecting windows, one of the tallest buildings in the area. You couldn't take it in without craning your neck and shading your eyes.

The lobby was equally imposing, with a seating area the size of a millionaire's living room. It was furnished with comfortable-looking sofas and chairs next to low tables where you could put your leather briefcase and your latte. A security guard stood a few feet from the entrance next to a potted plant that was as tall as he was and probably weighed as much. Off to his left were some stairs leading to a Starbucks on an open balcony. At the back of the vast space, another man in a brown uniform sat behind a long counter that blocked access to the elevators. You apparently needed permission to ascend to the offices of the important people on the floors above. There was a huge reader board on the wall behind the counter listing the locations of the companies housed in the building. I had no doubt that the higher you went, the better the view, and the more expensive the rent.

Between the front entrance and the elevator blockade were artistically placed plants in gigantic pots alongside expensive-looking pieces of sculpture. My eyes were drawn to a stone creation that looked like three rocks mating. As I walked by, I read the plaque describing the work: "Three Rocks." Got it.

The man at the counter said he would call Mr. Treemont and let him know I was there. I was instructed to sign in with the required information so he could print me a visitor's badge. Then I was invited to "make myself comfortable" in the waiting area. Given all the glitz, you'd think the least they could do was provide free coffee instead of making visitors walk up a flight of stairs and wait in line at Starbucks.

It was 10:22 when I finished signing in.

It was 10:23 when I tried in vain not to stare at a young woman's legs as she lowered her rounded body onto a low couch across from me. She had to tug at her short skirt to keep it from revealing even more smooth flesh. When she noticed my interest, she gave me a disdainful scowl, and I reluctantly shifted my attention to the shiny leaves on the plant next to my chair.

It was 10:35 when I was summoned to the elevators by a conservatively dressed middle-aged woman who said she was my escort.

By the time I reached the offices of Bushmole, Treemont, and Greenleaf on the 25th floor, I was expecting more than a medium-sized law firm tucked at one end of a hallway shared by several other businesses with names I didn't recognize. The entrance may not have been eye-catching, and the reception area unimpressive, but Benjamin Treemont's office didn't disappoint. The first thing that caught my attention was a large painting of blue and gold swirls with a spooky-looking village at the bottom that dominated one wall. It was probably a reproduction, but the frame alone most likely cost more than my living room couch. Granted, my couch wasn't real leather, but still—

Next, my eyes were drawn to the spectacular view of the waterfront from the floor-to-ceiling windows. The voice that said "Mr. Smith" finally got me to focus on the figure standing next to an expanse of table composed of glass and brass. Benjamin Treemont definitely belonged in the lavish setting. He was tall, slim, and held himself ramrod straight, like a butler about to serve royalty. My guess was that his suit was custom-made to accentuate his broad shoulders and tapered waistline. And he wasn't wearing shoes from Nordstrom Rack.

"Please sit." He waved me to a chair I assumed had once adorned a cow rather than manufactured from synthetic materials. It was placed at a slight angle in front of his desk/table, so the person seated was looking at the man rather than at the view. Seeing the view upon entry was apparently all you got.

"I wanted to give you this before we meet with the family." Treemont slid a sealed envelope with my name on it across the table. He didn't explain what was inside. When I opened it, I found a handwritten note from Delia:

"Mr. Smith. Your mother says that you are absolutely trustworthy and reliable. And I appreciated your tactful assessment of my insurance needs when we met. If you are reading this, my worst fears have been confirmed. My lawyer will explain what is required of you. But I wanted to personally thank you in advance and assure you that you will be fairly compensated for your services. Sincerely, Delia Flowers."

My inner voice screamed: *Mother—what have you gotten me into?* Yet somehow I managed to remain outwardly calm as I looked at Treemont and said, "The letter refers to services she expects from me and says that you will explain everything." I couldn't imagine that any services I could provide were worth five million dollars, so I suspected I was about to be disinherited.

"Yes. We don't have much time before the meeting with her relatives. But the bottom line is that Mrs. Flowers has entrusted you with her entire estate."

"What does that mean?" *Entrusted* was a slippery word. It could mean any number of things. And should I mention that she didn't like to be called *Mrs. Flowers*? Or did it matter now that she was dead?

"You will, of course, receive payment for your duties." I didn't like the sound of *duties* either. In my experience, a duty involved work, usually something you didn't want to do.

Treemont swiveled his chair around to retrieve a folder from a wooden cabinet along the wall behind him. I could see my name on the label. He swiveled back and said, "Mrs. Flowers had extensive assets, including a term life insurance policy, a home on a valuable piece of property, and considerable savings. You are in charge of deciding who receives what. You can designate specific individuals, divide it up equally among family members, or you can give some or all to nonprofits and charities. She's left a list of her preferred organizations if you decide to do the latter, but the list is only suggestive. Anything you decide to do with her estate is at your discretion."

I heard what he said, but was having a hard time taking it all in. "I'm not sure I understand."

"I thought I was clear." He didn't bother to mask his irritation at my failure to comprehend what he had told me. "Everything in her estate will be distributed according to whatever you decide to do with it." Unfortunately, it didn't sound as if I could retain a chunk of change for my personal use. But my "services" would be compensated. That was something.

"But why? Did she tell you why she...*designated* me for this responsibility?" I'd almost said "saddled" instead of "designated." Even if I was fairly compensated, the task sounded onerous.

"She trusted you."

"But I only met her once. And the family..." I began.

"You will meet them all shortly." He glanced at what looked like a very expensive watch.

"Something you said to Delia's sister Dorothy made them think that I'm the beneficiary of her term life insurance rather than some kind of executor with superpowers. And they're very angry about that."

"She must have misunderstood what I said in a brief telephone conversation that she insisted on having with me instead of waiting for the reading of the will. She specifically wanted to know about the status of the term life insurance policy, and I told her she would have to talk to you about that."

"She definitely misunderstood. She thought you meant I was going to get the five million all to myself." Did it occur to him that it was possible that sometimes he didn't make himself entirely clear? I wanted to say more, but my mind was swirling in an effort to get a handle on the situation. And on "my" place in it. "You do realize that although me being the executor isn't as bad for the family as what they originally thought—at least I don't think it is— they aren't going to be happy campers."

"All I can say is that it's what Mrs. Flowers wanted. And as her lawyer, I'm duty-bound to carry out her wishes."

"Ah, she didn't like being called *Mrs. Flowers*." I couldn't sit there and let him keep referring to her by a name she'd disliked.

"Excuse me?" His tone said that he not only didn't understand what I was saying but had already decided he didn't appreciate my comment.

"She said it was her late husband's name and…" It occurred to me that this might not be the best time to argue about what she did and didn't like being called. "Never mind," I said.

"Do you have any other questions?" It was clear that he thought I shouldn't.

"Just one—is this legal? I mean, as I said, I only met her one time."

"I made certain it's all legal." The statement was a firm declaration: the gods of legalese had spoken. I couldn't think of any other issue to bring up or anything else to say in order to avoid having to comply with Delia's wishes as communicated through her lawyer. The Fates, with the help of my mother, had stuck me with a duty I definitely didn't relish doing, no matter how well compensated.

Treemont handed me the file. "Here's a list of assets and ongoing expenses. I've also included my fees for setting up the arrangement and your fees for managing it. Of course, if I have to do more work to defend her decision, I will need to be paid for my time." He stood up and gestured toward the door of his office. "They will be waiting for us in the conference room. Shall we?"

As I preceded him out of his office, I felt fairly certain I was about to be attacked for the second time that morning. Some of my new attackers might even be wearing sweaters. I only hoped their bark was worse than their bite.

The conference room was large and filled almost to capacity with relatives of the late Delia Flowers. They were clucking and burbling like a flock of cranky chickens. I've always been intimidated by chickens. They don't respect boundaries, have sharp beaks and clawed feet, and you can't tell what they're thinking.

Everyone was seated around a long, highly polished wood table. You could see distorted faces reflected in its glossy surface. There were three silver trays with pitchers of water and empty glasses placed equidistant from each other on the table, but no one was drinking. They were too busy complaining, and they hadn't even heard the worst of it yet. I was relieved there wasn't any fruit for them to hurl at me. Although maybe once they knew what my role was in distributing their inheritance, they would douse me with glasses of water.

Treemont and I took seats at the head of the table at the far end of the room, and everyone fell quiet. If looks could kill, I would have died on the spot. I lowered my eyes to stare at my funhouse facial reflection in the tabletop while Treemont called the meeting to order. I was forced to look up when he suggested that they go around the room and introduce themselves by name and their relationship to the deceased. I wasn't sure if he was doing it for his benefit or for mine, but in anticipation of the animosity that would be unleashed by the lawyer's reading of the will, I knew that I needed to be familiar with the names and faces of my enemies, so I snapped to attention. Well, maybe I didn't quite "snap," but I did start paying more attention.

A young man muttered something about how they all knew each other, but Treemont ignored him and asked the woman to his left to begin. Like Mother had said, there were Flowers, Plovers, and Dicks. They ranged in age from young to old. Great-nieces and nephews of Delia's appeared to be in their twenties and thirties, with nieces and nephews in their fifties. The sister and brother were most likely in their early seventies. It didn't take long for me to lose track of the names and relationships of the fourteen relatives of Delia seated around the table. By the end of the introductions, all I saw was one merged angry face.

When Treemont introduced me, I heard a few muttered curses that he ignored, but it made me consider making a break for it before things escalated. It wasn't until he got to the actual reading of the will that the chorus reached riot levels. It didn't seem to matter that they had been wrong about the five million dollars and that it was still up for grabs, along with the rest of her estate. They didn't like the fact that she had given *me* the power over *their* inheritance. Like I'd warned Treemont—they weren't happy campers. And I was the target of their unhappiness.

As a lawyer, Treemont had undoubtedly encountered dissatisfied clients before. Despite their obvious displeasure, he exuded confidence and calm, acting as if their response was nothing unusual, explaining a few random details before concluding with: "I'm sure Mr. Smith will want to meet with each of you individually before he makes his decisions." He didn't ask if anyone had any questions, and, after a brief pause during which he stared them down with steely eyes that did not encourage further complaints, he said, "Mrs. Flowers also provided information about each of you for me to pass on to Mr. Smith, along with a list of her favorite charities and nonprofits."

The reference to charities and nonprofits caused a tidal wave of discontent aimed in my direction. I wanted to point out that this whole thing wasn't my doing and that I, too, was an unhappy camper. Like I'd been when Mother sent me to Boy Scout Camp when I was a kid—plagued by bullies and mosquitoes, forced to sleep on hard ground in a leaky tent, and made to eat runny eggs fried on tin can Bunsen burners we'd made ourselves. Now, once again, it was my mother's fault that I found myself in such an unpleasant if not downright nasty situation. Why did she have to tell someone that I was trustworthy and reliable? Couldn't she have said I was a philandering playboy?

"I can't believe my sister intended to give a complete stranger control over her estate." The older woman who made the comment at first glance looked like a softer version of Delia, but the family resemblance quickly faded as I noted her overall appearance. She didn't seem to be wearing any makeup, her hairdo was old-fashioned and not stylish, and her conservative, casual attire would have looked very out of place with a pair of dead animals hanging around her neck.

A chorus of "me neither's" filled the room, rising to a crescendo like the last line of a finale for a Broadway musical.

"May I say something?" I interrupted.

Treemont nodded, and all eyes locked onto mine with laser-like precision, as if they were preparing to shoot me down.

"I'm as surprised by this as you are." I had to wait for the murmurs of disbelief to subside before continuing. "I only met her the one time. And she gave me no indication that she intended to make me the executor of her estate. Under the circumstances, I believe I understand how upsetting this must be for you."

"No, you don't," the woman next to Brandon said. The pronounced wrinkles around her thin mouth furrowed deeper as she pressed her lips together in disdain. Everyone quickly and loudly agreed with her. I remembered Brandon from his visit to my office, and the woman arguing that I didn't understand had been introduced as his wife. I couldn't quite remember her name, but I thought it began with an "M." She looked older than Brandon, her neck sagging under a pointy chin. I could picture her in a black witch's hat, chanting a curse aimed at me. It was an unkind thought, but I was feeling unfairly put upon.

"You can think of me what you want," I said to the group. "But, ah, Mrs. Flowers..." Calling her Delia might make it sound like I knew her better than I was saying. "...has tasked me with distributing her estate, and I intend to do the best job I can." Another wave of complaints rose up, merged simply as noise in my ears.

If they weren't prepared to listen to what I had to say, did it make any sense for me to stay? I'd had enough abuse for one day—it was time to get out of Dodge. I stood up and started down the gauntlet toward the door. "I'll have my admin call to set up appointments with each of you," I said. Actually, since I didn't have an admin, I was going to have to do that myself, but I thought it made me sound more important if I implied that I had someone reporting to me.

Even though my knees were trembling and my brain was pinging stress signals, I thought I was about to escape with my body and ego intact until I stumbled over my own feet and reached out to steady myself by grabbing the shoulder of the young man at the end of the table. He reacted to my touch by jumping up and shoving me back against the wall.

"Keep your hands off me." He didn't need to add "or else."

"Sorry, I...I tripped." With that, I rushed out of the room to safety, still clutching the folder Treemont had given me.

As I hurried past the front desk, a woman called my name: "Mr. Smith." I almost didn't stop. What if the voice belonged to one of Delia's family members who had followed me from the conference room? She could have a gun pointed in my direction, determined to look me in the eyes when she took her shot. Although it was more likely that she simply wanted to deliver one last warning or one more comment about how despicable I was. Under the circumstances, maybe I owed it to her to take whatever abuse she wanted to dish out.

I turned around. Instead of one of Delia's relatives from the meeting waiting to verbally or physically annihilate me, the voice belonged to a young, nicely dressed woman holding out an envelope with a slight bulge in it. "Mr. Treemont wanted me to give you this." When I hesitated to take it from her, she added, "It's a USB flash drive with information from Mrs. Flowers about family members and a key to her house."

"Thank you." I accepted the envelope even though I was afraid I already knew everything I needed to know about the Flower-Plover-Dick family members. Based on my interactions with them so far, they were an offensive and aggressive bunch, and I questioned whether any of them deserved a share of Delia's estate. Knowing that it was within my legal right to ignore them completely and bestow her net worth on the charities and nonprofits of my choice was both exciting and frightening. *Exciting* because I'd never had that kind of power before, and a tiny part of me wanted to use it to get back at them for the way they'd been treating me. *Frightening* because of what might happen if I didn't give them everything. Even so, if they didn't start behaving like normal families were supposed to act, I would seriously consider that possibility.

As soon as the thought of defying them crossed my mind, I began to mentally backpedal. It would be easier, and probably safer, for me to simply swallow my pride and acquiesce to family demands. Making enemies of that lot didn't seem like a smart thing to do. After all, there *was* the tiny matter of Delia's demise to consider. Someone had murdered her, and I didn't want to join her in the near future. I was hoping for at least the thirty-year term life insurance plan, preferably longer still.

Chapter Seven: Twice Bashed

When I got back to the office, I called Bruno. "I told you…" I began.

"Before you tell me what you told me, let me tell *you* something: I talked to the lawyer for Delia's estate." He paused. "I know what you *told* me, and I didn't really believe you murdered her for her term life insurance policy."

"You sure acted like you did."

"Well, the police officer in me said I couldn't discount the possibility. It wouldn't have been professional if I'd let the fact that I've known you most of my life bias my opinion."

We had not only been friends when we were growing up in the same neighborhood, we'd stayed in touch as adults. Our lives weren't as connected as when we were young, but we were drinking buddies, and Bruno was a regular at my poker parties. "Rather than *bias,* I would call it using common sense. But I understand that you did what you thought you needed to do."

"It's kinda like beating you at poker. I have to do it." He laughed.

"Putting that aside for now, can we meet after work for a beer? I need some advice."

"Sounds good. Also, you may want to think about getting a bodyguard. According to everything I've heard, that family is something else."

They were indeed "something else." But a bodyguard? Could I rent a Doberman until this was over?

During my lunch break, I called Laney to report on the visit with the lawyer and the family. "It was ugly," I concluded, muffling the word ugly by taking a bite of a tuna sandwich while trying to talk. "Really ugly," I repeated after swallowing. "Bruno suggested I hire a bodyguard."

"He wasn't serious, was he?"

"I think it was his way of telling me to be careful." I took another bite and swallowed before chewing long enough. I turned my head away from my phone to cough.

"You okay?"

After a few sips of Coke, the coughing stopped, but my voice came out funny, like I had inhaled helium out of a balloon. I managed to say: "Yes. Just swallowed wrong."

"I could stay in your spare room for a while."

"You'd do that for me?" My voice had come down an octave but wasn't quite *my* voice yet.

"Of course. Or, you could stay at my place."

"Let me think about it." Both were good ideas, but how long could we do that?

"You could also upgrade the locks on your houseboat and on your windows."

"And get a gun, take shooting lessons, and wear disguises going to and from work."

"Now you're getting the idea."

"I'll think about it. But the reason I called is to see if you will go with me tomorrow to check out Delia's house. I don't feel comfortable going alone."

"Sounds like fun."

"Not how I would describe it. But it would be good to know you had my back."

"Always."

* * *

By comparison to my morning spent with Delia's family and lawyer, the rest of the day was as boring as vanilla ice cream without chocolate sauce...and sprinkles...and nuts. I fell asleep at one point, waking up when I heard

Emma drop some files in my inbox. They landed with a loud PLONK, like she had dropped them from about five feet in the air. I opened my eyes just in time to see the swish of her knee-length plaid skirt as she slipped out of my office. I didn't have to see her face to envision the look of disapproval for having caught me sleeping on the job.

How I missed not being able to lock my door. Maybe I should have a locksmith come and make a new key—after Emma left for the day, of course. Although, if as I suspected, she'd confiscated my original key on the sly, she would just do the same thing again. If only she hadn't seen the bottle of whiskey I used to keep in the bottom drawer of my filing cabinet. Maybe I could get a new key and wear it on a chain around my neck. On the other hand, Emma could hire a locksmith, too. It was a cold war in which both sides avoided any direct confrontation. I was probably wise not to do anything to upset the delicate balance. Even if it meant not having a door that I could lock against unexpected visitors and intrusions into my space.

Bruno and I met at what was once our favorite bar and pizza place. Unfortunately, it's changed hands after being a thriving business since the early 50s. The new place is a bit on the seedy side, but the pizza is good enough, and the red vinyl booths are comfortable—as long as you avoided the occasional torn or lumpy spots on the bench seats. I could understand the tears, but what on earth created the lumps?

I noticed Bruno was slowly and gingerly lowering himself onto the seat on his side. "Hemorrhoids bothering you again?" I asked.

He glanced around. "Don't say that so loud."

"It's nothing to be ashamed of."

"That's easy for someone who doesn't have them to say. Anyway, my doc is talking surgery, so I may not have the problem for much longer."

"Is your situation getting bad enough so that the surgery will be covered by your insurance?"

"Not quite, but getting close. It makes you wonder about the sadists who write these policies."

"You need a donut pillow that you can carry around. If you want to be secretive, get one you can inflate on demand by running a tube up the inside of your clothes. No one would know; anyone who saw would just think you were sucking on a straw."

"Not funny. Let's change the topic." He sounded more sad than mad. It isn't often that I get a chance to tease Bruno instead of the other way around, although at the same time, I felt bad that he was suffering. Bruno had saved *my* butt on more than one occasion when we were young. He'd been big and strong even then, acting as a buffer between me and the bullies who otherwise would have made my youth even more miserable than it was at times. I owed him.

"Okay, let's talk about *my* problem. Being in control of assets that fourteen people would like to get their hands on. Fourteen obnoxious, pushy people— one of whom may already have committed murder."

"I don't envy you that. Can't you refuse to accept her request? Turn it over to the lawyer?"

"I don't care for him actually. Kinda officious. A big fancy office with a view. And he has his meter running all the time so he can be sure he'll get paid for every minute of work."

"So? Lawyers have big egos and charge exorbitant fees for their services; that's no surprise. What difference does it make to you?"

"Delia could have appointed him as her executor, and didn't. She trusted me to do the right thing."

"Where's my tiny violin?"

"I know, I know. But I want to honor her request."

"I think you're being naïve, but I do understand."

"So, tell me about her murder."

"Well, you're still technically a suspect…although not anywhere near the top of the list at this point. So, I don't mind sharing some information with you, but you need to keep it under your hat."

I don't wear a hat, not even a cap, but I agreed to his terms with a nod anyway. I've always regretted that men no longer wear fedoras. I think I'd look good in one. Especially tipped forward, like a noir character from a detective novel. Cool.

He took a deep breath before delivering the punch line. "The first thing you need to know is that her death definitely wasn't an accident. There's evidence that suggests someone bashed her head against the concrete block *after* she fell and hit her head."

"Couldn't she have tried to get up and fallen down a second time?"

"Not impossible, but highly unlikely. Especially since her head hit in almost the exact same spot the second time."

"So, the theory is that the first injury didn't do the job, and the killer had to try again. Do you think they thought a second whap couldn't be detected?"

"That would be my guess. Criminals aren't the brightest bulbs. The goal was obviously to make it look like an accident. But they may have panicked when she didn't die from the fall. I doubt they turned on the lights to perfectly align the two wounds, probably couldn't have done that even if there had been a light on. And they couldn't have fooled the experts anyway."

"Why didn't *she* turn on the lights in the first place?"

"We think someone messed with them so they wouldn't come on when she tried."

"But they were working after her death?"

"Like I said, someone tried to make it look like an accident."

"I assume you've checked out the alibis for the family members."

"Most people are sleeping in the middle of the night. Even her brother, who was out of town, wasn't so far away that he couldn't have made it back in time to commit the murder and then return to his hotel. Although with his arthritis, he might not be the most likely suspect."

"He could have had help. As near as I can tell so far, there wasn't much love lost between Delia and the rest of her family. And based on how they've treated me, I think most of them are more than capable of violence."

"Name-calling and making threats can also be a way of letting off steam. It's a big leap to planning and executing the murder of someone you know."

"I thought most murders were committed by friends and relatives."

"That's true." He nodded. "And we still don't know why she went down to the greenhouse in the first place."

"No texts or messages from anyone asking to meet her? No handwritten notes? Nothing?"

"You got that—nothing."

"I hope you can turn *nothing* into *something* soon. I would hate to give money to a murderer."

"I'll do my best to make sure you don't."

* * *

In general, I felt safe enough on my houseboat. I have close neighbors, an inconvenient location for intruders, and a cat who doesn't like visitors. Also, apparently, there were cameras too. In the final analysis, it seemed like overkill to have Laney stay over or go to her place as a precaution. Still, having Brandon break in to look for who knew what had made me uneasy. As had the uncomfortable encounters with Delia's family members. Laney was right—it wouldn't hurt to install deadbolts on my front and back doors and replace the flip locks on my windows with something better. She'd learned a lot about that sort of thing when she was a full-time PI. I relied on her for that kind of knowledge. Although if someone wanted to get in, all they had to do was break a window.

Maybe I should find out how much it would cost to install a subscription home security service. Although, since I'm not good at remembering codes, I would probably pile up fines for accidentally calling in false alarms. I could get a gun instead. Then again, I would probably just shoot myself. Deadbolts and better window locks would have to do.

* * *

When I finally turned in for the night, I found that I couldn't sleep AGAIN. This whole situation was really getting to me. I went through the entire litany of tools suggested online for insomnia, finally getting desperate enough to try drinking a glass of warm milk. I hate drinking milk by itself under any circumstances, and warming it up made it as appealing as a pre-colonoscopy cocktail.

I slogged my way through the thriller to page 34 before setting it aside.

Nothing was working. At one point, I managed to doze off on the couch but woke up when I turned over and rolled off onto the floor.

By morning, after a sleepless night, I was exhausted. I got up earlier than usual—why not? Wild Thing seemed pleased to be fed early, but that was the only bright spot. Then, when I was on my third cup of coffee, he wanted more. After all, by then it was his "usual time" for breakfast. What the hell, I thought. Someone in the household deserved to be happy. I gave him a somewhat smaller version of his earlier breakfast, and he didn't complain about the portion. Afterwards, he wandered off to either exercise or take a nap.

Laney and I were meeting at Delia's house at 10:00, but by 8:00 I decided to run by the hardware store to pick up a couple of deadbolts and some better locks for my windows. I'm not handy with tools, but how hard could it be to install a few locks?

The woman who helped me at the hardware store also talked me into buying the tools she said I would need to put up deadbolts for my two doors and gave me some lengthy instructions for installation. Then she started telling me about all the different kinds of window locks there were, as well as the additional things one should do to effectively burglar-proof your windows. I could feel the energy draining from my body, thanked her for all her help, and made my escape. I would start with the deadbolts and worry about my windows later.

In spite of my hardware stop, I still arrived at Delia's early. I decided to take a look around outside the house and maybe check out the neighborhood. Surely I would be okay on my own for an hour.

Chapter Eight: The Neighbor

I'd looked up the house online and thought I had a pretty good idea what to expect based on satellite pictures, but I was surprised when I pulled up in front and saw the real thing. It was much larger than I'd realized. It was, in fact, huge, the kind of Victorian home built for wealthy families at the turn of the century, families with half a dozen children and live-in servants. With its large bay windows, wraparound porch, steep roof, and colorful gingerbread trim, the three-story structure made quite an impression.

There was even an octagonal tower with windows on each of its eight sides. It peeked up from behind the porch and the second-story windows, its pointed roof extending higher than the house's third story. The whole place was straight out of another era. I couldn't imagine one person living in a house this size.

According to the information in the materials given to me by Delia's lawyer, the estate used to include another twenty acres. Most of the surrounding land had been sold off, leaving the house on two standard city lots ringed with tall fir trees that had obviously been there for a long time. The land sales probably accounted for at least some of the money Delia had in her bank accounts.

As I studied the house from the safety of my car, I couldn't help but think about how much my mother would love the porch with its decorative railing spindles and ornate corner posts that ran all the way to the porch roof. She was wild about Victorian houses, and this one was classic. I could picture her sitting on the front porch in a lounge chair, surrounded by aromatic flowerbeds and the scent of fir trees, gazing at the view while drinking a glass of sherry. She didn't like sherry, but that seemed appropriate for the vision.

At the same time that I was admiring the intricate design features of the house, I couldn't help but think about how difficult it would be to paint everything. Rich people of that era had servants to do the work, but I wondered how Delia had managed to keep everything looking so good. It must have cost her a bundle.

I got out and walked over to look at the house to the left, and then to the one to the right. Both were smaller than Delia's, but still three-story super-sized. And although both appeared to need a lot of TLC, they were reminiscent of the formal elegance of a bygone era. Still, if I owned one of them, I would probably be looking to sell.

There was an older man standing in the front yard of the house to the right. He was studying a push lawn mower as if willing it to take on the tall grass in his front yard on its own. I wasn't sure even a John Deere riding mower could tame the overgrown mess. Maybe a blow torch made more sense. Although what do I know? I'm no expert on grass; the water around my houseboat takes care of itself.

With him standing there, I hesitated to walk up to his house without permission, so I called to him from the sidewalk: "Hey there." When he looked over at me, I waved. He didn't wave back. Nor was there any change in his facial expression. Nor did he say anything. He just stood there looking at me, looking at him. He was wearing a tattered pair of jeans and a denim work shirt. Like he'd really been seriously thinking about giving the mowing thing a try. I couldn't tell his age, but he was definitely a senior citizen. If I looked in his mailbox on the right day, I had no doubt I would find an AARP Magazine. And probably some ads for cremation. My mother says she gets those all the time.

"Hey," I yelled again. Not an imaginative opening line, but it was a start. I went up his sidewalk until I was close enough to talk in a normal voice. He still hadn't changed position or said anything, but he'd followed me with his eyes, his head moving imperceptibly to keep up with them.

58

"I hope you don't mind the intrusion, but I've been given the task of deciding what to do with your neighbor's house." I pointed toward Delia's. He took several steps in my direction, and one hand went to a device hanging from a chain around his neck. He pushed a button and said, "I had the dang thing off because I was going to mow. What'd you say?"

I wasn't sure if a hand mower made noise, but I now realized that he had hearing aids in both ears, and the device was probably a volume control. "I'm John Smith…" I said in a strong voice. He quickly reached down to adjust his volume. Now I didn't know what to do. Should I keep talking louder than usual or let him adjust one more time to a normal speaking voice level?

"Who did you say you were again?"

I compromised by talking a little louder than usual, but not as loud as my first blast. "I'm John Smith, Delia Flowers' executor." It was as if I'd flipped a switch; he immediately went from "couldn't care less about what you have to say" to "eager to engage." As he adjusted his volume one more time, I said, "Would you mind answering a few questions?"

"You really 'John Smith'? Or are you pulling my leg?" He frowned to let me know he didn't like to have his leg pulled.

I stepped off the sidewalk and handed him my card. His lips moved as he read it.

"That's a mouthful." He paused a moment, then added. "I like the part about a *company with a heart.* Though I doubt it's true." Before I could respond, he added, "And shouldn't that be *in*surance and not *as*surance?"

"*In*surance provides compensation for covered events, whereas *as*surance policies provide financial support. But the terms are often used interchangeably. And there is overlap in services provided by assurance and insurance companies." I could see he wasn't getting the distinction I was trying to make, and I really didn't want to get sidetracked by trying to explain something that wasn't totally clear in my own mind. So before we could get too bogged down in a philosophical discussion about company names, I said, "Do you mind if I ask if you're the neighbor who found…ah, Delia?" I hated to refer to her as "the body."

For a moment, I thought he wasn't going to let me change the topic, but thankfully, the esoteric *insurance* versus *assurance* topic wasn't nearly as interesting as one in which he was the star of the show. "Yeah," he said, straightening his shoulders and puffing out his chest a quarter of an inch. He had a narrow, flat chest that probably wasn't easily puffed. "I went over to complain about the smell and found her lying there. The smell, it was unbelievable. I half expected to find a pile of dead animals rotting in her back yard—"

"You called 911 right away?"

"Yes. Well, not immediately. I had to come home to make the call."

"Did you look around?"

"Hell, no. The smell was nauseating."

"That bad, huh?"

"Ain't smelled anything quite like it before."

"Well, I'm sorry you had to go through that." I paused. "Other than seeing her lying there, did you notice anything strange?"

"Like what?"

I wasn't sure what he might have seen that the police hadn't noticed, but it seemed like something I should ask. "Anything out of the ordinary."

"A body is out of the ordinary for me."

I stepped back to the sidewalk. "Well, thank you. I'll let you get back to your mowing."

"What's going to happen to her house?" he said.

"Not sure yet."

"Those two relatives that came by seemed to think *they* would be inheriting it."

"Oh?" That was interesting. "Did you catch their names?"

"No. They didn't say. He was a little shorter than her. She had kinda sharp features. Both were pretty intense. Wanted the name of the developer who wants to buy up the neighborhood."

From his description, my money was on Amanda and Brandon as the two who had asked about the developer. They seemed determined to get their share of Delia's estate one way or another. "All I can tell you is that nothing has been decided yet."

"Well, if you have anything to do with it, now's the time to sell. Before they decide to go elsewhere."

"You mean the developer?"

He pointed at Delia's house. "She was the only holdout. Everyone else has agreed to sell. Most of us are happy to sell. They've offered a lot more than we could possibly get on the open market. But they want all or none. And she refused. No concern for the rest of the neighborhood."

"Well, in fairness to her, the house has been in the family for several generations. And it looks well-maintained. It's probably worth quite a bit."

Suddenly, a dog came racing toward me, barking and snarling. It was a German Shepherd, a large German Shepherd with a mean face and even meaner disposition. It stopped about a foot away, lowered his head, neck hairs standing up, body rigid. Then he began circling while staring me down.

"Call off your dog," I begged.

"Not mine. Belongs to a neighbor."

"Nice dog," I said to the animal. "Nice doggy."

"He either likes you or he doesn't," the man said. "Looks like he doesn't in your case."

"What should I do?"

"Don't turn your back on him. Show him who's alpha."

"His teeth are bigger than mine."

The man actually laughed. "Here, Snooky," he said, holding out his hand. The German Shepherd glanced at him for a moment, then turned back toward me and bared his teeth. "Try backing away."

My knees were quivering as I slowly tried to get my feet to obey. The dog followed, step for step.

"Watch out for the steps," the man called.

I paused, explored the walkway behind me with the toe of my right shoe. One more step and I would have stumbled. "Thanks," I said. Before I could start the descent, I heard someone come up behind me.

"Hey," Laney said as she stepped past me. "Nice dog." The German Shepherd started wagging its tail and let Laney rub his head.

"That's Snooky," I said.

"Well, Snooky, you're a handsome beast, aren't you?" Snooky beamed love at Laney and glared at me as I quickly retreated down the steps.

Laney said goodbye to Snooky and waved at the neighbor. "What's the rush?" she asked as she caught up with me.

"That dog hates me."

"What did you do to him?"

"Why would you ask that?"

"He seems like a great dog. Very friendly."

"He hates me for no reason at all."

"He probably senses fear."

"Is that supposed to make me feel better?"

"It's an instinctual predator response to go after an animal that is afraid of them."

"Now you're calling me an animal?"

Laney grinned. "A real beast."

I was fairly certain she was teasing, but being referred to as a beast could imply that I was wild and dangerous. That wasn't all bad. But I wasn't an alpha.

When we reached Delia's house, we paused. "It's really somethin', isn't it?" I said.

"Definitely the jewel of the neighborhood. I can't wait to see inside."

We started up cement steps sandwiched between two brick pillars. The house was set back about a hundred feet, looming over us as we approached, majestic in size, almost otherworldly with its complicated roof lines and ornate trim. I could picture Delia's ghost zipping out of shadowy corners, fluttering from one of the windows in the tower. It wasn't a place I would have trick-or-treated as a kid.

"So, this is Delia's home," Laney said. "Wish I was in line to inherit it."

"Could you imagine living here by yourself?"

"No. But you could rent out rooms. Turn it into a B&B."

"Is that something on your bucket list? Run a B&B?"

Laney laughed. "No, I'd probably sell it and use some of the money to spend a year traveling the world."

"According to the neighbor, some developer wants to buy it. They're trying to buy a group of houses in the area."

"What for?"

"I didn't get a chance to ask. Snooky interrupted our discussion."

"Maybe you should carry pepper spray. The trick is to make certain you point it in the right direction."

I had a vision of spraying myself instead of an attacking dog. "Maybe." We walked up the brick steps to the porch, pausing to take in its incredible length and width. There was a wicker rocking chair and a matching table at the far end, next to a few small plants in colorful pots. But for the most part, it didn't look as though Delia had made use of the porch. It certainly wasn't set up for entertaining guests.

The vintage skeleton key to the front door was a work of art. I was a bit surprised that Delia hadn't updated the locks, but at the same time, although I'm not sentimental in that way, I could understand wanting to use the same key as generations before had done. It was a connection to the past, a symbol of lineage.

Holding the key in my hand reminded me of my own security issues. "By the way, I bought some deadbolts, but I have some questions about the window locks. Maybe we can talk about that later."

"Are you pausing for dramatic effect before opening the door?"

"Sorry." I slipped the key into the lock, turned it first this way, then that, finally finding the magic formula, and we stepped inside. It was like taking a step back in time. Geometric tiles in the entry gave way to an expanse of hardwood flooring. The hardwood planks were wider and longer than you see in today's houses. I wasn't sure what kind of wood it was, but it had probably darkened with age. Still, it appeared to be in perfect condition.

The first room we came to was what I assumed to be a formal living room. There was dark wood furniture with upholstered fabrics that reminded me of *Downton Abbey*. Spindly end tables holding complicated lamps with fringed lamp shades. Formal pictures of people in oval gilt frames alongside peaceful landscapes with moody skies. An ornate fireplace dominated one wall. A couch and two chairs with rolled arms and deep button tufting were clustered in front of the fireplace. On the wall across from the fireplace, there was a shelf near the top of the wood paneling lined with fancy plates and figurines.

"Would I hate to dust this room." Laney said. "Look at all those knick-knacks. And that crystal chandelier—imagine being the person assigned to cleaning it."

"That's what you see? How much work would it take to keep this place dust-free?"

"My working-class roots are showing, huh?"

"Well, my first thought was that, except for the furniture in front of the fireplace, everything looks uncomfortable or fragile."

"You worry about comfort, and I worry about cleaning. What a couple we'd make."

We wandered through the rest of the rooms on the ground floor. There was a modern kitchen and bathroom at the back and an "L"-shaped sunroom with glass sliding doors facing the greenhouse and side yard. The other rooms looked like stage sets for a period drama.

At one point, we thought we heard creaking coming from the second floor.

"Old houses make noises," Laney said. Then she whispered, "The ghosts of past residents. Maybe Delia is threatening to haunt you if you don't do a good job of distributing her wealth."

"Not funny."

"You've seen too many horror movies," she said.

The second floor had four bedrooms and a library. Only one bedroom appeared to be in use. "This must be Delia's," I said. There was a window that looked out over the back yard with a view of the greenhouse. "Maybe she saw someone out there and went out to check."

"I thought we agreed that was unlikely."

"I do think it's unlikely, but not impossible."

"I can't imagine sleeping in a bed with a canopy." Laney ran her fingers up and down one of the posts and looked at her fingers and laughed. "Dusty"

"You know what we haven't come across," I said. "A way into the tower. Did you see a downstairs entrance?"

"No, we'll have to take a second look." Laney opened a door. "Hey, it's a bathroom. This one hasn't been updated much. Check out his classy clawfoot tub." I went in and stood beside her, unimpressed with the tub. But I liked the view from the window. I stepped closer to get a better look.

"It's too bad the window is so small. It might be nice to look at trees while taking a bath," I said. I was envisioning dim lighting, a glass of wine, and a sexy blonde in the tub with me when the door slammed shut so loudly the sound reverberated throughout the house. Startled, I lurched to the side, banging my arm against the sink. "What was that?"

"One feisty ghost," Laney said, grinning. Then she got serious. "I don't remember seeing any windows open, although there's no wind anyway. Maybe we did hear someone…" She went over, twisted the doorknob, and pushed. It didn't open.

"Did it lock itself?" I asked.

She jiggled the knob. "I doubt it. There *is* a keyhole, though." She bent down and put her eye up against it. "Something's blocking the hole."

"Could someone lock us in without a key?"

"It's more likely that they've put something in front of the door."

"If there is someone in the house and they didn't want to get caught being here without permission, why not just leave?"

"Maybe they haven't found what they came for yet."

Chapter Nine: The Intruder

"I didn't tell anyone I was coming here, did you?" I asked Laney.

"No, but I don't think being locked in here is about us. Someone probably wants us out of the way."

"For how long?"

"Don't panic. We'll either find a way out, or we can call someone to come and let us out."

"I'm not panicking, but this is a pretty small space." I'm not normally claustrophobic, but I could imagine the walls closing in, manipulated by Delia's ghost.

"I'd rather find a way to get out on our own. It would be embarrassing to have to explain to someone what happened."

I pictured the smirk on Bruno's face if he knew we'd been trapped in a bathroom.

"Besides," she continued, "...at least we can bathe and take a leak."

As soon as she mentioned it, I had to pee. "Could you turn your back?"

"What? Can't you hold it for a while?"

"You're the one who said we could use the toilet."

"But I didn't mean right away. It was a joke." She shook her head. "Let's check the window."

The window opened with a loud squeak. I poked my head out and yelled, "Help." My voice seemed to lose itself among the trees, drifting off as a whisper.

Laney said, "Let me look." She nudged me aside and leaned out the window. "I think we can get down from here. The roof's rather steep, but there are some vines coming up near the corner."

"Great. You plan to swing down like some demented Tarzan?"

"No, I'm hoping for a trellis. They were popular at the turn of the century." She gave me a once-over. "Demented? That you are at times, but Tarzan?" She turned back to the window. "It will be a tight fit for one of us, but we can do it." She poked me in my paunch. "A few too many beers of late?"

I admit that I don't like exercise. Laney is athletic and has never met a vegetable she didn't like. Whereas I tend to shop in the ready-made meals frozen food section at the grocery and frequent drive-throughs and food trucks. On the other hand, Mother does make me the occasional healthy meal. Healthy by the standards of the 60s, that is. A bit heavy on the sauces and cheese, but very tasty.

"Let me look again." I leaned out, assessing not only the width of the window but where I would land if I managed to force myself through. "You think that roof is *rather steep*? More like a ski jump, I'd say. And I don't see anything to hold onto."

"We don't both have to go. Why don't I try it? I can either wave you on or come back through the house and see whether I can get you out from the inside."

"What if someone's still here?"

"I'm willing to take the chance."

I considered it, but only for a moment. "Okay, you go first. I'll follow." As much as I didn't want to leap from a window onto a roof with no visible way to get from there to the ground, I wasn't going to let Laney face an intruder on her own. Especially an intruder who had tricked us like this.

With the ease of a cat, Laney slipped out the window onto the roof. "I'll steady you," she said, turning back to the window. "Come on."

I tried to do it the way she did, climbing on top of the toilet seat next to the sink, sticking one leg out, twisting around, and pulling the second leg out while holding onto the sides of the window frame. In her case, the other leg seemed to follow naturally, like the two belonged together. But not mine. My legs acted like they didn't know each other. The first went out as planned, but the second resisted. I bent the leg still inside and tried to guide it over the sill to join the other leg, but it kept refusing, sending a sharp pain down my calf. Suddenly, I felt Laney's hand on my ankle. "Got you," she said.

The next thing I knew, I was standing on the roof with my feet bent at a forty-five-degree angle, and Laney was steadying me. When she let go, I took a deep breath and turned awkwardly to the side, sliding my feet around rather than lifting them. She was already making her way across to the corner of the roof. I waited until she waved me over, taking tiny steps, arms spread out for balance. "You can do this," I told myself. "You *have* to do this." I felt like a baby penguin walking on ice for the first time. Or what I imagined it was like for them.

When I reached Laney, I thought I'd won at least a Bronze Medal in the roof climbing event. Then I looked down and almost fell. I hate heights. "Steady," she said. "This will be easy. I was right—there's a trellis. The cross bars are level side to side, which is good. But I can't tell from here how far apart they are. There's too much foliage in the way. It feels sturdy, though. Made to order for climbing. Just don't get your foot caught in the Wisteria vines."

"What if the trellis won't hold me?"

"I think it will. But it isn't that far down. And there are thick bushes at the bottom to break a fall." She quickly added, "Not that you will fall. Just do what I do."

She made it look easy. Turn, kneel, put one foot over the edge, then the other. Slide down until your foot touches the first crossbar. Then take it one step at a time. She accomplished the entire descent in under a minute. I was equally as fast, although not as controlled. About halfway down, I missed my footing and failed to grab the trellis as I went into freefall, landing on my back in the bushes.

"You okay?" Laney sounded concerned.

Except for feeling like a beetle flipped on its back and unable to roll over to right myself, I seemed to be fine. My arms and legs felt functional at least. "I'm stuck. But I don't think I broke anything."

"Let me give you a hand," Laney said. She reached across me, grabbed my arm, and pulled. I can't say my performance was graceful, but I landed it on two feet without faltering. Another bronze medal.

After testing my limbs and ability to breathe, Laney and I crept along the side of the house and up the steps to the front porch. I pushed open the door, and we charged inside like two FBI agents on a raid. There was no one visible. We stood still, listening. "I think they're gone," I whispered. Laney nodded.

Before heading upstairs, we checked out the downstairs rooms, one at a time. We didn't yell "clear" like they do in the movies, and I admit to being relieved each time we didn't come face to face with an intruder. Nor did we find an entry into the tower, although we weren't actually looking for one.

There were three stories, so there was a lot of space to check. And not knowing who or how many might be lurking somewhere didn't leave me feeling all that confident. "I could call the police and report a break-in," I said softly as we crept up the stairs to the second floor. It was then I noticed that Laney was holding a pistol. I wasn't sure if that made me feel better or worse. I knew she owned a gun and was proficient in its use, but I hadn't realized she had one with her. Where had she been hiding it? Had she anticipated running into trouble? Did she bring it because I told her that Bruno mentioned I might need a bodyguard?

"Let's hold off on calling the police. I'll go first, you follow."

Although I didn't want to seem cowardly, in my mind, the person holding the gun should definitely go first, so I didn't argue.

We didn't find anyone on the second floor either, but we learned how we'd been trapped in the bathroom—there was a chair propped under the knob. I'd seen that done in movies, but I hadn't realized how well it would work in real life.

The third floor was also clear. That's where we finally found an entrance to the tower, but it was locked.

"Do you think there could be someone in there?" I asked.

"You mean like someone living in there, like Quasimodo in the bell tower? Or someone hiding in there now to stay out of sight until we leave?"

"Either."

"Okay, let me see what I can do." Laney extracted two metal picks from her pocket, crouched down, and started poking at the keyhole.

"You look like you're using chopsticks," I said.

"Some of us are pretty proficient with chopsticks," she said with a smirk. I've never been able to get a handle on using them. Except for shoveling takeout food with my mouth pressed next to the container. But why bother when a fork works better?

"What's usually in a tower like this?" I asked, keeping my voice low.

"It's coming back to me. I think they are called turrets in Victorian homes. They aren't like a full-sized tower and don't go all the way to the ground. They were originally built as lookouts and eventually became a standard part of the architectural design for a classic Victorian. So, it's probably a single room and could be used for just about anything."

"Maybe we'll find a woman inside with blonde braided hair long enough to climb up from the ground to her turret window," I said.

Laney giggled. "I'd like to see you shimmying up a braid."

"Okay, so I fell on the trellis."

"I don't love you for your athletic prowess."

"You love me?"

"As a forever friend, yes."

I was touched. "I'm not sure I know what a forever friend is."

"Can you picture us friends when we are old? Like in our 80s or 90s?"

"If we live that long, yes."

"That's *our* forever." She straightened up and said "Voila!" and turned the handle on the door, pulled it open a few inches, and stepped back. "You first." She said it loud enough for anyone inside to hear.

I wasn't sure I wanted to be first, but she had done her part by picking the lock. I reached for the door knob as Laney put a hand on mine and held a finger to her lips. We both stepped back, and she held up fingers to indicate a countdown. Three, two, one. She pulled back the door, and I held my breath for a moment before peeking around the door into the turret room.

"Empty," I said. "Except for some furniture."

We went in, me in the lead, still cautious, but not as concerned about

70

finding a transient resident. There were sheets over what looked like two chairs in the middle of the room. A curved bench ran past the three windows facing the back yard.

Laney went over and looked under the sheets to make sure there was no one hiding there. "Dusty, "she said with a small laugh.

"Great view."

"We can come back later and explore a little more, or maybe just sit and have a cup of coffee." She looked around. "This is a lovely space."

"It doesn't look like Delia spent any time here. But then, with so much space, why would she?"

Laney pulled the door shut after we exited. "I checked out Victorian house floor plans online last night," she said. "There might also be an attic and some sort of basement in this house."

We walked around the third floor, looking for access to an attic. Laney spotted it first.

"Hey, there's a pull-down stair." Before I could stop her, she reached up and yanked on the cord dangling from a metal ring in the ceiling. Then she scampered up the steps, pausing at the top to reach up to another cord. It was attached to a single light bulb that blinked on when she pulled on it.

"What do you see?" I asked.

"A lot of stuff. A LOT of stuff. Oh, there's a flashlight right here. I'm going in."

"Maybe you shouldn't," I said as I started up the ladder. "Maybe *we* shouldn't." Even if there wasn't anyone trying to hide in the attic, there could be rats or big spiders or all sorts of creepy crawly things up there. Next to heights, I dislike any critters that could be classified as creepy-crawly things.

By the time I climbed into the attic, Laney was already partway down an aisle between the towers of "stuff" she had mentioned. "There are no footprints in the dust," she said over her shoulder. "I wonder when Delia was last up here. Or anyone else, for that matter."

Looking around at the jumble of boxes and piles of discards from the past, I felt a bit overwhelmed. "I probably need to inventory the contents of the house, don't I? Otherwise, how would I know what to do with everything?"

Laney turned and headed back in my direction. "If the family keeps the house, they can figure that out. It's their ancestors' accumulation of memories and junk. Probably more junk than memories at this point. It's been several generations, after all."

"They would undoubtedly haggle over who gets what and how much each item is worth."

"Not your problem. All you have to come up with is a plan for distribution. It would be a huge job to go through the contents of this house, let alone the things stored up here. I did see a lot of antiques piled up back there. And think of all the artwork, knick-knacks, and antiques in the main rooms. You don't want to take responsibility for valuing everything."

"I could hire it done. We do that at Universal for insurance premium estimates. But, you're probably right. Depending on who gets the house. If I decide to sell it, someone will have to figure out what goes to family members and what is sold as part of the property."

"Even if they are a disagreeable lot, it wouldn't be right to sell family memorabilia without giving them a chance to look things over. If it comes to that, maybe you could let them take what they want and then sell the rest."

We climbed out of the attic and put the stairs back up.

"At least it seems like whoever was here took off after locking us in the bathroom," I said.

"The only place we haven't searched is the basement. If there is one. I don't remember seeing any way down, though. Did you?"

"No. Maybe there's an outside entrance. Like a place to store coal, that kind of thing."

"According to the plans I've looked at, a lot of Victorian homes had cellars for storing coal or food. We can check the perimeter for a cellar after we finish up inside."

"This time, if we think we hear a noise, let's not blame it on an aging house, okay?"

"The intruder could have been a burglar...or a family member who wanted a jump on picking up a few valuables in case you give everything to charity."

"My fear is giving everything to the wrong family members. I mean, what if one or more of them conspired to murder her? Delia wouldn't be happy if I gave part or all of her estate to someone responsible for her demise."

"Hopefully, we will learn who murdered her before you have to make any decisions. Meanwhile, given how little time we had to look around before getting locked in the bathroom, I doubt we'll be able to tell what, if anything, the intruder took."

"Maybe Delia's friend or one of the family members could tell if something was missing. Although I hate to have them poking around at this point."

"First, you need to secure the place. In case the intruder didn't get everything they wanted."

We went back to the second-floor bathroom where we'd been trapped by a chair. "I didn't think that really worked," I said.

"You need just the right chair and the right door knob." Laney glanced around. "I wonder where this chair came from?"

We checked out nearby rooms. There was a matching chair in the library.

"The person who did this had to know where to look for a chair that would do the job. We weren't in there long," I said.

"Definitely someone either very lucky or familiar with the house."

"I think I *will* get an appraiser in to give me an idea about the overall value of the house and its contents. Maybe they will spot something particularly valuable. Like those pictures on the wall there. Since I've been handling insurance claims for art, I've learned that sometimes the bland or the bizarre can be worth a lot."

Together we studied the paintings on the library wall, mostly landscapes in muted tones. Laney stopped at one featuring a barn and some houses covered with snow behind a barren tree with a few rocks piled in front of it. Not my cuppa.

"I think it's a Maxwell Parrish," Laney said. "Obviously not the original, but nicely presented."

"Huh?" I turned toward her and raised my eyebrows.

"I go to the occasional art show and museum. You should try it." She poked me in the ribs. I hoped she didn't make poking me a habit. Although it did seem friendly. "Maybe you would see something you'd like for your houseboat to replace that black velvet painting you have on the wall."

"You don't like my dogs playing poker painting?"

"It's tacky, John."

"There's a museum in New Mexico entirely devoted to paintings on black velvet. That's where the famous one of Elvis is."

"You're serious, aren't you?"

"Only a little. One of my poker buddies gave me the painting as a joke. It grows on you, though."

Laney brushed at her arms: "I hope not!"

"Maybe I should exchange it for one of these exciting landscapes."

"Okay, you win. I can't picture any of these in your houseboat, no matter how expensive or classic they are. But there are other nautical paintings that would look good there. Maybe Santa will give you one for Christmas."

"I don't have a fireplace."

"Santa can be creative." She shook her head. "Meanwhile..."

"Meanwhile, I have decisions to make. And considering the amount of stuff in this house, the bottom line is that I can't divvy everything up without knowing more about its value."

"Personally, I think you should give everyone an equal share of the whole and let them duke it out." Laney looked at me and rolled her eyes. "I know, you don't think that's what Delia would want. But you have to admit it would be amusing to watch."

Without warning, a loud metallic voice began blasting instructions. It sounded like it was coming from a surround system from the heavens: "Evacuate, EVACUATE."

Chapter Ten: Evacuation

Evacuate? Laney and I looked at each other for a moment, then simultaneously turned and ran down the stairs and raced for the front door. We didn't stop until we reached the steps to the sidewalk. Then we turned around and looked back at the house. Over the sound of our breathing, I could still hear a faint voice continuing to demand that we evacuate.

"I don't see any smoke," I said.

"Maybe it was a carbon monoxide detector."

"My first thought was a bomb," I confessed.

"That crossed my mind, too. A gas explosion, maybe. At any rate, it's the loudest alarm I've ever heard."

"Maybe it's made for the hard of hearing."

"Maybe Delia set it up to scare off intruders."

"The question is, what do we do now? Go inside to see what's happening?"

"That doesn't seem like a good idea to me. It could involve deadly fumes of some sort. And if it *is* a fire, we don't want the place to burn down. I think we should call 911."

The person who answered my 911 call advised us to stay away from the house; they would have someone there within five minutes. As soon as I made the call, the metallic voice commanding us to evacuate had fallen silent. There were no flames shooting out of the windows, no strange odors wafting from the open door, and not a single wisp of smoke to be seen anywhere. We paced back and forth on the sidewalk, second-guessing our decision to place an emergency call to 911.

As promised, five minutes later, a fire truck pulled up, lights flashing, a high-pitched siren blaring. It was followed by a second fire truck and two police cars. Neighbors were spilling out onto the sidewalks as if attracted by the possibility of witnessing a disaster. Dogs were barking. Everywhere there was noise and chaos...except inside Delia's house, where it was as silent as snow falling.

After we explained what had happened, several figures dressed in full hazmat outfits headed for the entrance. Outside, everyone waited, all eyes glued to the house. I still half expected it to blow up and wondered if that was the kind of spectacle some of the neighbors were hoping for. It would certainly resolve the issue about whether their houses could be sold to the developer who wanted to buy all or none of their properties. And between the insurance and what the land was worth by itself, the family—or some organizations—would still inherit a bundle. It would be incredibly sad, though, if the place were destroyed, given the lovely Victorian structure and the contents accumulated by generations of Flowers.

Unfortunately for the neighbors hoping for drama and an end to the controversy about whether Delia's house would be sold to the developer, the verdict was: "Defective alarm." I started apologizing for the unnecessary fuss to the first responders nearby, but one of the firemen interrupted me: "You did the right thing by calling us. You just never know."

Another said, "This was a good outcome, not a bad one."

A hazmat-suited individual took off her hood and came over to talk to us. She was a very attractive woman with long reddish-blonde hair. "We disconnected the alarm," she said. Still wearing most of the bulky white outfit, I couldn't tell if she had the kind of voluptuous body I lust after, but I was attracted to her full lips like a hummingbird to sugar water. Then Laney gave me a look that I sensed meant to "back off." I wasn't sure what that was all about, but I trust her instincts, so I kept my pheromones in check.

"What do you think caused it to go off?" Laney asked the hazmat woman. Laney's eyelashes quivered, on the verge of batting like butterfly wings in slow motion.

"It was hard-wired, so it wasn't a battery problem. Could be vent dust, moisture, electrical problems. Although it looks like someone may have messed with the wiring recently. You should have it checked out." The woman in the hazmat suit and Laney appeared to be exchanging silent messages—tiny eye movements signaling mutual attraction? Is that why she hinted that I should back off?

"Thanks for the prompt response," Laney said with a full-mouth smile, white teeth sparkling like a toothpaste ad.

"Any time," the hazmat woman replied, bouncing a big smile back at Laney.

After the trucks, cars, and neighbors disappeared, Laney and I went back inside. "I'm surprised you didn't invite her up to see your etchings," I said.

"That obvious, huh?"

"She was hot."

Laney sighed. "It didn't feel like the right time and place."

"We could set off another alarm…"

"Thanks, but no thanks."

We scanned the ceiling. There were wires dangling next to an alarm neither of us had noticed before. "Maybe I *should* have someone check out all the wiring. I wouldn't want the house to burn down on my watch."

"Maybe the person who was spooking around earlier tampered with it."

"Why would they do that?"

"Maybe to scare us off or create a distraction?" Laney didn't sound like she believed what she was suggesting.

"To what end? And why didn't it go off earlier?"

"You're right. It was probably just a coincidence, an actual coincidence. They do happen. This is an old house. And like the redhead said, it could have been caused by dust or moisture."

"Or, maybe it went off by accident sometime in the past, and that's why it looked like someone had messed with the wires. I've had that happen before."

"That's a possibility. We might be trying to make more out of this than it is."

"Okay, I'll call an appraiser *and* an electrician."

"I also think we need to consider how we're going to keep an eye on this place in case our intruder comes back."

Laney continued looking around while I made calls to set up times for an appraisal and for an electrician to come by. After that was done, I joined her in the library.

"Delia obviously used this antique roll top desk as a mini-office," Laney said. "There are financial records, her checkbook, miscellaneous paperwork, including insurance coverage. She must have spent considerable time here. The curious thing is what I found in the one locked drawer."

"You got into a locked drawer?"

"This is an old desk. The lock wasn't very sophisticated. And I didn't damage anything."

"What was in there?"

"A cigar box containing a few random receipts. That was all."

"Do the other drawers lock?"

"No, that was the only one."

"Strange."

"Yes, and I noticed one other strange thing," Laney said.

"Other than some of the weird knick-knacks?"

"Which weird knick-knacks?"

"That shelf of teensy sculptures over there: dragon heads, octopus, rabbits, people with pointed hats. Strange."

"Those are netsukes. Miniature hand-carved Japanese sculptures. Some of them could be quite valuable. Depends on their age, what they are carved from, and the intricacy of the carvings. Although I doubt that she would have left them out like that if they were worth a lot. Unless she simply wasn't worried about being burgled. But with a skeleton key lock on the front door and no security system—"

"Netsukes?" I said, hoping I was saying it right. "You into Japanese sculpture?"

Laney shrugged. "I read a novel about them once."

"What about that row of cutesy figurines on the top shelf?"

"Hummel. My grandmother collected them."

"And the boats in bottles on top of the bookshelves? And all the old books.

The room feels like a museum. Do you think Delia collected these things or inherited them?"

"Hard to say. Although my guess is that most of this was here when she moved in. Unless she was an avid collector who liked variety." She gestured for me to look around the room. "What I find odd is that there are no pictures of family members. Except for those two in the hall, which I assume, given their age, are formal family portraits, probably her mother and father. And another out there that looks even older, maybe her grandparents."

"I wonder if she was close to her parents or just left their pictures up out of inertia."

"Wait, I hadn't noticed this before." Laney pointed to a shelf next to the desk. "Here's a small photo propped against this candle. It looks like a school picture."

I stepped closer to get a better look. "That's Amanda's daughter. I think her name is Bethany."

"And here's a framed picture of a child. Looks to be about two, I'd guess."

"I think Bethany has a child. Maybe that's her."

"So, where are the pictures of the rest of Delia's great-nieces and nephews? Do any of the others have kids?"

We took a turn around the room, poking here and there, but we didn't find any other family photos.

"Let's take a closer look at the stuff in her desk," Laney said. She pulled out a ledger and started thumbing through it while I examined her checkbook and some of the receipts kept in the cigar box from the locked drawer.

"This cigar box is cool," I said. "It's part wood and says 'Charles Thomson. Five cents.'"

"That makes it pretty old—five cents for a cigar." Laney turned another page in the ledger she was browsing. "For a wealthy woman, she didn't seem to spend much on pleasure. No theater tickets listed, no spa time, no cruises. At least not that she has noted in her accounts. Find anything interesting in her checkbook or receipt box?"

"There are only blank checks in her checkbook, no transaction register."

"Maybe we'll come across bank records someplace. Her ledger seems to only track larger purchases and payments."

"Well, she did travel a little. There are a couple of receipts for a hotel in Vancouver, BC. And a few from Vancouver restaurants. Not that many. One from a pharmacy for Tylenol and some prescription pills. And another that could be from a clinic or hospital."

"Maybe she got sick in Vancouver."

"I wonder if she was visiting someone there."

"Too bad she didn't keep a diary."

"Maybe she did, and we just haven't found it yet."

"Well, given what we've found so far, it doesn't seem like she was exactly extravagant."

"All the more to leave to her loving family."

After we gave up on the library, we checked out her bedroom. I felt uncomfortable looking through her bureau drawers and the dark wood armoire that stood on curved legs in the middle of the wall opposite her canopy bed. The armoire had ornate carvings of flowers on both doors and a row of tiny sculpted vines followed its curved top. While I stood there staring at the woodwork, Laney was in her element, not hesitating to plow through drawers of underwear and assorted clothes or fingering the garments in the free-standing closet. "She has a collection of vintage clothes," she said. "Some great items."

"Have you come across the mink heads yet?"

"Yes, they're on a hook beside the armoire. Handsome piece."

"Ugly." I couldn't help but shudder.

"Well, I wouldn't want to wear them, but it's a classic stole."

I started feeling antsy. There was just too much to look at, and I didn't see how it was helping me make my decision. Nor were we learning anything about Delia's death. "We could spend days going through the things in this house," I said. "Let's do one last run through the first floor and then take a look at the back yard and the greenhouse, okay?"

"Okay." She held up a key ring with several odd-shaped keys on it. "Not sure what these are all for, but this small one looks like it might be to that desk drawer in the library. Wish I'd seen these earlier. They were in the top drawer of her bureau under some lovely silk scarves. Did the lawyer say anything about a safety deposit box or a safe?"

"No, nothing."

"Let's keep our eyes open."

Before heading downstairs, we stopped off at the library to see whether the smallest of the three keys fit the desk drawer where we'd found the receipt box. It did. "Maybe she liked it because it's a cool antique key," I said. "Like the cigar box. Collecting things seems to have run in the family." We glanced around one last time in case there was another box or drawer to unlock with the keys we'd found. But we didn't find anything.

The kitchen was so unlike the rest of the house that it was jarring to step from the old-fashioned hall into its modern ambience, like walking into a stage set on a movie lot. "She may have been a miser, but she spent a bundle on this remodel," I said.

There were floor-to-ceiling cupboards, more drawers than I'd ever seen outside of a big box kitchen display area, and all sizes of containers and appliances for this and that lined up on a vast expanse of countertop. It looked like a kitchen designed for someone who liked to host large parties instead of meals for a party of one. The thought of searching such a big and complicated space was a showstopper for me.

"Remind me what we're looking for again," I said.

"Anything of interest."

"That covers a lot." I opened the refrigerator and looked in the freezer compartment. "No ice cream," I noted.

"A woman of few pleasures."

"This should probably be cleaned out."

"Now you're the maid, too?"

"I could hire someone to come in."

"You're pretty free with someone else's money."

"Well, when five million dollars slips through your fingers, you tend to cling to what might have been."

"You're right," Laney said, looking around. "There's too much here to search without knowing what we are looking for. Let's go outside and see what's there. We can come back to this if we feel a need."

"That sounds good to me. I could use some fresh air."

We went out the front, pausing on the porch to take in the view. "It's really a lovely location," Laney said. "And a lovely house. It would be a shame to tear it down." She glanced around. "And if the house goes, then all of those big trees would go too. Sad."

"I'm not sure the neighbors appreciate the view or the trees. Not if they're itching to sell. Of course, it's largely a question of economics."

"Hey, I have an idea. As long as we have their attention, why don't we check out the neighborhood and maybe chat with a few neighbors. It's good timing. They're probably dying to know why all the firetrucks and police were here."

Chapter Eleven: The Neighborhood

"Which way do you want to go first?" Laney asked, looking from left to right as we reached the sidewalk in front of Delia's house. I pointed to the right, away from the house where I was attacked by Snooky, the German Shepherd. Although I was probably safe with Laney at my side. Why did dogs and cats hate me lately? Was it my aftershave lotion? Not too long ago, I switched from something I'd worn for years because of a comment Emma made. Instead of the "bold, masculine fragrance" it was advertised as having, Emma said it smelled like something you found under a pile of wet leaves. Not very diplomatic of her, but it made me rethink whether that was the reason I didn't have women chasing after me. I'd read that scent plays an important role in attraction between the sexes. So I switched to "musk," supposedly a "rich, alluring scent" with "sensual undertones." When I asked Emma what she thought, she wrinkled her nose and shook her head. She finally gave "sandalwood" two thumbs up. Since Emma's a little older than the women I want to attract, I'm saving the musk for a special occasion.

The first house we came to was, as I'd noted earlier, a poor relation to Delia's. Although not a lot smaller, it lacked the decorative design touches that made Delia's house attractive. It was vanilla to Delia's spumoni. The front yard was also vanilla, mostly grass, but at least the grass was mowed. There was a small porch to get out of the rain when entering, but no comfortable place to sit and watch the world go by.

As we got closer, I could see how much the house desperately needed paint, and the railing for the steps had some rot in it. The cap rail was cracked and sunken at the ends. I knocked on the door. We heard movement inside, but were just about to give up when the door opened a few inches and a wedge of wrinkled face peeked out at us. "Can I help you?"

My mother always corrects me when I use "can"—a word suggesting capability—instead of "may"—which asks permission. Although in this instance, perhaps "can" *was* the better word.

"We're handling the estate of your neighbor, Delia Flowers," Laney said. "We have a couple of questions if you have a few minutes."

The door came open until we could see her entire face, but she didn't invite us in. As an elderly woman confronted by two strangers, I'm not sure I would have either. I was tempted to praise her for her caution, but then, we didn't want her to close the door on us.

"I didn't really know her." She looked fragile, but her voice was strong. Suddenly, a cat peered up at us from the space between her leg and the doorframe. Laney immediately knelt and reached out to pet the cat.

"Hello, there," she said. "Aren't you a pretty kitty." She looked up at the woman. "What's her name?"

"Priscilla."

"Priscilla," Laney said, continuing to make over the animal. It was a very average-looking brown cat, the kind I've heard referred to as a "tiger," even though they are the wrong color for a real tiger and totally lack the majestic demeanor of their namesake.

"She's *prissy*," the woman explained. "About her food, her bed, her toys—everything."

Laney stood up. "Well, she's lovely."

The woman smiled at the compliment.

"So, you didn't talk much with Delia Flowers?" Laney asked.

"No, she wasn't what you'd call a friendly person." She pressed her lips together in a scowl. "Not friendly and not particularly nice either."

"Oh?"

"I don't let Prissy out much, but on a couple of occasions when I did, she went next door, and that woman screamed and chased her away. One time with a shovel." She leaned down and picked up her cat. "Poor Prissy."

"I understand that most of the neighbors are hoping to sell their houses to a developer, but that Delia Flowers was against it."

"We had a neighborhood meeting at the local school. The developer explained the situation and gave each of us an envelope that contained information about the project and what they were willing to pay for our houses. Then we voted. Mrs. Flowers and a few others weren't there; we didn't learn until later that she was the sole dissenting vote."

"Did anyone try to get her to change her mind?"

"Yes, several neighbors got together and went to see her. But it didn't do any good."

"Can you give us their names? We'd like to talk to them."

She gave us their names and I wrote them down: Graham Denton, May Greely, and Terry Winslow.

"They weren't the ones who painted the graffiti on her sidewalk, though. Pretty sure that was kids."

"Someone painted graffiti on her sidewalk?" I asked.

"Tempers were pretty hot after she refused to cooperate."

"Anything else like that happen?"

"Someone knocked down her mailbox. And there were rumors about dead squirrels left on her porch, but I can't confirm that."

We thanked her and were about to leave when she asked: "What's going to happen to the house now that she's dead?"

"That's what we're trying to decide."

As we reached the sidewalk, Laney said, "Well, that was interesting. I wonder how much of that sort of thing went on and if she reported it to the police?"

"I'll see what Bruno knows." I punched in his number while Laney got out the plat map she'd printed and started looking for the lot numbers associated with the names of the three neighbors who had talked to Delia about selling her house.

Bruno answered on the first ring. "You do know it's Saturday?" he said.

"How do you know this isn't a friend call?"

"Let's say that I have a feeling."

"Well, your feeling is right, but I just have a short question—did Delia Flowers report any vandalism or kids leaving dead animals on her porch, that sort of thing?"

"I take it someone told you these things happened."

"Yeah, we were wondering if you knew anything about it."

"We? You and Laney?" Bruno knew that Laney and I had worked together on another case not long ago. In addition to being friends, our styles complement each other. Like Sherlock and Watson. Or Calvin and Hobbs.

"Yes, we've been checking out Delia's house and talking to some of the neighbors. Oh, and an alarm in the house went off earlier, and I had to call 911." I left out the part about getting locked in the bathroom, falling off the trellis, and being attacked by a German Shepherd. It had been a busy day.

"Everything okay?"

"Yeah, it was most likely a faulty alarm."

"So, no one was hurt and nothing was damaged?"

"No."

"Okay, I'll do it."

"Do what?" I hadn't asked for anything yet.

"I'll see if she made any kind of a report about vandalism, and if so, what they found out."

He'd read my mind. "Thanks, Bruno. I knew I could count on you."

"You buy next time we have pizza."

Laney had circled the plat map lot numbers of the three people we wanted to talk with. Graham was the neighbor next to Delia's on the other side, the one I had already talked to. May and Terry were a few houses down from him.

"Want to do a circuit of the block or go back now and talk to May and Terry about their interaction with Delia?"

"We can drive around the neighborhood later if we decide we want to see more of it. I say we visit May and Terry, if either of them is home."

We walked past Graham's. The lawn mower was where it had been before. The grass was still standing tall. Maybe Graham was taking a bathroom break, a long bathroom break.

May and her husband lived two houses down from Graham in what appeared to be a well-kept, although much smaller, house than the others on the block. A woman peeked out from behind a curtained window when we knocked, then said "Yes?" through the door without opening it. Laney said loudly, "We're handling the Flowers' estate and have a few questions."

We waited while the woman made up her mind. Finally, the door opened with the chain door guard stretched across the space between the door and the door jamb. "Do you have any identification?" It wasn't a very trusting neighborhood so far. I took out my card and handed it to her through the narrow space.

"Is this about insurance?" She sounded puzzled.

"No, I work for an insurance company, but I'm the executor for Delia Flowers' estate. I'm trying to find out more about the development project and why she didn't want to sell her property before making a recommendation."

A car drove into the driveway, and a man got out and headed toward us. The woman inside took the chain off and opened the door. "I'm May, and this is my husband." Laney and I shook hands with him, and he slipped past us and positioned himself next to his wife as if it was them against us. She whispered something to him that I couldn't make out, then turned to us and said, "What do you want to know?"

"I understand that you, Graham Denton, and Terry Winslow talked with Delia Flowers about selling her house to the developer, but you didn't manage to convince her to go along with the neighborhood vote to sell. Is that correct?"

"Yes, but your description of the conversation doesn't capture what our very brief encounter with her was like." Her eyes flashed self-righteous anger.

"Bad, huh?" Laney said. "We understand she was pretty adamant about not selling."

"Adamant? That's not how I would describe her response. Rude and high-handed is more like it. Arrogant. Unreasonable." Her husband put his hand on her arm. "Sorry," she said. "I get mad every time I think about it. She wouldn't listen to our concerns, wouldn't even consider what it meant to the neighborhood to get good prices for these deteriorating houses. She didn't care one whit that she was the only one who voted not to sell."

"Her house is rather nice," I said. "And it's been in the family for generations."

"But she lived there all alone. In that huge place."

May's husband jumped in. "It was a bad situation. She knew that the developer said it was all or nothing; he needs the whole neighborhood to meet the space demands for his project. And she wouldn't even talk about it. Just said it was our problem, not hers."

"We tried to get her to see it from our perspective," May said. "It's an aging neighborhood, both in terms of the houses and its residents. If she had been willing to talk to us, maybe we could have come to an agreement."

"It's too bad the developer wasn't more flexible," Laney said.

"There's a ravine to the west, and new housing to the south. There's also a strip mall and a park to consider. Unfortunately, he needed her house included in the deal for his plan to work," May's husband explained.

"She didn't say *why* she didn't want to sell, just that she refused to do so. The exchange did not begin or end well."

"One other question—we understand that there was some vandalism by neighbors or neighborhood kids. Was that before or after you talked with her?"

May nodded. "There was always some tension between the kids in the neighborhood and Delia, but it got worse after it became clear she wouldn't cooperate. Someone even smashed one of her greenhouse windows with a rock or a brick or something like that. That really ticked her off."

"Did the police find out who did it?"

"I don't know if she reported it. But no one in the neighborhood took responsibility. Even though they would have been applauded." May shook her head. "Sorry, that's a bit harsh under the circumstances." Then she asked, "What's going to happen to the house now that she's, ah, gone."

"We don't know yet, there's a lot to do before making a final decision." We thanked them and headed to Terry Winslow's.

"I have two observations," Laney said on the way. "First, this is not the friendliest neighborhood I've ever been in. Second, Delia seems to have been as popular with her neighbors as she was with her family. What a gal."

"Even so, I'm not sure it was fair of her neighbors to try to bully her into selling. And graffiti on a sidewalk is one thing, but destroying property is going a bit too far in my opinion."

"Sidewalks are property."

"True."

Where do you stand on the dead animals on the porch approach?"

"She could make another stole."

"Seriously?!"

"Okay, it depends on how the squirrels died. If it was by natural causes..." I paused. "Why don't we ever see squirrel corpses around?"

"Maybe you aren't looking in the right places."

"This time I *am* serious. Where do dead squirrels go?"

"Oh, oh. That's an opening—"

"Before you say something about small animals being raptured or that their bodies are instantly reincarnated..."

"How about they are eaten by owls or eagles, or people make squirrel stew out of them?"

"I still think there should be the occasional dead squirrel sighting."

As we walked a little further down the street, we passed even more large old houses in need of repairs, yards overtaken by tall grass and weeds. That wasn't true of Terry Winslow's, though. His white house with red trim was immaculate, the lawn mowed and edged, and flower beds ready for the spring planting. There were two children in the front yard playing on a swing hung from a limb on a large, nicely shaped tree. They paid us no attention as we went up to the front door and pushed the doorbell. Chimes echoed from inside. They reminded me of church altar bells. A young woman opened the door and said, "*May* I help you?" My mother would have been proud.

"We would like to speak with Terry if he's home," I said. "I'm the executor of Delia Flowers' estate and want to talk with him about the meeting the neighbors had with her regarding the proposed development project."

"Your home is lovely, by the way," Laney said.

"Thank you. It belonged to my parents. Just a minute, I'll get Terry."

While she was gone, I peeked inside. "This is nice. I'm surprised they would vote to sell."

"Well, there must have been a lot of pressure on all of the homeowners from those who definitely wanted to sell."

Terry came to the door with his wife. "Please come in," he said. "I understand you're the executor for Delia's estate."

We were ushered into a large living room. On the way, Terry picked up a few toys and tossed them aside. "The kids don't pick up after themselves," he said with a smile. He bent down again and grabbed a chewed rawhide bone. "Nor does the dog, obviously."

After we were all seated in some very comfortable chairs in front of an old stone fireplace with a wood mantle, I asked about the meeting with Delia.

"It was, ah, unpleasant. She kept us standing on her porch while we tried to ascertain if there was any hope of talking her into going along with the rest of the neighborhood. We might as well have saved our breath. Not only wasn't she interested, she berated us for even asking."

"She was a disagreeable woman," his wife said. "I made the mistake of taking our children to her house on Halloween last year. Her porch light was on, so I assumed it was okay. She answered the door, took one look, said she didn't believe in pagan holidays, and told us to get off her porch. Our little girl was terrified. Thought she was a witch and won't walk past her house anymore."

"Some of the teenagers egged her house the night after Halloween," Terry said.

"She was always complaining about tricks the kids in the neighborhood played on her," his wife said.

"Like what?" I asked.

"Well, after she yelled at them for sneaking into her yard to pick a few apples off her tree—she let most of them rot on the ground—they put a dead rat in her mailbox."

"We're not saying they should have done that," Terry quickly added. "But she was always yelling at the kids about something. Like when one of the girls down the street tried to sell her Girl Scout Cookies. She told her in no uncertain terms that her teeth were going to rot from all the sugar and slammed the door in her face. That was typical behavior for Delia."

"We understand that after the group talked with her, there was some vandalism to her property. Any idea who did it?"

"We didn't ask because we didn't want to know. Sorry."

I looked around the room. "This is such a nice home, why would you want to sell it?"

"It's too big, even for us. Too much to clean and take care of," Terry's wife said. "It was my grandmother's. She left it to me when she died."

"And, who wants to be *that neighbor*?" Terry said. "I mean, most of these older, oversized houses are rundown and difficult to sell. No one wants them. And prospective buyers consider the entire neighborhood when looking for a house. Even though we've maintained ours, our property value is impacted by what happens around us. We felt like the offer from the developer was a good opportunity that might not come along again."

＊ ＊ ＊

As we headed back to Delia's, I said. "I don't think we need to talk to Graham again, do you?"

"No, I think we have a pretty good idea about how the neighbors and the neighborhood kids felt about her. It sounds as though a lot of people might have wished her ill. But that doesn't mean they killed her or even that they thought killing her would get them what they wanted. Unless they were convinced that whoever inherited her estate would sell the house to the developer."

"I hate to admit it, but I'm afraid I'm rooting for the murderer to be a family member, not a neighbor. It sounds like she was pretty mean to them. Definitely not neighborly."

"I'm rooting for it to be the developer. I don't like developers on principle."

"You can't stop progress."

Laney opened her mouth and pretended to put a finger down her throat.

"Hey, I believe in the need for good urban planning and the preservation of trees. But I think this neighborhood is doomed by the size of today's families, not having servants, and just the cost of remodeling and maintenance. You agree, don't you?"

"I also believe in the right of the individual to own property, no matter how mean or nasty they might be."

Suddenly, a large furry monster leaped out from behind a tree and came charging in our direction. I started to hyperventilate. It was Snooky!

Chapter Twelve: Venus Fly Traps

Laney intercepted the dog moments before I started to run away. "Snooky," she cried. "Good dog." Snooky immediately hunkered down and put his head out for an ear rub, and Laney knelt down and obliged. "Come over here," Laney said to me. "Make friends."

I was cowering behind her, afraid to show myself. Maybe she was right; I needed to let Snooky know that I wasn't afraid. If Wild Thing could stand up to a German Shepherd, I should be able to. I bent over and started to reach for Snooky's ears, but his head jerked up and he snarled. One look at those incisors backed up by pointy canine teeth, and I backed away.

"He knows you're afraid."

"Well, he's right about that."

Laney gave Snooky's ears one last rub and stood up. "We'll have to work on this, John."

"Maybe later. Not now. Not with *this* dog."

As we walked away, I couldn't help but look over my shoulder. Each time I did I saw Snooky watching, baring his teeth to let me know that *someday*— I sincerely hoped that Creedence Clearwater Revival was right and that "someday will never come." At least for me and Snooky.

When we got back to Delia's, we decided to do a perimeter check before exploring the greenhouse. We started to the left. It was a beautiful, well-tended yard. Although I can't tell one plant from another, I had no doubt that at some point the garden beds would be a blaze of color. Like an English garden on the cover of a British cozy mystery novel. Delia obviously liked plants more than people.

"Hey, there's the apple tree the kids got caught trying to steal from. It's an old one. Wonder what kind of apples it produces?" Laney said.

"I think there was a picture in one of the hallways that showed an orchard on the original estate property."

"At one time, this was quite the place. Still is, actually. I like the perimeter of trees. Lots of privacy."

"Privacy for murdering someone?"

"I was thinking of a hot tub, but you're right. You can't see the greenhouse from the street, so unless you knew it was there, you wouldn't come up with a plan to murder someone in it. Obviously, the family knew about it. And probably the developer did. He would have checked out the property in order to make an offer. But I wonder how many of the neighbors knew it was there?"

"The kids certainly did. And whoever broke the window in it."

Not too far beyond the apple tree, there was a cedar garden shed. We estimated it was about 8 x 6, not particularly big, but very attractive. It had a vertical cedar door with a fancy black door handle and one window with a window box for flowers underneath it. There was a bird feeder hanging from a black hook on the corner.

"You don't suppose…?" I said.

Laney got out the key ring and tried the smaller of the two unidentified keys. Then, even though it didn't look like a fit, she tried the larger one. "No, neither works." She reached out, grabbed the door handle, turned it, and said, "Too easy. It isn't locked."

Everything inside was neatly categorized and organized. There were garden tools, a weed wacker, a pile of patio pavers, a couple of buckets, a coiled hose, grass seed, and an array of supplies for fertilizing plants as well as for controlling weeds and eliminating every kind of insect pest you could possibly imagine.

"It looks like this is all yard stuff," Laney said.

"No lawn mower though."

"She probably hired someone to do that as well as the pruning and trimming, that sort of thing."

After giving the shed a cursory search, we continued our perimeter review. It was on the tip of my tongue to say that I didn't see any sign of a basement, not even an opening for a crawl space, when Laney said, "Look over there. I think I see something behind those bushes."

She was right—there was a boarded-up space in the foundation. "It doesn't look like much of an entry, does it?"

"They could have filled in the space where the steps went down into the cellar when they decided to board up the entrance."

"You think the cellar is still there, only blocked off from the outside?" I stood back and looked at the house. "Isn't this below the kitchen? I wonder if you could get into it from the house before the remodeling was done."

"Maybe there's still a way in," Laney said with a glint of the explorer in her eyes.

"You read too many Nancy Drew books as a kid."

"I love hidden rooms and secret tunnels. Don't you?"

"Okay, let's look for a way in from the inside. If we don't find anything, we can get these boards removed and take a look."

"That's not part of your job description." Laney grinned. "Come on, admit it, John. You love the idea of a secret room as much as I do."

Of course I did. I'd read the Hardy Boys and could still remember the thrill when Frank and Joe discovered a secret room in a mansion in one of the books. Still, I hesitated to admit to childhood fantasies that persisted into adulthood.

We hurried back inside and started tapping walls in the updated kitchen, searching for breaks in the plasterboard as well as scrapes on the floor produced by the opening and closing of hidden panels. I felt silly, but it was fun looking for something that probably wasn't there but *could* be.

"This is odd," Laney said. "Check out the inside of the pantry—it looks original. Even the shelving. Not even the paint matches the rest of the remodel." She started moving things around, examining the back wall.

"Hey, look over here," I said, pointing at some faint scratches in the wood floor. "Is it possible there really is a secret panel that hides an entrance to the cellar?"

"Oh ye of little faith. I'll make you a Nancy Drew convert yet."

It didn't take long to find it. To be honest, I must have brushed up against something inadvertently that made one side shelf move towards me, almost knocking me over. "Hey, very good," Laney said. I accepted the compliment without revealing what I'd done because I didn't know what I'd done. If asked to do it again, I might be forced to admit it had been a lucky accident. But for the time being, I was willing to accept credit for the discovery.

Behind the shelving was a door with an ornate old-fashioned keyhole. "You don't suppose...?" I asked for the second time. Laney whipped out the keys from the bureau and, sure enough, the smaller old-fashioned-looking key opened the door.

"Why would she keep a key to the cellar in her bureau under some silk scarves?"

"Maybe the third key is to her wine cellar."

"Dream on."

Peering inside, we saw a flight of stairs leading down into a dark abyss. "You stay here," Laney said. "I don't want to get trapped a second time." Using the flashlight on her phone, she started down, her figure a quavery silhouette on the wall. I watched until she disappeared around a corner.

Waiting impatiently at the top of the steps, I worried that I should have gone with her. I agreed that one of us needed to guard the entrance, although what if the person who had been creeping around earlier was hiding down there and ambushed her? Would I be able to hear if she called for help? Why hadn't we decided how long I should wait before I went down to see what was happening? Would she have cell service down there? Should I call to make sure or wait a few minutes before panicking? It was too late—I was already panicking. But that didn't mean I would leave my post. I could panic in place.

I leaned forward as if I would hear better if I got a few inches closer. No sounds were coming from below. Nothing. No thuds or other indications of a struggle taking place. No scrabble of tiny rat feet. No gunshots. Just heavy silence weighted down by my anxiety.

When I finally heard her returning and saw the flickering light from her cell, I literally did a little happy dance.

She looked up at me and said, "Hey, what's that all about—you get a bug down your shirt?"

"Just glad to see you."

"I've only been gone a few minutes. And we were right, it's a root cellar. The entrance from the outside is boarded up, all the way to the floor. It looks like the opening was at one time big enough for normal steps leading to the yard outside. They probably filled that in when they quit using the cellar."

"What's down there?"

"Not much. A few jars on a shelf, some boxes. No coal; fairly clean overall. But a good place to hide a body."

"The murderer could have arranged for her to have an accident on the cellar stairs instead of in the greenhouse. If they had done it that way, it might have been some time before her body was discovered."

"I can think of two reasons why the cellar wasn't the locale of choice," Laney said. "First, they may not have known about the secret passage. Second, if they did know about it, they may have thought the body would be too well hidden there. Settling the estate without proof of death could have taken a while."

"So, if the killer was hoping for an inheritance, wanted to buy the land for a development project, or wanted to eliminate the remaining holdout for the sale of houses to the developer…"

"Precisely."

"Even so, although I assume family members knew the cellar existed in the original house, I wonder if they were aware that the remodel left the cellar intact?"

"It's the kind of thing kids love. I bet Delia and her siblings played there when they were young. And there may have still been access to it for the next generation."

"Turrets, cellars, an apple tree. It's too bad they weren't a close family. It would have been a great place for a kid to play."

As we pushed the shelving back in place, I saw the button I must have pressed to trigger the hinge mechanism. Not as sneaky as pulling out a book like you see in the movies, but just as effective.

"It feels like there should be answers down there," Laney said.

"To what questions?"

"You're right. This whole house and family situation seems whacko. But to what end?"

"I agree. Let's check out the greenhouse. See what whacko thing we find there."

"Lead the way, Sherlock."

This time we went out through the sliding doors in the sunroom, the shortest route to the greenhouse. We were surprised to see that there was a break in the trees between Delia's and Graham's houses. Delia's lot was higher, so the space between the two houses was on a slope. But Graham definitely had easy access to her greenhouse. On the other hand, the row of trees in back and around the other side were encased in bushes, making access through them difficult.

"Someone could have sneaked along the edge of Graham's property and come up this way," I said.

"But they would have had to know about this opening."

"True. I wonder if Graham ever hosted neighborhood parties in his back yard."

"Do we know if there is a Mrs. Graham? I didn't see her name listed on the property ownership chart."

"She may not be an owner, but that doesn't mean she doesn't exist. Although so far she's been invisible."

"Aha," Laney said. "The least likely suspect—the invisible wife."

We studied the greenhouse from the outside before going in. It was about 20 x 30, placed far enough away from the tree line to get some sunshine. In spite of its size, unless you were peering through the gap in the trees from the neighbor's yard, there was no way a passerby would know it was there.

"It would be nice if we could narrow the suspect list by figuring out who knew about the greenhouse," I said.

"Even if they never came physically on the property, they could have spotted it by looking at satellite footage. Or they could have used a drone to scope out her back yard. There is no such thing as total privacy these days."

"A neighbor could even have wandered into her back yard chasing after a lost dog or cat and seen it."

Laney reached into her purse and took out a tin of mints. "Here, have one."

"No thanks."

"Seriously, it will help mask the smell."

"I don't have bad breath...do I?"

Laney gave me a snort laugh, her way of letting me know I had said something she found amusing. "The senses of taste and smell are related, so sucking on a mint should help minimize reactions to the lingering bad aroma inside."

"Oh, thanks." I quickly accepted a mint and popped it in my mouth.

Entering the greenhouse was like walking into another world. A world of jungle-like greenery. Benches ran along both sides and across the back. There were plants of all sizes and shapes in pots nestled together on the benches. I can't tell one plant from another except by size and color, but the pink flowers in the pots near the entrance were nice. I almost forgot for a moment that I shouldn't be sniffing the flowers.

"Phew," I said. "Hand me another mint. Make that a fistful."

"Nasty."

Bruno told me that the Voodoo Lilly had been removed to make it easier to search the greenhouse, but inside it still smelled a bit like a slaughterhouse, or what I imagined a slaughterhouse would smell like. My worst experience with bad meat smells was with a moldy steak hidden behind some take-out cartons at the back of my refrigerator that I'd forgotten about until it made its pungent presence known.

"Imagine how bad it must have been and how far the smell traveled for the neighbor to come over to have a look. I wonder why she was growing a Voodoo Lilly in the first place? I mean, if they smell that bad, why have one?" It made no sense to me.

"The leaves are beautiful, and they only bloom once or maybe twice a year for a couple of days."

"Bruno said they attract flies and that the place was filled with flies."

"No wonder that poor police officer couldn't handle it."

"Even with beautiful leaves, why bother growing one? Seriously, I don't get it."

"I think some people are attracted to unusual or strange plants because it makes them feel like they are doing something unique and special."

"You mean like dying spiked hair hot pink? Or getting lots of face tattoos?"

"Like that, yeah."

"But those things call attention to yourself, and according to those who knew her, Delia was a recluse. She wasn't trying to make an impression on anyone."

"Who knows why people choose the hobbies they do? But keep in mind, even the way she dressed suggested a woman who had a strong sense of self."

We fell silent, staring at the dark stains on the vinyl plank flooring near the entrance.

"This must be where it happened," I said. The police had removed the pot she tripped over as well as the concrete block she'd hit her head on. Both were evidence. There was still a pile of bricks and several decorative pavers stacked near the door. I wasn't sure if the pavers were what the police were referring to as concrete blocks, but they could have been. Various garden tools and bags of plant food were also stashed under the benches on either side, some spilling out into the aisle.

"Why would there be a concrete block sticking out from under a bench?" I asked. "I mean, the killer obviously put it there. But what made them think it would look like an accident?"

"Maybe that's why there are other things not stashed neatly *under* the benches. To make it look like she was sloppy. But I don't buy that for a minute. Do you? I mean, everything in her house was so neat and tidy."

"No, I don't buy that, and I don't think Bruno does either."

"It probably felt less personal than confronting her face to face with a weapon."

"Until a second whap was required. That made it personal."

We walked down the middle aisle, looking at the plants. Even though I'm not a plant person, I could appreciate all the work that must have gone into growing and maintaining the crush of green and flowering plants in Delia's greenhouse.

"These gentians are gorgeous," Laney said, fingering a deep blue flower with a tiny tuba head. "They have a variety of medicinal uses."

"What's this odd-looking green plant, do you know?"

"Club moss."

"And this creepy thing?"

"I believe it's a sundew. I think it's also carnivorous."

"Delia had strange taste in plants."

"I agree. But look over there, there's a lemon tree." The tree had several yellow orbs of different sizes weighing down its limbs.

"Maybe she liked lemon with her tea."

Laney pointed again, this time to an empty spot on the back bench. "That must be where the Voodoo Lilly was."

I paused to check out a grouping of similar pots containing plants with clusters of what looked like tiny traps lined with thin fiber teeth balanced on leafless stalks. "Now these are really bizarre. What are they, any idea?"

"Venus Fly Traps."

"Do they actually trap flies?"

"Yes, and I think I've read that they're difficult to grow. Both light and temperature sensitive."

"It *does* feel warm in here."

"Now that you mention it, I think most of these plants are quite temperature sensitive."

"Maybe she came out here because of a power outage. We can check to see if there was an outage in the neighborhood. Or...maybe our clever killer triggered a power failure in the greenhouse. But how could they be sure she would notice in the middle of the night?"

"It looks like she has both electric heating and a propane heater. Maybe there's a remote monitoring alarm setup," Laney said. "Serious gardeners often have them."

We started looking for monitors on support posts, behind plants, and under the benches.

101

"Maybe she got a call from a neighbor who thought they saw a prowler," I said.

"I doubt many of her neighbors would bother to call her even if they saw someone setting her house on fire. Sorry, that's unkind."

"Couldn't we see the greenhouse from her bedroom?" We both looked back at the house. "Maybe someone made noise and flashed a light around to attract her."

"But would an elderly woman come down by herself to check something like that out?" Laney said. "Even a gutsy woman like Delia had to have second thoughts about confronting an intruder on her own."

"Maybe she had a gun with her."

"Did Bruno mention anything about a gun?"

"Not that I recall."

"Aha," Laney said. "Here it is—behind this pot."

"A gun?"

"No, an alarm attached to a temperature gauge."

"How would it work?"

"If there was a drop in temperature, she was probably notified either on her phone or by an alarm."

"But if she came out to check on the electrical system, wouldn't she have brought a flashlight? I don't remember Bruno saying anything about a flashlight."

"Maybe if she knew there was one handy at the entrance—" Laney started looking around, checking behind pots.

"I noticed a row of low solar lights in the flower beds alongside the house. They might produce enough light for her to see well enough to get to the greenhouse in the dark."

"There's a flashlight." It was standing upright between some plants about a third of the way in.

"Why would she have left it there?" I asked. "She was so meticulous."

"Maybe she was examining a plant in this location."

"Or maybe the meticulous Delia Flowers always left it near the entrance, in case she needed to come out to check on the temperature in the middle of the night. And…"

"You think the killer moved it in advance so she wouldn't see the pot on the floor," Laney said. "Let's see, sabotage the alarm system, move the flashlight, and place a pot in just the right place so she would trip on it and hit her head on a concrete block strategically placed for her height. Pretty elaborate planning."

"And even thinking it through like that, I don't see how they could be sure it would work. They must have been waiting nearby, just in case. If she didn't trip, they might have been prepared to push her from behind."

"Wouldn't that show up in the autopsy?"

"Not necessarily. And not if she was pushed with a pillow." I'd seen that done on some TV program once.

"You think her killer was savvy enough to bring a pillow to prevent bruise marks on her back in case she didn't trip and they had to push her, but didn't realize a second head bash would show up?"

"Maybe they believed the original fall *would* do it, but when it didn't work as planned, they had to improvise."

Laney steepled her fingers in mock contemplation. "You are very wise," she intoned. "But…even though all of this makes sense, it doesn't get us any closer to identifying the killer. The only thing this tells us for sure—and we can't be 100 percent sure— is that whoever was responsible for her accident most likely knew not only about her greenhouse but also about its monitoring/alarm system. I think that narrows the suspect field a bit."

"I wonder why they tried to hide the fact that the alarm went off?"

"Maybe they didn't have the skills to make a temperature fluctuation look like an accident, so instead, they tried to hide the reason she came down to the greenhouse at night."

"I wonder if Bruno's team is working on this scenario as a possibility." Bruno hadn't mentioned anything about a monitoring system to me, but he might have decided it wasn't something he wanted to share, at least not yet. *If* they were hoping the police would write off her death as an accident, they will soon know that even without any evidence that the alarm system was tampered with, the police are considering it murder."

Laney frowned. "And if the killer was the one who locked us in the bathroom, there must be something they want from the house, something that either blows the accident theory or that gives away their identity."

"Playing the Devil's Advocate for a minute—it could also have been a neighbor taking advantage of an empty house to steal valuables."

"In either case, if we fouled up their plan to get what they were looking for, they might return."

"But we won't know unless they come back and we catch them in the act, will we?"

Chapter Thirteen: Caught!

"Okay, here's the plan," Laney said. "I suggest we stay here tonight. I'll move your car so it isn't right out front. Then I'll run home and·pick up a couple of spare security cameras I have that we can put up here temporarily. You may want to have the estate pay for some better ones, though. When I come back, I'll park a couple blocks away and come in through the back door. We don't want to advertise that we're here. And since our goal is to catch the intruder inside the house, I say we set up surveillance in the comfort of the living room. I can pick up some food and snacks on my way back. What do you think?"

"Buy those cheese curl things. And a six-pack of Coke."

"So, you agree we should spend the night here?"

"Yeah, but..."

"But?"

"This is a killer we're talking about catching. Think we should tell Bruno what we're doing?"

"Any doubt what he'd say?"

"It's a job for the police," I mimicked in my best Bruno voice. "And he'll promise to put a police car out front to protect the place. Although that might prevent another intrusion, it wouldn't catch an intruder. Okay, I cast my vote for junk food and vigil."

* * *

Four hours later, I was questioning the wisdom of our decision. I was nauseated from eating most of the bag of Cheetos and washing them down with two Cokes. Shadows were filling the front yard, giving the entire setting a Halloween atmosphere. Not the kind featuring cute kids in costumes carrying sacks of candy, but like in the movie Monster House or Halloween II. Even without an intruder, the place had old house noises, creaks, and squeaks and ghost-like swishes. To top it all off, I was sleepy. After several nights of insomnia, I could barely keep my eyes open.

Laney, on the other hand, had snacked on apples and celery and Cran-Grape juice. She was feeling good and was wide awake. "Go ahead," she said. "Take a nap. I'll be fine for a while."

The next thing I knew, she was shaking me, waking me up to tell me I was snoring. "I don't snore...zzzz."

What seemed like only minutes later, she was shaking me again, this time with a hand over my mouth. "Shush," she said softly. "Someone's here."

Although I usually wake up slowly, remaining groggy until after my first cup of coffee, the words "someone's here" produced a shot of adrenaline that snapped my eyes open wide and sent my heart rate soaring. Someone was here? It was what we'd hoped for, but now that it was happening, I wasn't really sure that what we were doing was a good idea.

Our plan that we'd agreed upon was to stay quiet until the intruder was fully inside and then to turn on the lights—shocking them into submission. There was one small catch, though, one tiny detail that Laney may have considered, but I hadn't thought about: the light switch for the room was on the far wall! In order to turn on the lights, one of us had to sneak over to it. Before I had time to figure out how we were going to accomplish that, Laney was on the move. She was fast and silent as a panther, and in seconds the lights came on, like theater floodlights capturing our little drama in progress.

Amanda Dick, Delia's niece, was frozen in place like a butterfly pinned to a board. She didn't need Laney's admonition to "Don't move."

"Who? What?" Amanda said, blinking against the overhead glare, sounding even more confused than I felt.

"Search her for weapons," Laney said, a pistol aimed at the woman. Amanda was visibly trembling, as if she might faint from fright. "But don't get between us."

I edged up to Amanda from the side. Once next to her, I was unsure where to start.

"Torso first, then legs." Laney was good at reading my mind.

"Excuse me," I said. "Please raise your arms." I reached out to feel Amanda for weapons, and she screamed and pulled away.

"Don't touch me!"

"See this gun?" Laney said, taking a few steps closer. "We aren't going to talk until we are confident you are unarmed. Let John check you for weapons, or…we could call the police. Your choice."

Amanda only hesitated a moment before raising her arms in the air. I quickly patted her down. She was softer in some places than others, and definitely had no gun or knives concealed on her person. "Clean," I said, trying to sound professional.

"Sit," Laney motioned to the couch with her gun. The directive was so authoritative that I almost obeyed by sitting down next to Amanda. At the last instant, I caught myself and took a seat on the nearby ottoman. Laney chose to remain standing, projecting a commanding presence for someone who usually looked like the innocent girl next door. "Want to tell us what you're doing here?"

Amanda's lower lip started to quiver. "Am I in trouble?"

"Let's see, two break-ins within 24 hours. Caught in the act, both on camera and in-person. With two witnesses to your illegal entry. You tell us."

"*Two* break-ins? I don't know what you're talking about."

"We know that you were here earlier in the day." Laney acted like it was a fact and that Amanda had no choice but to confess. However, Amanda surprised us by firmly denying the allegation.

"No, you're wrong. I wasn't here before now."

There was something about Amanda's denial that seemed credible to me, and I could see doubt spark in Laney's eyes. "Let's say you weren't here earlier, why are you here now? What are you here to steal?"

107

"I haven't taken anything."

"Let me rephrase that—if we hadn't caught you, what would you have left with?"

"I'm not a thief. She owes me something."

"Who?"

"Aunt Delia. She told us we were named on her term life policy. She…she lied to us."

"And that justifies you stealing from her estate?" I asked.

"Not when you put it like that. I mean, I don't think of it as stealing exactly."

"How else would you put it?" Laney said. "And if you weren't here earlier, who was?"

"How should I know?" She sounded truly puzzled by the question. "I thought you said you had cameras?"

"There were some issues earlier. But they are fully functioning now."

"Does Brandon also feel that he is owed something?" I asked.

"Well, it shouldn't be up to you to decide what to do with the estate." She stared at me with venom in her eyes.

"If you had to guess who would break in to pick up a few items for themselves, who would you suspect?"

"We're all angry about what Aunt Delia has done."

"What about what was done to *her*?" Laney asked. "Anyone upset about her being murdered?"

If Amanda was faking her surprise at the comment about murder, she was a good actress. For a moment, her lips moved, but no sound came out. Then she managed a whispered, "I thought the police said it was an accident."

"You know they're still investigating her death, right? Why do you think they're doing that if it was ruled an accident?"

Amanda started blinking, then stopped as a few tears trickled down her face. "They didn't tell us. I didn't know."

I was feeling a few tickles of sympathy when, without warning, Amanda's husband erupted into the room, wielding a baseball bat, freezing in place when he saw us. "What's going on?" He looked from Amanda to the pistol in Laney's hand that was currently pointed at him.

"Gun beats bat," Laney said. "Put it down and take a seat." She glanced at me, eyebrows raised in question.

"This is Travis, Amanda's husband," I said.

"I demand to know what's going on." The words were strong, but his voice wasn't. When Laney gestured with the pistol to put down his bat, he obediently dropped it and took a seat on the couch next to his wife. The bat clattered noisily as it rolled toward us on the hardwood floor.

"Now then, let's take it from the top. The two of you are here to steal what?"

Travis and Amanda looked at each other.

"I'll make you the same deal I made your wife," Laney said. "Tell us the truth and do it now, or we'll call the police. Which is it?"

Amanda nodded at her husband, apparently giving him permission to speak. "We didn't come to *steal* anything," Travis said. "We only want a few things that are rightfully ours.

"We've already been down that argument. Tell us the 'what' or John will call his detective friend." I guessed that she deliberately used the phrase "detective friend" to make sure they understood the police would believe us and not them.

Amanda sighed a sigh of resignation. "There are a couple paintings Aunt Delia promised me. They have sentimental value."

"Really?" Laney said. "Sentimental value, huh? Like the Flemish painting in the living room? Or the Maxwell Parrish in the Library?" I wasn't sure whether Laney was guessing or knew they were pricey paintings, but I was fairly certain there was no sentimental value involved in whatever the husband-and-wife team had come to claim as theirs.

Amanda looked down at her hands cupped in her lap. "Maybe those. Or some of the others. She said I could have whichever paintings I wanted. Honest."

"I'm not sure why we should believe you." Laney took another step toward them and pointed her pistol at Amanda's head. "Which one of you pushed your aunt down in the greenhouse? Or did the two of you lure her out there together and stage a fall?"

Amanda's eyes opened wide as did her mouth, but no words came out. Her husband looked equally shocked, "We didn't...we wouldn't...did someone...?"

Laney lowered her gun and motioned me over to the corner for a confab. "I don't think they did it," she whispered. "What do you think?"

"I don't think they did it either."

"We have them on camera sneaking in, but we can't prove they were here to take anything, even though we know it's why they're here. We should have let them try to actually steal something."

"You're not suggesting we let them go?"

"Want to call Bruno?"

I thought about it for a moment and quickly decided against it. "No. But we need assurance that they won't say anything about this to anyone, especially other family members. If they know we're looking for a murderer, we lose any leverage we may have."

"You mean you don't want them to tell the other family members they were going to rip off valuable paintings for themselves instead of sharing?"

"I mean, we don't want to leak the part about Delia being murdered.

"I agree."

Amanda and Travis were holding hands, like lovers from warring families awaiting their fate. Laney and I went over and stood in front of them, two judges about to deliver their verdict.

"Okay, Amanda, Travis," Laney began. "First off, give me the keys you used to get in."

"How did you know...?"

"I didn't hear you fiddling with the lock."

"Mother gave them to me—"

"We aren't accusing you of stealing the keys, but using them to help yourself to whatever you want in the middle of the night wouldn't sound good to a judge."

I got up and held out my hand. Amanda handed me a skeleton key like the one we used to get in, and I put it in my pocket.

"Now then. We'll let you go if you agree not to say anything to anyone about tonight. After all, your family wouldn't be pleased to know you were trying to steal part of their inheritance. And the police won't want you blabbing about a murder investigation. By staying mum, you don't tick off the police, and John and I can continue looking for your aunt's killer. Deal?"

"You believe us then?" Amanda asked, her eyelashes wet with a hint of tearing.

"We believe you tried to take advantage of your Aunt Delia and are willing to steal several valuable paintings rather than wait for a division of the estate. And...we're gambling that you didn't kill her."

"But," I said. "If we find evidence that you did, we will show you no mercy." It felt good to have the upper hand.

The two lovebirds couldn't leave quickly enough, like zoo animals suddenly finding the door to their cages open.

"Hope we are right about them," Lacey said.

"I think they are guilty of greed, but murder?"

"Well, let's turn off the lights just in case someone else shows up—assuming they didn't come while we were having our little lights-on party."

When we were once again sitting in the dark, the silence of the house hanging over us like a shroud, Laney said, "John, there's something I've been meaning to talk with you about." She kept her voice low, the disembodied sound echoing in the large room.

"It's a good thing we aren't dating or I'd be worried with that lead-in that you wanted to break up."

"Just the opposite actually."

"I don't follow..."

"Do you want children? I mean, I know your mother wants grandchildren, but what about you?"

"I don't really think about it."

"Well, I do. And it puts pressure on me to meet the right person."

"You want me to help you find the right person?"

"No, I want you to father my child."

"What?" It was the last thing I was expecting Laney to say. "But..."

"Don't worry. Not right away." She laughed. "And with IVF."

"IVF?"

"In Vitro Fertilization. There's no physical contact between the two people involved. The egg is fertilized outside of the body, and the embryo is transferred to the mother."

"Okay, I've heard of it. But why me?"

"Because you're my *forever friend*. I trust you. You're a good person. Smart. Caring. And I think a child should know their father."

"You mean you would want me to be a *parent*?"

"Only if you wanted to be involved in parenting. I wouldn't ask you to do anything you didn't want to do. But knowing you, I think after the child was born, you would want *some* involvement."

"Like doing something with the kid on weekends, that sort of thing?"

I heard Laney chuckle. "Something like that."

"No diaper changing or pushing a stroller down the sidewalk?"

"You could be as involved or as uninvolved as you wanted to be. But I can picture you wanting to take on a variety of parenting duties."

Being a theoretical parent had a nice ring to it, but my mind immediately went to the practical issues involved. "You would want to share costs."

"Costs? You mean child support or IVF fees? In either case, I have enough money of my own."

"I would want to contribute."

"That would be fine. We could work something out."

"Would we live together?"

"I hadn't thought about that. I have my house; you have your houseboat. We're not that far away from each other."

"What about a name?"

"That's jumping a bit ahead, isn't it?"

"I mean, a last name."

"I was thinking Drew."

"We could hyphenate: Drew-Smith."

"Or Smith-Drew. Although that sounds funny. How about blending our names: Dreith? Or Smiew?" She chuckled again, this time louder.

To me, the first sounded like a mythical monster and the second a sneeze.

112

"You're really serious, aren't you?"

"Yes. If we agree in principle, we can figure out details later."

"You didn't plan this with my mother, did you?"

"No, but think how happy this would make her."

"She wouldn't need to know right away, would she? About a possible arrangement, that is."

"No. I'm suggesting this because if neither of us marries, we may still both want a child. I would like to think it's a possibility."

"I'll think about it," I said. But I was already picturing a mini-me running around my living room, Wild Thing complaining loudly.

"Take your time. It will be a while before I'm ready to take on being a mother. And who knows, maybe you'll meet the love of your life. That could change how you feel about sharing a child with me."

To be honest, I was not necessarily looking for a wife, just someone to date and enjoy. Preferably someone curvy. But I did consider Laney my *forever friend,* even if I hadn't given much thought to what that meant. And having a child with a friend might be a good option.

My mind was restlessly conjuring up images of Laney and me as parents interspersed with images of confronting a killer, a strange combination of good and evil, when…we heard someone rattling the front doorknob.

Chapter Fourteen: What a family!

We heard two voices when the door opened. Although our revised plan was to wait until we knew what the intruder was up to, when we realized there were two of them, we didn't have to discuss it to make still another change of plans. We couldn't take the chance that they would split up and make it difficult for us to corner them together. They ended up getting the same treatment as Amanda. Only this time, I was standing next to the light switch so Laney could focus on making sure neither got away.

As soon as they were halfway into the room, I flicked the switch and bathed them in light while Laney covered them with her gun.

Luis and Gabe, Brandon's stepsons, were quicker to respond than Amanda had been. They started to turn back to the door, but I was there holding Travis's bat in what I considered the combat position: wide stance, knees bent, bat pointed upward. "Make my day," I said, giving it my best Clint Eastwood imitation. Both men stopped and stared, but didn't appear to be impressed by either the bat or my impersonation.

Gabe took a step in my direction as Laney yelled, "Stop, or I'll shoot you in the leg." The specificity of Laney's threat did the trick. They froze. "Hands in the air and turn toward me." They slowly did as they were told.

"Who are you?" Gabe asked.

"Someone not afraid to shoot an intruder. And I believe I could get off two shots before you could disarm me. Consider yourself warned. Now, want to tell us what you're doing here?"

They both shifted from foot to foot, like two kids caught stealing candy from the corner grocery rather than two adults wearing all black, each with a large bag dangling from their raised hands. Probably containers for the loot they were intending to pick up.

"These are Brandon's two sons," I said to Laney. "Gabe and Luis." Since I might decide to give some or all of them huge chunks of change, I'd been brushing up on the family tree.

"You, Gabe, step to the side so John can pat your brother down for weapons."

I put the bat on a side table and reached out to frisk him. "Luis, hold still," I said as he resisted. He glanced at Laney's gun and let me proceed. Unlike Amanda, he was lean. I found tape in one pocket, a box cutter in another. "Planning on removing a few pictures from their frames?" I asked. He shrugged, his hands still in the air. I grabbed the bag he was holding and tossed it on the couch.

"Your turn, Gabe," Laney said. Gabe had on a large backpack. I had him lower his hands so I could slip off the pack. Then, after patting him down and not finding any weapons, I took his bag and put it on the couch with his brother's. Then I emptied the contents of his pack on the couch. There was a toolkit in a zippered pouch. Bubble wrap. Cloth bags. An angle grinder for cutting through metal. A makeshift lock pick made out of a paper clip. And a pack of Blackjack gum.

I held up the gum. "For pleasure? Or do burglars use this for something?"

Gabe shrugged. "I like gum."

"Given all the padding you brought with you, I assume you were going mainly for the small but priceless stuff?"

"No comment."

"What's the angle grinder for?" Laney asked.

"No comment."

"Just so you know," Laney said, "we have you breaking in on camera. So why don't you take a seat on the couch next to your tools of the trade while John calls his detective friend to let him know the trap caught the rats." Laney motioned with her gun toward the couch, and they obediently found space and sat down.

"We didn't break in, we have keys."

"Which you should have handed over after Delia died," I said.

"You don't need to call the police, do you?" Gabe said. "Can't we work something out?"

"Like what?"

"A share of the profits?" Luis said, his voice a not-very-hopeful wheedle, like a kid asking for candy before dinner and knowing he probably won't get it.

"I already have access to everything," I pointed out.

"But you can't really give it to yourself. The whole family would go after you in court."

"It isn't about the money," Laney said. "It's about Delia's demise."

"She was old. She died. So what?"

"I take it from that comment that you weren't close to her."

"She told us time and again that we weren't 'blood.' So how were we supposed to feel about her? Still, our dad made us mow her lawn and do repairs on the house. We even hauled supplies for her precious garden. But she said we wouldn't be included in her will because we weren't real Flowers. Even though Dad officially adopted us when we were young."

"You sound bitter."

"Of course, we're bitter. Who wouldn't be?"

"Bitter enough to kill her?"

They both assumed blank, neutral expressions, no tells that I could discern. But they didn't exude innocence either.

"She fell and hit her head," Gabe said. "End of story"

"Who told you that?"

"Dad. He was told that by the police."

Laney raised her eyebrows in question. I agreed with what I thought she was thinking: it wouldn't do us any good to question these two more. And it might be construed as interference with a police investigation. I nodded and punched in Bruno's home number. It was almost 2:00 a.m. Maybe I should have dialed 911, but I thought he would forgive me for the inconvenience.

He didn't answer until the fourth ring. "What the hell, John. Do you know what time it is?"

"Sorry, Bruno. If you want, I can call 911. Laney and I are at Delia's. We've just caught two of Delia's sister's grandkids breaking into her house. The equipment they have with them suggests they were going to rob the place."

There was silence on Bruno's end. He doesn't handle robberies, but under the circumstances, it didn't take him long to decide. "I'll have a couple of my men there shortly. Give me the address." After I gave him the address, he warned me not to leave before he got there and hung up.

"You didn't have to do that," Luis said in an unpleasant whiny grumble, as if he had a phlegmy throat. Maybe I shouldn't have gotten so close to him.

I stepped back a way. "You think I should stand by and let your family empty the house before I make my decision about who gets what?"

"No one would miss a few knick-knacks."

"And a valuable painting or two?" Laney added.

"Where did you get the key?" I asked. Did all the family members have keys?

"She gave us one. As I said, we did some work around the house for her."

"And she trusted you with a key. Were you ripping her off while she was still alive?"

"She would have noticed. She probably counted the number of grapes in a bowl on the kitchen table. Besides, we assumed our dad would get a share, and we knew he would be generous with us."

"Among other things, you were counting on getting a piece of the five million from the term life insurance, weren't you?"

"Mom and Dad would have gifted some of it to us, sure."

"Why were they counting on their aunt dying within five years. Any ideas?"

"No comment," the two said in unison. It made me wonder how many family members might have conspired to knock Delia off.

When we heard the sirens in the distance, Laney and I stepped aside and whispered back and forth, quickly deciding on the story we were going to give the police just seconds before two officers came bursting into the room, weapons at the ready. Laney had already pocketed her gun, and it didn't take a genius to figure out who the two thieves were—they were the ones in black with guilt written on their faces. But the officers weren't taking any chances. One covered the two young men who had put their hands in the air again, while the other told us to hold up *our* hands.

"I'm the one who called," I said as I put my hands in the air, one hand still holding my phone. "You can check my phone if you want."

"He's the estate executor for the woman who owned this house," Laney said, raising her hands. "It's a matter of record. These two are related to the dead woman. They have a key to the house, but that doesn't give them the right to be here in the middle of the night."

"What are *you* doing here in the middle of the night?" the officer asked Laney and me. It was the question we'd expected, so we were prepared.

"We had reason to believe some family members were going to rob the house, so we decided to spend the night in order to protect the premises. Tomorrow," Laney added, "he's hiring an appraiser to catalogue what's here and adding some security measures."

They looked doubtful. But at least we weren't dressed in black. The two officers were still trying to sort out the situation when Bruno arrived and told them to put away their weapons. "It's okay. They called me about these two," Bruno said, motioning toward Gabe and Luis. Then he checked out the contents of Gabe's backpack on display on the couch, along with the tape and box cutters from Luis' pockets. "Pack that up," he said to one of the officers. "Then take them to headquarters. I'll be along shortly."

Once it was just the three of us, Bruno sat down on the couch, and in a tired voice said simply: "Explain."

We gave him the same brief explanation we'd given his two officers. But Bruno has known me almost all my life, and as a detective, he has a suspicious nature.

"So, tell me the truth, were you safeguarding the house or hoping to catch a killer?"

Laney looked completely innocent, but I felt blood rushing to my face. I'm a terrible liar. "Maybe a little of both."

"John. Laney. Killers are, by their nature, dangerous people. Why didn't you give me a heads-up. I would have…"

"Put a car out front," I finished for him.

"Now you have four suspects," Laney said. "Although we don't think Amanda and her husband, Travis, are the killers."

"Amanda and Travis?"

We explained that they were there earlier to "pick up a few items they felt were promised to them," and Bruno said, "And you just let them go?"

"They didn't even know Delia was murdered."

"You gave them lie detector tests?"

"We didn't want to waste the opportunity. We thought someone else might show up...and they did," Laney said.

"Maybe we should turn out the lights and wait for more family members to show," Bruno said.

Before I realized he was being sarcastic, I almost said out loud that it was a good idea.

"My advice is for the two of you to go home and get some sleep. I'll have a car out front."

If he caught the irony of his offer of a car out front, he didn't show it. And somehow Laney and I managed to keep our faces neutral. Although a teensy smirk may have slipped out of the side of my mouth for a second or two.

We didn't talk much as Laney walked me to where she had parked my car. Some might say we were making progress, but it didn't feel that way. We'd managed to save some of Delia's possessions, but we weren't any closer to finding her killer.

Once back home, I crawled into bed, exhausted, but still unable to sleep. I kept thinking about the many family members with motive and opportunity. Even if we didn't include Amanda and her husband, that left quite a few, especially when including spouses as suspects. There were also the neighbors who had reason to want Delia dead. And the developer.

There were just too many suspects. I kept going over and over what I knew about each of them, one at a time. The process didn't produce answers or make me sleepy. Eventually, I gave up trying and started fantasizing about a life with Laney and our baby. I certainly hoped it looked like *her*. Then I started worrying about all the logistics of raising a child with someone who was a friend and not a wife. Sleep didn't seem to be an option. It was time to read my page-turning thriller.

Chapter Fifteen: Complaints

Sunday was apparently National Complain to John Day. It started with Wild Thing. I'd finally managed to get to sleep around 5:00 a.m. and selfishly did not get up at 7:00 to feed my high-maintenance cat. He waited until 7:30 before getting in my face and yowling his discontent with my behavior. I have no idea how he got into my bedroom; maybe through a secret panel.

At first, I tried to ignore him by rolling over in bed, poised precariously at the edge, but he was not about to give up. He climbed across my shoulders and leaned over to head butt me. When that didn't work, he started pummeling me with his paws. Before he decided to unleash his claws, I dragged myself up, staggered out to the kitchen, and served him his usual breakfast fare before heading back to bed. He didn't bother thanking me.

It seemed like I'd only been asleep for a few minutes when there was pounding on my door. I grabbed my extra pillow and held it over my head to block out the persistent "whap, whap, whap." Then I heard a muffled voice through my pillow yelling, "We know you're in there." I was afraid they would damage my door trying to get in, so I finally gave up, grabbed a robe with tiny cartoon horses and dogs on it to hide my boxers that were emblazoned with hearts, and headed for the door. The robe had been a gift from my mother. Originally, I'd intended to donate it to Goodwill, but it was kinda cute. And very comfortable.

The first person I saw was Brandon. As soon as I opened the door, his wife, Marcy, stepped out from behind him. They were flanked by five other members of Delia's lovely family: Bud, his wife Marigold, and their two children—Heather and Harold—and Amanda's daughter Bethany. I recognized them from the tiny pictures I'd placed next to their names on the family tree I'd created on poster board, using the pictures Delia had provided on the thumb drive she'd left for me. They didn't look like a group who had come to engage me in dialogue. Rather, they looked more like a lynch mob or a gathering of rioters on the rampage, eager to exact what they thought was justice.

While I was standing there trying to decide whether I could get away with slamming the door shut on them, Wild Thing slipped past me and took off. "Oh no," I groaned. Pushing Brandon aside, I started after him. But it was like running a gauntlet, several of them trying to knock me off my feet, only using their hands without the aid of weaponry. "Please, you don't understand. I have to keep Wild Thing away from the neighbor's dog."

Before I could break free, Heather and Bethany yelled, "Save the cat" and raced off. Little did they know that their rallying cry should have been "Save the dog."

My robe had slid open, revealing my bare chest with its scant smattering of hair and my Valentine shorts. Marigold snickered and rolled her eyes. "Hope you didn't buy those for yourself." Everyone laughed. "Although the horsies and doggies on your robe are definitely *you*." There was more laughter. A man can only take so much ridicule. I pulled my robe shut and went inside. The group trailed in after me, leaving the door open for the return of the two young women who were chasing down Wild Thing. Hopefully, they would catch up with him before my landlord did.

My uninvited visitors were apparently prepared to talk instead of fight after all. They all found places to sit and made themselves at home while I remained standing. "Okay, why don't you tell me why you're here. I assume it isn't because you've heard I make good coffee."

"I'd love a cup..." Marigold started to say before being cut off by her husband.

"Not now," he whispered loud enough for everyone to hear.

Brandon cleared his throat, and all eyes turned to him. He was apparently their spokesperson. "We're here to let you know that we don't like how you're going about this, not one bit. First, you take over our inheritance, then you have four of our family members arrested. We demand to know why."

"Have you talked to the police?"

"They say they're being processed. Processed for what?"

I didn't see any reason not to tell them what they wanted to know. I was surprised the police hadn't been more specific. Maybe they'd asked the wrong person or ticked someone off by how they went about asking. "For breaking and entering," I said.

"Where?"

"At Delia's."

"How can it be breaking and entering when they had keys to her house? Most of us have keys."

"Well, when the owner is deceased and you let yourself in without permission in the middle of the night with the intent to steal things that don't belong to you—I guess that qualifies you as a burglar."

The group started whispering back and forth to one another until Brandon spoke again. "You called the police on them, didn't you?"

I hesitated. They outnumbered me, and I wasn't sure how much I wanted to share. Or how much Bruno would want me to share. I could hear Laney's voice in my head saying that I should turn this on them by asking them questions. But I couldn't think of what to ask. I was saved from saying the wrong thing by Bethany and Heather making their triumphant return.

"We got him," Bethany said. Wild Thing was snuggling in her arms, looking happy. Traitor, I thought. How could you?

"Thank you," I managed. I went over and closed the door. "Now, where were we. That's right, I was about to ask you if Louis and Gabe were acting on behalf of the entire family or if they were there to help themselves to a few things they personally wanted." Laney would have been proud.

Brandon stretched his neck and looked uncomfortable as the other family members waited for him to speak. "They must have made the decision on the spur of the moment. I'm sure they intended to tell the rest of us after the fact."

"A spur-of-the-moment thing in the middle of the night, you mean. Wearing black and carrying burglar bags." Brandon looked even more uncomfortable, but apparently the family wasn't about to challenge him in front of me. "What about Amanda and Travis? Does the same go for them?" I asked.

Bethany, their daughter, spoke up to defend her parents. "They were only there to get some things that were rightfully theirs."

That was beginning to sound like a family mantra. "Such as?" I asked.

It was Heather's turn to jump in. "Let's be honest, we all considered doing the same thing—removing art or keepsakes that rightfully belong to the family." Her eyes turned cold. "Before *you* had a chance to give them away to some charity."

"I told you that I intended to ask for your input before deciding who was entitled to what. Why would you automatically assume I would make decisions you wouldn't agree with? Delia trusted me to be fair; she did not instruct me to deprive you of your inheritance."

I thought I'd made a pretty solid case for my good intentions. But they had tried and convicted me in advance. They were convinced that I was the enemy and that Delia and I had somehow plotted to disinherit them in the most humiliating way possible. They also assumed that I had schemed to get four of their family members arrested. Most importantly, they believed that I was all that stood between them and a fortune that would make them all millionaires. To them, I was the devil incarnate hiding behind cartoon horsies and doggies.

After making it clear that they would fight for their rights all the way to the Supreme Court if necessary, they finally ran out of epithets and complaints and departed. Wild Thing made another attempt to escape, but this time I was quick enough to snatch him up. But not quick enough to avoid a few scratches of protest. As soon as I closed the door behind the disgruntled family members, I put him down. He arched his back, black fur standing on end, and hissed like an angry snake before scampering off.

Although I disapproved of his attitude, I had to admit that he had been the distraction needed to break up the mob when they arrived and later to prevent me from saying something I'd regret. My gratitude was, however, diminished somewhat by the scratches on my hand.

I decided against coffee with my eggs and toast, hoping to catch a few more zees after breakfast to make up for all the sleep I'd been missing. After gulping down my food, I stretched out on the couch with a lap blanket and a pillow in an embroidered pillow sham my mother had made during one of her craft phases. I hadn't bothered to get dressed because I wasn't expecting more company, and miraculously, I quickly dropped off.

It was a young girl's giggles that woke me. I should have anticipated Valerie's daily visit to play with Wild Thing and locked myself in my bedroom.

"You dress funny," she said. Wild Thing was rubbing himself against her legs while she examined the cartoon characters on my robe.

"Mother bought this for me," I said. Since she knew my mother, I felt that ought to explain everything. I should have realized that she had no way of knowing that my mother bought things on sale, whether they were needed or appropriate to the person she bought them for. Mother simply loved a good sale.

"She must still think of you as her 'little boy.'" She giggled some more. I hadn't thought of it like that. Valerie was sometimes insufferable but also wise beyond her years.

"Something like that," I said. "Now, go play with Wild Thing in the other room and let me sleep."

I closed my eyes, but the magic of sleep had vanished. Counting all the sheep in the continental United States wasn't going to help. Not even if I also included China—I'd read that China was the country with the largest sheep population in the world. Instead, I lay there thinking about Delia's mercenary family, wondering if they really were going to come up with some way to take legal action against me for something I hadn't chosen to do in the first place. Delia's lawyer claimed to have done everything by the book, but you never knew what loophole some ambitious legal counsel could come up with.

When Valerie left, she yelled, "Bye, Mr. John." Had she known that I was awake, or was her loud goodbye a glimmer of the spiteful little girl I knew before she bonded with Wild Thing and agreed to leave my mailbox alone in exchange for visiting rights with him? I certainly didn't miss the dead fish, smelly marine life, and melted popsicle sticks mixed in with my mail. Hopefully, she was getting too old for that kind of mischief anyway. She'd told me she was about to turn nine. That was just one year away from ten and four away from becoming a teenager. Then again, as she aged, she might graduate to more sophisticated trickery.

I wiled away the rest of the afternoon doing this and that, mainly avoiding chores that I should have been doing but didn't feel up to tackling. Before leaving for my mother's condo for Sunday dinner, I put out Wild Thing's dinner, one of his favorites, chunk tuna canned in oil. I'm grateful he doesn't prefer the more expensive whole albacore, but I don't like the fishy smell that hovers in the air even after he's licked his bowl clean.

When Wild Thing didn't come running at the sound of the can opener, I called out his name and loudly announced: "Dinner is served." Still, no cat appeared. Since he loves his meals, I knew he was still mad at me for twice thwarting his rush to freedom. "Fine," I said out loud. I grabbed a bottle of wine, tripped over a rug Wild Thing had scrunched, and left him there to dine alone.

As I walked to my car, it occurred to me that I had at least one thing to be thankful for—I was no longer being dive-bombed by crows on the way to my car. Either they had forgiven me for knocking down one of their nests from a tree next to my parking space, or they had moved on to warmer climes. Either way, it was a relief. Now that I didn't have to constantly deploy defensive moves against their attacks, the walk to my car in the parking area on the street above the marina was pleasant. That particular evening, the air was crisp but hinting at the summer to come. It was like an oven's preheating stage.

Mother had invited Laney to join us for this Sunday's meal. She had finally accepted that Laney wasn't interested in me romantically and settled for enjoying her company. They both loved reading mysteries and frequently shared recommendations. And apparently, they both loved children. Although there was no way I was going to tell Mother about Laney's IVF proposal, I would have liked her opinion on some of the finer points of managing a lifestyle with Laney and a child. However, tonight's conversation wasn't about my personal life or any fictional mystery; rather, the topic over dinner was Delia and who we thought most likely ended her life.

"My money is on the neighbor," I said. "Graham—the one who has a view of her greenhouse."

"But didn't he find the body?" Mother asked.

"That doesn't eliminate him. Maybe it was a return to the scene of the crime thing."

"There are too many suspects," Laney said. "Way too many."

"Maybe family members conspired to murder her." Mother is a great Agatha Christie fan. At her urging, I read Murder on the Orient Express, so I knew what she was referring to—a group of people agreeing to take part in the murder of someone who deserves to die.

"I'm not sure *that* family could cooperate long enough to plan and pull off a murder," I said.

"I still think Amanda and Travis were truly surprised that Delia didn't die in an accident," Laney said.

"Maybe what you interpreted as *surprise* was their disappointment that the police had changed their minds about it being an accident," Mother said.

Laney and I thought about that for a moment, and both said "no, I don't think so" at the same time.

"Well, assuming Amanda and Travis weren't involved, how about Brandon on his own?" Mother asked. "He and Amanda were both willing to bet that Delia was going to die within five years. Maybe he talked Amanda into going along with him to suggest it to Delia because he wanted to deflect from his own selfish interest in making it happen."

"It would have been smarter for them to suggest she ask for the standard ten-year policy."

"When you're young, you don't realize how precious a few years can seem to an older person. That could have been part of the reason they suggested the five-year policy. And didn't you say someone thought she was a penny pincher?"

"That's what Gabe said."

"Maybe they thought a cheaper policy would appeal to her."

"If it wasn't a family member, maybe the developer did it," Laney said. "He undoubtedly checked out the property, including the greenhouse, when he was deciding how much to offer Delia for her property."

We gave the possibility some thought, then tossed around pros and cons. "We need to talk to him," Laney concluded. "Can you take off some time tomorrow afternoon?"

Since I was getting paid for acting on behalf of the estate, maybe I didn't need to double-dip but simply ask for the afternoon off. There was a lot to do, like getting some security cameras installed and talking to the lawyer about the keys we found. He could probably tell me whether she had a safety deposit box or something else that might fit the remaining key. Talking to the developer was also a priority, but I didn't want to do that on my own.

"How about you, Laney, can you go with me to talk to the developer?"

"Wouldn't miss it."

"I don't suppose you want to make it a threesome?" Mother asked. "You two can do the talking; I'll just listen."

Fat chance, I thought. But they say there is safety in numbers; whoever *they* are. It's amazing how certain alleged truths become part of one's reality. "Okay. Let's meet in front of my office at noon."

Chapter Sixteen: Pioneers

Things were pretty slow at the office on Monday morning. Emma hadn't left a huge stack of minor accident cases for me to handle like she usually does, so I assumed most of our insurance clients had been home watching TV on the weekend rather than out driving around playing bumper cars on the freeway. It's hard to predict in advance. Although whenever it snows, there are always accidents caused by people who don't know how to drive in the snow or who don't have the right tires on their car or who have the bad luck to encounter someone else who either doesn't know how to drive in the snow or has the wrong tires on *their* car. And if it rains hard, there are accidents caused by people improperly applying their brakes on slippery pavement. Of course, there are also accidents if it's sunny—people claim the sun was in their eyes. That's possible, but they also might have been distracted by whatever they were passing by, like scantily clad women or shirtless men with great abs. That's something they usually don't want to admit.

When you come right down to it, there are almost always enough auto accidents to keep me busy. Still, slow days sometimes happen. And today was one of those rare days. As a result, when I told Emma that I was taking the afternoon off to run my mother on some errands, she didn't give me any pushback. And although I wasn't exactly telling the truth, I could hardly explain what we were doing without providing a lot of details about my involvement in investigating a murder I wasn't supposed to be investigating, and that I had no doubt Emma would disapprove of me doing in the first place.

"You're a good son," was all Emma said. I suppose in some ways it's true, but in this instance, I was using my mother as an excuse. I didn't think that qualified me for any kudos.

Both Mother and Laney were right on time. As usual, Laney was prepared. She had looked up the address for our destination and had a phone app ready to go with directions for the shortest route with the least traffic. But my mother had other ideas. She wanted some lunch first. Neither Laney nor I was opposed to getting something to eat, although we argued briefly about which fast food place we would bless with our presence. I basically love junk food by any name, but I had a hankering for a hamburger and fries, Laney wanted a salad, and Mother wanted a fish sandwich. We were still arguing when I spotted a McDonald's and pulled into the line for their drive-thru. We ate in their parking lot with our windows cracked to dissipate the smells that always seemed to hover over their takeout meals.

Less than a half hour later, satiated with trans fats, I drove us to our destination on the shortest route with the least traffic, except for one slip-up where I misunderstood what the preachy female voice on the app commanded me to do. To get back to where I should have turned, I had to drive around a city block. One stoplight and two stop signs later, I was back on track.

"What's the name of the company again?" Mother asked.

"Pioneer Development Enterprises," I said.

"I like that name," Mother said. "*Pioneer* is a good, positive word. It makes you think of risk-takers and the entrepreneurial spirit that makes our nation great and..."

"And settlers taking away the lands from indigenous people," Laney interrupted.

"That too," mother conceded.

"Sorry," Laney said. "I would prefer they call themselves what they are."

"Like 'A Big Company Interested in Profit'?" I asked.

"It seems to me that big companies always have more power than they should." Laney smiled. "Like big insurance companies."

"And big law firms," I countered.

"Big anything," Mother said. "Although I do love Costco." We managed a moment of silence in honor of Costco before Mother asked, "So, what's our plan?"

"I made an appointment to talk with Leland Kelsey about the Flowers' property. He seemed quite excited when I explained that it might soon be on the market."

"That was a bit misleading, wasn't it?" Laney said. Then added with a smile: "Good for you."

"What are you going to tell him about us?" Mother gestured to her and Laney. "Who are we?"

"Who do you want to be?"

"Your financial advisor," Mother said without hesitation.

I was tempted to ask why. Instead, I said: "Done."

"I'll be your paramour," Laney said.

My mother smiled, but I didn't. "Seriously?"

"Okay, how about your bodyguard?"

Mother shook her head 'no.' "You don't look like a bodyguard."

"Isn't that the best kind?" Laney asked. "Okay, how about you tell him that I'm your legal consultant. That might come in handy." She looked at my mother for approval, and my mother nodded "yes."

I pulled into a crowded parking lot for the building Pioneer Development Enterprises shared with a number of other businesses listed on a crowded monument sign at the entrance. I wondered how many accidents were caused by drivers suddenly slowing down to try to read whether they were in the right place. It wasn't a problem for me because as we got close, Laney was repeating every direction her phone gave. There was no doubt when I'd "arrived."

There was a row of "Visitor" signs just to the left of some reserved parking for specific people. Kelsey had his own spot filled with an expensive-looking blue Corvette. I managed to squeeze into the last visitor space. I don't like putting Bee in such close proximity with other cars, but if you have to do it, being between a new Tesla and a Mercedes-Benz is the way to go. Obviously, the building had some upscale clientele. The lesser vehicles belonging to the employees who did the actual work were most likely parked further out; in my experience, that's the way it usually was in corporate lots.

The building was a bit fancier than I'd expected. The four-story structure looked like a corporate headquarters, albeit not a tall one. I'd anticipated the kind of office I associate with overalls-wearing contractors. But then, we were going to be meeting with a developer, the big picture moneybags, not a worker bee. The actual jobs required to get the development built were most likely handled by independent contractors and subcontractors housed in more functional, less upmarket buildings. This office complex was the honey hole where the deal makers performed their magic. Even though it wasn't as fancy as some of the downtown office buildings, the parking was a lot easier to navigate.

When we went inside and looked at the reader board, we learned that Pioneer Development Enterprises occupied the top floor. We took the elevator up. The doors opened onto a spacious area with a reception desk that looked like a bunker against the wall facing the elevator. From that desk, the short-haired male wearing a dark blue jacket and light blue shirt was able to monitor everyone's comings and goings. No visitor could sneak past as long as someone was seated there. The space was bookended by wood doors in both directions.

I stepped up to the desk and explained that I had an appointment with Mr. Kelsy. When I didn't refer to my "colleagues," the man asked: "Are all three of you meeting with Mr. Kelsey?" I said "yes." It made me feel important to have both a financial adviser and a legal consultant with me.

The receptionist dutifully had each of us fill out an information card for our visitor badges. I wasn't sure why badges were needed when the entire floor belonged to the same company and was guarded by a stylishly dressed male who, for all I knew, had a panic button under the counter. Or a weapon. The setup suggested they didn't like surprise visitors and were prepared to make sure any unwanted guests didn't get past the keeper of the gates.

I glanced over and saw Mother write "financial advisor" under her name. Laney simply wrote her name: Laney Drew. The receptionist studied my form the longest. The name "John Smith" does that to people. About half are suspicious that it's an alias, and the other half are trying to come up with a clever comment. When it comes to Pocahontas jokes, I've heard them all.

Once we had our badges, the man behind the desk finally smiled, a weak half-smile to let us know we were accepted, but only conditionally. "You may go back now." His hands disappeared under the counter, and the door to our left slowly started to open. "Turn right at the end of the hallway. His office is the last one on the left."

The place wasn't exactly bustling with activity. We passed quite a few shut doors and didn't see any sign of life before arriving at the open door to Leland Kelsey's office, the last one on the left as promised. It was fancier than I'd anticipated. Even though he had a designated parking spot with his name on it right out front, it hadn't occurred to me that he was anything more than a glorified contractor. But apparently, when you deal with very large development projects, you are an important honcho and entitled to all the trappings that go with it.

The receptionist must have warned him that there would be three of us because there were three chairs lined up in front of a long wooden desk that looked like it had recently been polished. The entire room looked picture-perfect. Even Kelsey looked picture-ready in casual attire that might have passed muster for a Brunello Cucinelli ad. I wasn't actually familiar with the line, but I'd seen an eye-catching ad in a magazine I'd browsed at the dentist's office not long ago. The heading was: *The Evolution of Neutrals.* Until then, I'd been unaware that colors evolved. It made me wonder about the shades of gray Kelsey was wearing—were they "evolved"? To me, his light gray sweater looked like, well, light gray. The collar of the dark gray shirt that hugged his neck was, well, darker than his sweater. Then, when he came around the end of his desk to shake hands, I forgot about the gray evolution and became fixated on his charcoal gray slacks—they didn't have even a hint of a wrinkle. Either they were made of some incredible material, or he knew how to sit without creasing his pants. If the opportunity arose, I needed to ask him about that. Still, gray was gray in my book.

After brief introductions and some hearty handshaking, Kelsey started the conversation by telling us how pleased he was to hear that the Flowers' property might be available. Then he quickly added, "I'm sorry to hear of her passing, of course."

I opened with "I have a few questions." It was kind of what I assumed a chess game was like, only I didn't have a name for my opening strategy and no game plan for winning. Rather, my opening move might have been called *right to the point.* Not about the potential sale of Delia's property, but about what I wanted to know to uncover a murderer. "Have you talked with any family members other than Delia Flowers about an offer on the property?"

Kelsey's eyelashes flickered at the unconventional move, but he recovered quickly. "I may have. I'd have to check the notes in my file." His counter seemed to be to stay on track, to respond as if the situation was a normal one.

"Would you mind doing that? We'd be happy to wait."

He only hesitated a few seconds before picking up the phone and asking for someone to bring him the Flowers' file. "Would you like coffee or tea or water while we wait?"

"No, thank you," I said before Mother could ask for a cuppa. There was no need to get chummy that I could think of.

"While we're waiting, I have a question too," my mother, the financial adviser, said. "Is the offer for the property still the same as you made to Mrs. Flowers?"

"Yes, but we may have some wiggle room."

Wiggle room? Was he talking down to us, or was that simply his way of saying that he was prepared to sweeten the offer?

"Wiggle room?" My mother said sweetly, too sweetly. "Would you care to expound on that?" The jowls that were just starting to form on both sides of her face hardened, and her gray curls were absolutely still. Kelsey didn't know the signs, but I did; he was about to be taken down a peg or two, maybe even three or four.

"Ah, I'm more than happy to discuss the sale price."

I decided to spare him my mother's attempt to play tough financial advisor. At this point, knowing there was "wiggle room" was almost as important as knowing how much. But I wasn't there to negotiate a price. I wanted to poke a potential murderer to see if I could get him to reveal himself. "I'm afraid that all of the family members will have to agree to sell before we can talk money," I said. "I don't have everyone's approval yet."

"Oh." A tiny flicker of worry ran across his forehead before he got his face under control. "Are any of them as sentimental about the property as Mrs. Flowers was?"

"One or two may be." My lies were compounding. Too bad there was no interest involved.

His admin brought in a file labeled Delia Flowers and placed it on his desk, barely glancing at us as she left. He picked it up and leafed through a few pages. "I talked briefly with an Amada Dick and a Brandon Plover." I suspected he'd already known he'd talked with them. Was the delay so he could assess the situation and decide on an approach?

"And you told them what you thought the property was worth?"

"Yes. They seemed to think it was a fair assessment." The neighbor had indicated the prices Kelsey quoted everyone were above market, but I doubted he was privy to what Delia's offer had been. I wondered what the appraiser would think of the offer. I would find out soon enough.

"I'm seeing an appraiser tomorrow. And I haven't met with all of the prospective heirs yet. So, there is still some question about whether the property is for sale." I watched his chin fall almost imperceptibly.

"I certainly hope you will give me a chance to make our case to the heirs before any final decisions are made." He was hiding his disappointment fairly well, like someone trying to be a good sport when he wanted to cry "foul."

Laney leaned forward. "When did you talk to Amanda Dick and Brandon Plover?"

He glanced at his notes. "Two months ago."

"Did *they* contact *you?*" she asked.

"I believe so."

Of course they did. Maybe we were thinking about the wrong grouping of people as murderers. Rather than several family members getting together to plot Delia's demise, perhaps it was one developer and two family members motivated by different short-term goals but with the same end in mind. "Did they say they represented the entire family?" I asked.

"They implied they could make the sale happen."

Laney jumped in again. "You're certain they didn't mention any family member who was reluctant to sell?" Laney made it sound like they both knew there was at least one member of the family who wasn't on board.

Kelsey paused a little too long before saying, "I believe they were confident that they could get all of the family members to agree."

I wanted to ask who the outlier was, but didn't want to admit that we didn't know. When I talked to each individual family member, I would find out...unless they had recently been persuaded to go along with the sale.

"It's a lovely house," my mother said. "I can see why the kids might want to keep it in the family." 'Kids' could refer to several different generations, but if she was hoping he would give something away by her making the comment, she was wrong.

"The Flowers' house is in good shape, but the neighborhood as a whole is deteriorating. Sometimes you have to sacrifice one or two nice homes for a development that will benefit the majority who live in an area." He gave me a hard look and added. "We've started looking for other possible locations, so the sooner you can let me know whether they are going to sell, the better."

"What kind of development are you looking to build?" Laney asked.

"Townhouses, a retail center, and a specialty market. It will be convenient and modern while having the advantage of being close to the city." He started to warm to the sales pitch, then apparently reconsidered whether it was appropriate for his audience of three and abruptly stopped.

I glanced at Mother and Laney to see if they had any more questions. When they didn't respond, I stood up. "Well, Mr. Kelsey, I will let you know what is decided as soon as I can. Thank you for your time."

Mother and Laney followed suit. Instead of heading to the door, however, Mother went over to look more closely at a picture on Kelsey's desk, turning it slightly to get a better view.

"Is this your family in front of the family home?"

"Yes." He seemed surprised that she would ask. So was I.

"And the pictures on the wall over there are they all development projects you've handled?"

"Ah, yes."

Mother smiled at Kelsey as she turned to leave. Laney, too, was smiling. Kelsey wasn't. But he remained cordial. "I look forward to hearing from you soon."

I bet you do, I thought—there were dollar signs in his eyes when he talked about the property. The question was how far he would go to ensure the success of a project the size of the one he hoped to build in Delia's neighborhood. For instance, would he have conspired with family members to do away with Delia? Would he have lured an elderly woman to her greenhouse in the middle of the night and knocked her down, then given her head one final smash for good measure? And, if there was another holdout in the family, were they too in danger?

As soon as we were in the car, Laney said, "I'll check out who his backers are. See how anxious they are to get this project underway."

"And see if you can find out how Kelsey is doing financially," my mother said. "He lives in a pretty fancy place with an expensive-looking family. And we saw his pricey car. Maybe he's overextended. Maybe he needs this project to stay afloat."

"I thought *you* were the financial adviser," I said. "Shouldn't that task fall to you?"

She gave me a "don't be ridiculous" scowl and changed the subject. "Maybe we should think of Leland Kelsey as the latest addition to the Clue board game. I understand they've added some new characters to give it a more modern feel. If we did add him, I would say, *Kelsey did it with a concrete block in the conservatory.*"

"No one says *conservatory* anymore, Mother."

"It sounds better than *greenhouse.*"

"And technically, I think she tripped on a pot and her head struck a concrete block. So maybe the pot is the weapon."

"At least we know what we need to do next," Mother said, ignoring my corrections.

"We?"

"Well, Laney needs to check on Kelsey's finances. I don't trust him; he obviously wasn't eager to talk about certain things. And John, you need to talk to each family member, get an appraisal for the house, and then tell us everything so we can decide what to do with Delia's estate."

I wanted to protest that the decision regarding Delia's estate was mine to make. But she was right; I would definitely want to run what I found past Mother and Laney before making my final proclamations about the distribution of estate assets. Laney was not only my technology superior, she balanced my conservative and sometimes wing-it approach to investigations with an aggressive, analytic perspective. As for Mother, she often had hunches that proved helpful. We were a good team.

In the meantime, in addition to making a decision about Delia's inheritance, I was also hoping to solve a murder.

Chapter Seventeen: Last of the Flowers

Tuesday morning, I got a call from a woman who identified herself as Candy Sprinkles. At first, I thought it was a joke, but when she said she was with Climate Synchronicity, the organization's name rang a tiny bell somewhere in a shadowy part of my brain. She was in mid-sentence about what sounded like a sales pitch for donations to her organization when it hit me.

"Sorry," I interrupted. "But are you calling me because I'm in charge of the Delia Flowers' estate?" If I remembered correctly, Climate Synchronicity was a starred non-profit on Delia's list of possible recipients for her estate distributions.

"Yes, we've been hoping to hear from you. Delia was such a lovely person. I'm sorry for your loss."

"Well, I didn't actually lose her. I mean, I didn't actually know her. But…it's always sad when someone dies."

I could tell she didn't know quite what to say in response to my disjointed comments, although she recovered quickly.

"Yes, it is. Well, I'm calling on behalf of Eldon Cliffton. He's been the organization's contact with Mrs. Flowers. We understand that instead of leaving us the trust fund we were expecting, she has left the question of bequests in your hands."

"She promised you a trust fund?"

"We were going to name a research project in her honor."

"I'm afraid that hasn't come up."

"It's our understanding that her lawyer was advised of the arrangement."

"Sorry, no one told me. But I will look into it."

"We would appreciate that. Funding is important not only for our organization but for everyone's quality of life in the future."

Before she could launch another plug for her organization, I explained that I had a meeting but would call her back soon. As I hung up, it hit me how many people were looking for a piece of Delia's pie and how many people she had strung along in the hope of getting big bucks after her death. It had probably made her feel important. Dangling a carrot before the horse. And she'd had plenty of horses prancing around her, vying for her attention. Now it was up to me to sort through the deserving and the undeserving.

Even though Delia had starred Climate Synchronicity as a potential recipient on her list, I needed to do my due diligence and check on their bona fides. If they looked good, then I should either talk to Candy or Eldon or both to assess which camp they fell into—the deserving or the undeserving.

To save time, I had decided it would be nice if I could interview family members in the 2nd-floor conference room of Universal. The room wasn't in high demand, and I thought it would appear more professional to meet there rather than using my claustrophobic office or getting together at a coffee shop. I knew I should have checked with Emma before signing up for the space, but I'd convinced myself she wouldn't notice. Now that it was about to happen, though, I realized I couldn't spend time in the conference room without Emma figuring out what I was up to. So, like a Roman soldier preparing for battle, I girded my loins and went to break the news. In reality, I think the "girding your loins" phrase is a biblical reference to securing a robe with a belt. But that doesn't sound nearly as brave as a Roman soldier "preparing for battle." And to face the formidable Emma, I needed all of the bravado I could dredge up.

To my surprise, the usually stern, rule-abiding Emma was in a mellow mood. She must have had a lunch high in carbs or a little weed in her green tea because she didn't object when I explained that I was using the conference room for interviewing a few of Delia's family members. Even so, I quickly added, "I'll put in some extra hours to make up for time lost. And if anyone else needs the room, I will immediately turn it over to them and use my office for interviews."

"It *is* insurance-related," she said thoughtfully. "And your office is…ah, rather cramped for talking to what could be potential clients."

Was she actually making an argument on my behalf? That would be a first. She usually scrutinizes my every move as if suspecting me of being a Russian spy, or worse—a lazy employee. I admit to being lazy at times, but I would never spy for Russia. Then she surprised me even more.

"You talked to someone from Climate Synchronicity this morning."

She had transferred the call, but had she also listened in? At least long enough to identify the caller? "Yes, are you familiar with the organization?"

"I make annual donations to them. It's my small contribution to the health of the planet. Well, that and the other things I do personally."

"I recycle," I offered. Although admittedly, I'm not too consistent. But whenever I host a poker night, I contribute a lot of beer bottles to the local recycling plant.

Fifteen minutes later, I was inviting my first interviewee into the conference room. Harold Flowers was the young man who had shoved me against the wall at the meeting with the lawyer when he thought I'd grabbed his shoulder for some reason other than regaining my balance. He had also been with the group that swarmed my houseboat. We'd never had an actual conversation, though. In preparation for the meeting, I'd studied his place in the family hierarchy and listened to what Delia had to say about him on the thumb drive she'd left me.

Harold was the son of Marigold and Bud, and Bud was the son of Darby, Delia's brother. That made Harold the last of the Flowers' dynasty. At least until when—or if—he had children. Delia had called him "full of himself" but smart, good-looking, and charming when he wanted to be. That description seemed rather even-handed coming from someone who supposedly hated her relatives. It would be interesting to see if I felt the same after talking with him.

"You can call me Hal," he said as he shook my hand and gave me a glimpse of sparkling white teeth, displaying his charming side.

"Isn't that from a Paul Simon song?"

"No, that line is 'you can call me Al.' I'm Hal."

"Not Harry."

"Definitely not Harry."

"And not like Hal in the Space Odyssey." I don't know why I was going on and on about his name. There was just something about him that made me uncomfortable. Which in turn made me strangely chatty. He was young with preppy attractiveness, his chin tilted slightly up when he talked. It felt like he was staring down his nose at me from his soon-to-be elevated status in life. At the same time, he was all smiles with his "you can call me Hal" bonhomie. Did he think he could charm me into generosity?

"So...Hal, tell me why you think your great Aunt Delia set up her will and term life insurance the way she did."

"She was always a little weird. Liked everyone to bow down to her. And she led everyone to believe that her estate would go to her nieces and nephews. Leaving it to you came as a big surprise."

I didn't bother pointing out that she hadn't exactly "left" it to me. Instead, I asked, "She didn't mention leaving anything to *your* generation?"

"I kinda thought we would get a little something, a bit of cash. Maybe get an opportunity to choose some things from the house. Except for Luis and Gabe, of course."

"Because...?"

"Not blood. Aunt Delia made it very clear that she didn't consider them family in the strict sense of the word."

"And did you think of them as family?"

"They were around when I was growing up, but they were older, so we didn't actually have a lot in common."

"It sounds to me like Luis and Gabe had every reason to resent her and even to steal from her estate, but no reason to murder her."

The reference to "murder" seemed to penetrate what felt like disingenuous geniality. "Why would anyone in the family murder her?"

"For money?" I suggested.

"That's a serious accusation." He had gone from smiles to a menacing frown in a single blink of the eye.

"I'm not accusing anyone of anything. But someone murdered her. That's a fact. I'm just curious if you have any ideas about that."

"It's been verified, then—her death wasn't an accident?"

"Not an accident. Again, any ideas about who might have wanted her dead?"

"Some psycho, most likely."

"Some psycho who just happened to be in her backyard in the middle of the night?"

"I thought you were a claims adjustor. Why are you asking me these questions?"

"Because I have to decide who gets her inheritance. I'm starting to think that the best thing may be to give it to that nonprofit she liked so much."

"You don't mean Climate Synchronicity, do you? What a bunch of losers."

Hal's pleasant demeanor had totally vanished, replaced by a cynicism that seemed to come from a dark place in his personality. Had Delia been less than candid with me in her description of Harold, or had he kept that part of his personality hidden from her? "Why do you call them losers?"

"Aunt Delia offered to get me a job with them when I graduated from college. I thought, why not? They have a great mission statement. One interview and I knew it wasn't a good fit, though. They're more hype than substance."

I wondered if he'd opted out or if they failed to make him an offer. Perhaps Delia's request wasn't backed by sufficient funding. Or maybe she made it clear that her potential donation wasn't tied to them hiring Hal. It was also possible that he came across as too entitled or didn't interview well for some other reason. I would have to check that out.

"They do have an aggressive sales strategy," I admitted. "But as you said, a great mission."

Hal had slouched in his chair, like a surly teenager, and was apparently not amenable to talking more about Climate Synchronicity.

"One last question," I said. "How do you feel about selling the house to the developer who wants to buy it?"

That question got his full attention. He sat up straight and said, "I think it should stay in the family. The Flowers have lived there for generations."

"You're technically the last of the Flowers. In name at least."

"Like I said, it should stay in the family. I believe deep down, that's what Aunt Delia wanted."

Maybe deep down, that's what she wanted. But if so, she should have spelled it out. I'm kinda shallow; I don't read "deep down."

For the umpteenth time, I pondered why she had saddled me with the job of divvying up her inheritance. If she wanted to preserve the Flowers' lineage, why not just give the house to "Call me Hal" Harold? Was she teasing him with talk of keeping it in the family? Or was he lying? She could have given the house to him and designated that the rest of her money go to the other family members, with a set amount bequeathed to her favorite charities and nonprofits. If she sincerely couldn't make up her mind what to do with what she had accumulated, what made her think I was a better judge of character than she had been? Maybe she was toying with me, too. But why?

I had two more interviews with fourth-generation family members that afternoon. One with Heather, Hal's sister. And one with Bethany Dick, Amanda and Travis's daughter. Luis and Gabe were scheduled for Wednesday. They'd been hesitant at first to meet with me, as if it was my fault they'd been arrested. They were currently out on bail, and, from my perspective, it seemed only fair that I talk to them since I was also going to talk to Amanda and Travis. Four thieves in one family seemed like a disproportionate percentage, but it didn't necessarily eliminate them from being considered to receive some of Delia's money. Nor did it eliminate them as suspects in her murder.

Delia had described Heather as "flamboyant" and, although intelligent, lacking in interpersonal skills. Given Delia's own inability to make friends or to get along with her neighbors and relatives, that seemed like an almost laughable observation. Heather was two years older than her brother Harold, worked part-time as a barista, and was about to finish her M.A. in education. I hoped Delia was wrong about the interpersonal skills; otherwise, Heather's choice of profession might land her in that category of despised teachers

144

who earn their disparaging nicknames.

When Heather appeared at the door to the conference room, my first impression was that there was definitely a family resemblance to her brother. But unlike his preppy persona, she had that touch of flamboyance that Delia had used to describe her. Her hair was really short, almost a buzz cut, and she wore long dangly earrings that swung and winked as she walked. Her bright orange shirt didn't quite cover her stomach, and her jeans were positioned below her belly button. I tried not to look at the expanse of skin between her shirt and pants, but it was hard to keep my eyes from lingering there. At the same time, she seemed more down-to-earth than her brother, and our conversation started off cordial...until I mentioned that her brother was the "last Flowers" in the family.

"My last name is Flowers, too," she said crisply, her multicolored metal earrings flashing for emphasis. "And no one says that I have to change my name when or if I marry. That's no longer a *thing*. It isn't fair of him to claim a right to Aunt Delia's house because of his surname."

Oh, oh. Laney would tell me that I shouldn't have fallen for that misogynistic stereotype. Some ways of thinking persist like a bad toothache. You can't wish them away; rather, it requires some specific action. In this case, awareness and determination to do better. "Sorry. You're right. Have you talked with your brother about this?"

"Of course. But I'm not into old houses. My preference would be to sell the monstrosity and divide up the profit."

"Setting that issue aside for the moment, why do you think your great Aunt Delia assigned me the task of deciding what to do with her estate and term life insurance benefits?"

"We always just called her 'Aunt' Delia. Saying the 'great' part was too much of a mouthful. As to your question, that's all the family has talked about since our meeting with her lawyer. My dad assumed Amanda and Brandon would get the term life insurance benefits, and he would get the house. The rest of us would divide up any savings she had. That seemed fair to me."

"What about her brother and sister?"

"They don't need any money."

"Because they are wealthy?"

"Because they're getting up there in years. What are they going to spend it on?"

Oh, I don't know, a cruise? A new home in a retirement community? Health care? "What about the possibility of leaving everything to a charity or a nonprofit?"

"That wasn't her style. I mean, I was told she didn't even tip, let alone give money away to causes. It was only the last couple of years that she started talking about that climate group. The one she tried to get Hal lined up with. But recently, Bethany told me she was having second thoughts about them, like maybe they were trying to scam her. She was a tightwad but not stupid."

"I take it you're referring to Climate Synchronicity?"

"Yeah, that's the organization I mean."

"Your brother considered going to work for them."

"That was a joke. He thought it would be a slam dunk followed by an easy ride. Aunt Delia was stringing him along."

"Why would she do that?"

"Because she was a controlling...witch."

I thought I knew what she'd intended to say, and it was nice to know she had some boundaries. She had obviously not been fond of her Aunt Delia, and it sounded like she had some issues with her brother as well.

When I asked about Delia's death, she agreed with her brother's conclusion: she didn't think a family member killed her. "We aren't killers. More talk than action." Then she pointed at me, "Besides, you had more motive than any of us."

"I didn't know she wanted me to be an executor. And I can't keep any of the money," I said.

"We only have your word for that. Is there any legal reason why you couldn't? Some of the other family members seem to think that's what you're trying to do."

"I don't know about the legality, but there are ethical considerations."

"I've noticed that most people are willing to exchange their ethics for

146

remuneration."

"That's pretty cynical for someone your age."

"I take after my aunt in that regard.

"She was cynical?"

"Cynical, suspicious, domineering, and manipulative." After the briefest of pauses, she added, "And although I may not have *liked* her, I *loved* her dearly. Her death is a loss to the entire family."

I blinked at the blatant hypocrisy. Or was she pulling my leg? Maybe it was her directness and acerbity that made Delia say she lacked interpersonal skills.

"You look like you don't believe me. You *can* love someone you don't like," she said with conviction. Her phone started playing some upbeat tune I didn't recognize. Her fingers danced across the touchscreen keyboard, and the music ended. "If that's it, I need to run."

She was halfway to the door before I opened my mouth and said "Thanks for your time" to her retreating back. Her earrings waved goodbye.

Hal's initial exaggerated friendliness and eventual petulance had been off-putting. As was Heather's blatant hypocrisy. Bethany, on the other hand, did not appear to have any of the disagreeable traits of the other family members I had met so far. Although she had been with the group who had come to my houseboat to complain, letting Wild Thing out in the process, she had also chased him down and brought him back. If I was remembering correctly, the only time she'd chimed in was to defend her parents' right to take some of Delia's possessions without permission. You could attribute that to family loyalty.

Today, she was polite and seemed sincerely friendly—which was consistent with Delia's assessment that she was attentive, kind, and warm hearted, if perhaps a bit too trusting. Delia had also mentioned that she was fond of Bethany's daughter Clara and expressed the hope that Clara would take after Bethany rather than other family members. She hadn't passed judgment on Bethany's brief marriage other than to say that Bethany was doing a good job as a single parent. She apparently had a warm spot in her otherwise cold heart for Bethany. Maybe just a wee tiny spot, but a spot nevertheless.

During our conversation, Bethany patiently answered each of my questions, sharing special memories of her Aunt Delia in the process, pleasant memories that made her smile in the telling.

"I take it that you spent quite a bit of time with your Aunt Delia?"

"I went for tea regularly. With my daughter, Clara. She's two and a half, well almost—two years, four months, and fifteen days. But who's counting?" She smiled at her prideful-mother response. "Delia enjoyed seeing Clara. She was always buying her some little thing." She reached for her purse. "Let me show you." In her wallet, she had a picture of Delia holding Clara as the child hugged a teddy bear almost as big as she was.

"Did she give Clara the bear?" I asked.

"Yes, it's Clara's favorite."

The picture of Clara was a perfect match for the girl in the framed photo in Delia's library. "Adorable," I said, even though I wasn't sure that was true. Did I really want to be a parent?

"Sometimes I ran errands for her. She was very good to me, and I tried to help out in any way I could." She smiled wistfully as if she was going to miss time spent with Delia. If so, she was the only family member so far to express any real sense of loss.

Then I turned her smile upside down when I asked: "Why do you think your parents and your Uncle Brandon encouraged her to get a five-year term life insurance policy?"

"I know what you're implying, but you're wrong." A ripple of irritation pushed a touch of red from her neck to her cheeks.

Aha, I thought. She understood the implication but was once again loyal to her parents. I didn't bother denying my insinuation. "The normal range is from 10-30 years."

"There's a simple explanation."

I kept my face as neutral as I could and waited for her to justify their actions. I find it's best if you don't speak prematurely when you're trying to get people to say something they may be reluctant to admit.

"They have friends who got five-year term life insurance, so that's why they were thinking five years. It's as simple as that. They didn't want her to die within that time period."

I hesitated to disillusion her about her parents, but what she said didn't ring true with me. For whatever reason they decided to suggest a five-year policy, I believed they were hoping she wouldn't make it to the end.

"And did they know how often you visited your aunt?"

"They were glad I did."

I decided not to ask "why." It seemed to me that for them, it was probably all about money. I couldn't imagine them caring whether Bethany and Clara brought a little joy into Delia's life.

By the end of our conversation, I had mentally crossed Bethany off the list of murder suspects. She seemed to have been truly fond of Delia. And being loyal to her parents, though in my opinion misguided under the circumstances, was still overall a positive trait.

So far, Harold, with his "call me Hal," was at the top of my suspect list. Heather's "I loved her dearly" earned her second place. There were, however, a lot of interviews yet to do.

Chapter Eighteen: A Dysfunctional Family

Delia's sister Dorothy and her brother Darby declined my invitation to come to Universal Heartland Liability and Casualty Assurance Company of America for an interview, but they agreed to meet me at Dorothy's house after work. It was just as well because on Wednesday, I managed to book the entire afternoon with interviews of other family members, one after the other, including spouses.

Meanwhile, Laney was busy showing the appraiser Delia's house. I felt fortunate that Laney had accrued a lot of vacation time and that her law firm was okay with her taking a day off here and there. I needed help to get everything done in a timely manner, and having her support was like being in two places at once.

The appraiser's report would include a house valuation as well as a list and estimated value of any noteworthy pieces of art, furniture, and other collectibles. Laney was going to supplement the listing of valuables by taking lots of pictures to document the rest of Delia's possessions for purposes of deciding how best to dispose of them. The report was supposed to be delivered to me by Friday. Maybe the murderer would be revealed by then, too. But I wasn't counting on it.

I hired a PI friend of Laney's to stand watch Wednesday night at Delia's house just in case, although we felt it unlikely that any other relatives were going to sneak inside after what had happened to the four who had already failed in their attempts. The security people were scheduled to put up cameras and install an alarm system on Thursday. Someone was coming to check out the electrical system on Friday. And Laney continued to poke around into the developer's finances, as well as looking into the status of Climate Synchronicity.

Mother also had an assignment. She was going to talk with Mildred, her friend's friend—the one who recommended me to Delia—to get a better handle on what Delia was like as a person from a non-family member and non-neighbor perspective. She was also going to ask if Mildred knew of anyone else we should be talking with or be adding to our suspect list. The three of us were going to meet at Mother's for dinner that evening to discuss what we had learned.

Everyone had their role to play. Mine was to conduct interviews with the remaining Flowers, Plovers, and Dicks. Some people seem to easily remember names and family relationship, but I have trouble recalling the names and details of my own aunts, uncles, and cousins let alone those of Delia's family tree. That's why I had to create a chart to keep them straight. The pictures Delia had provided were definitely helpful, although I was slow to connect names with faces. At times they blurred together in my mind as one snarling mass of family members.

When I first created the tree, I'd been tempted to label it the Dysfunctional Family Divided by Greed and Murder. However, even though it was technically for my eyes only, it seemed more discreet and respectful to simply call it the **Flowers Family Tree**.

At the top of the tree were **Reba and Caleb Flowers**. It was their Victorian house that Delia had inherited.

Next came their children: **Delia Flowers** (deceased – no children), **Dorothy Flowers Plover** (divorced – two children), and **Darby Flowers** (wife deceased – one child).

The third tier: **Dorthy's two children**—Amanda Plover Dick (husband Travis Dick) and Brandon Plover (wife Marcy Plover). **Darby's son**—Bud Flowers (wife Marigold). They were all in their 50s with the exception of Marcy who was in her early 60s.

Finally, the youngest generation: Amanda's daughter—Bethany Hogg (divorced with one daughter, Clara). **Brandon's two stepsons**—Louis and Gabe (wives Louise and Gabriel), the "non-blood" relatives. **Bud's two children**—Heather and Harold (unmarried).

There were a lot of family members to be interviewed and evaluated in a short period of time. With three down, I had seven to go, not counting spouses.

Amanda and Travis came at 12:30. Delia's assessment of them on the thumb drive was that they were well-meaning but not very competent individuals—I would add that they weren't very competent burglars either. From her point of view, their greatest accomplishment was producing Bethany and, in turn, Clara. But just because they were Bethany's parents apparently didn't change Delia's overall impression of them as losers.

It quickly became clear that Amanda and Travis had agreed to meet with me because they had two agenda items of their own. First, they wanted me to know how upset they were that I had given their names to the police after suggesting I wouldn't if they agreed to stay mum about the details of Delia's death. After all, they weren't criminals—even though they had sneaked into Delia's home in the middle of the night. In their minds, the fact that Delia had "promised them a few things" made taking whatever they wanted on the sly acceptable. Second, they wanted to know if their little escapade had disqualified them from getting a piece of Delia's estate.

"You said you were letting us go," Amanda complained, a scowl forming a downturned arc with her thin lips.

"And we did," I countered."

"Then you reported us."

"When your brother's two boys broke in, all dressed in black and carrying two large bags, we felt like we had to call the police." I left out the part about them trying to bribe us. "After that, it was impossible not to mention your earlier, ah, visit." I held up my hand like a traffic cop to end the circular argument. "There are other more important things to discuss."

Before letting me continue, Travis got right to the bottom line, *their* bottom line: "Are we still being considered as possible recipients for some part of Aunt Delia's estate?" They shifted slightly forward in their chairs, and I could sense their leg muscles tensing in anticipation of getting up. I had no doubt they would simply leave if I said "no."

"No one has been ruled out," I assured them. "And nothing has been decided yet." At my announcement, they relaxed and leaned back, looking hopeful and disappointed at the same time. Pleased to still be in the running to win the lottery, but aware there was at least one strike against them.

"I invited you here to ask you a few questions related to Delia's death. Is that okay?" They glanced at each other to see if the other agreed to my request. Obviously, if they wanted to stay in the competition for a slice of Delia's estate, they had to cooperate, so they nodded "yes."

Moving on to *my* agenda, I went through the same litany of issues I'd covered with the others. It wasn't until I got to the point where I hinted that a family member might have been responsible for her aunt's death that I got any overt reaction. Amanda looked sincerely horrified, her eyes flashing disbelief. While Travis's furrowed brow suggested he was giving it some serious consideration.

It crossed my mind that Travis could be trying to determine whether he thought any family members were capable of such a heinous act, or he might have dismissed my hint and moved on, focusing instead on what he could say that would influence my inheritance distribution decisions. In any case, neither Amanda nor Travis was able—or willing—to give me the names of any enemies who may have wanted Delia dead. They did, however, point a weak finger at her next-door neighbor, suggesting it might be worth my while to check him out. But they quickly added that they thought he was more talk than action. It was the same argument Heather had made as proof that no one in the family would have killed Delia. I found it worth noting, however, that although Amanda and Travis obviously wanted to deflect attention away from themselves, there must have been some "well-intentioned" inner voice that held them back. Maybe they took to heart the Biblical saying "Judge not that ye be not judged." Some Sunday School lessons still echoed in my own brain.

When I asked them what they knew about Climate Synchronicity, they said that earlier that year, Bethany had mentioned something about Delia

153

considering a donation to the group. They hadn't been concerned, though, because they thought Delia was too tight-fisted with money to give any organization very much, if any, serious contribution. Then, later on, Bethany told them that Delia was questioning the organization's credibility. The same rumor also filtered to them through their brother Bud based on conversations he'd had with his son Hal. But they didn't know any details because they hadn't talked to Delia about it.

I switched gears and asked, "How did you feel about your daughter and granddaughter visiting Delia?" It wasn't a question from my list, but I was curious.

"We were supportive," Amanda said, and her husband nodded in agreement.

"Bethany seems to have been fond of her."

Amanda's lips twitched as if fighting a frown. "To be honest, I suspected Delia invited her over and gave Clara presents to annoy me. I can't picture her having a sincere fondness for another human being."

"Did you tell Bethany how you felt about your aunt?"

Travis leaned forward. "What does this have to do with anything?"

"Bethany and Clara are on the list of possible recipients of estate money." That didn't really answer his questions, but it shut him down.

"She didn't like it when we badmouthed Delia around her, so we avoided the topic." They didn't really answer *my* question either, but I moved on.

In the end, none of their answers got me any closer to determining who killed Delia. It did, however, leave me wondering about the relationship between Bethany and Delia. Was it real on both sides? Delia's notes, as well as the fact that she had pictures of Bethany and Clara in the library, suggested she had feelings for them. And Bethany had seemed sincere when she'd shared memories of time spent with Delia. But even if it was genuine on Bethany's side, caring about a family member certainly didn't fit the image of Delia as depicted by the others I'd interviewed. It made me wonder what the rest of the family thought about Bethany's visits with her great aunt. Did they assume she was simply sucking up to Delia? Or did they dismiss her visits as the act of a naïve young girl? It was even possible that they appreciated having someone on the inside to keep track of what Delia was up to.

It crossed my mind that in some ways, Delia was like Wild Thing, mean to many, but loving to a select few. Also, disliked by many but loved by a few. There was probably more to her story than I was going to uncover by talking to relatives whose perspectives were hardened by time or to those with a personal agenda. But then, I didn't have to either understand or like her to fulfill my obligation to her estate.

Bud and Marigold called to say they were running a few minutes late. I didn't mind; it had been a jam-packed day so far with much more to come. The delay had given me time to review Delia's notes and turn a fresh page in my notepad.

Delia's assessment of Bud was not high praise, but only included one negative comment. She acknowledged that it had been hard for Bud to lose his mother. It almost sounded as though she'd liked her brother's wife, Bud's mother, but since the woman was deceased, she hadn't said much about her. As for Bud, she noted that he had been a good student and a decent athlete, and always had steady employment. But...he had married Marigold for her looks and not her brains.

When they arrived, I understood immediately why Delia had commented on Marigold's looks. Attractive at fifty, I could see that she must have been stunning when younger. Bud, on the other hand, although not unattractive, sported a straggly beard that didn't make up for his receding hairline.

Since Marigold didn't have much to say, usually turning to her husband to answer my questions and then nodding in agreement, the interview went quickly. They labeled Delia as selfish and high-handed, but Bud remembered liking holidays at the family home when he was young. "Brandon, Amanda, and I played in the turret while the adults talked downstairs. Then, at some point, we stopped getting together as a family."

"What was your impression of her back then?"

Bud thought for a moment. "I can't really say. She was an adult we only saw on holidays. I don't remember her being that interested in me or my cousins. But she wasn't mean to us."

They had no idea why she named me as executor. They had never talked with her about Climate Synchronicity. They were aware that Bethany visited Delia frequently but thought Delia also favored their son Hal. And, no, they couldn't think of anyone who would have wanted to harm her.

When they left, I was none the wiser about anything. But I was starting to get a more nuanced picture of Delia.

Brandon and his wife, Marcy, came next. Delia's comments about them had started with her belief that her nephew's biggest mistake in life was to marry a woman who was both older than himself and who already had children. Their lack of progeny together seemed to be more than simply a bone of contention for Delia; she was obviously angered by it. In her message to me, she emphasized what I had already heard from several family members—that Gabe and Luis were not "blood" relations. In addition, she didn't find them particularly likable, although she acknowledged that they had helped with home maintenance tasks from time to time.

Other comments she made about Brandon and Marcy echoed her feelings about Amanda and Travis. Basically, she wasn't impressed. What she felt they *should* be doing with their lives wasn't clear. But by whatever standard she had in her mind, they weren't living up to expectations. The fact that both were gainfully employed engineers didn't apparently count for much in her book.

Given Delia's post-grave comments and the conversations I'd already had with family members, I wasn't surprised to find that one of the main reasons Brandon and Marcy had for talking with me was to make sure I understood how unfair Delia had been to always point out that their sons weren't "blood."

"We got married when they were young," Marcy said. "They were three and five at the time. The only father they know is Brandon, and they grew up as part of the Flowers' family. Granted, they were a few years older than Amanda's and Bud's children, but they're still cousins by any measure."

"Why do you think Delia felt so strongly about their status? Did she not get along with them?"

"Delia didn't 'get along' with people—adults or children. She was always a bit aloof and considered herself better than everyone else."

"That's not entirely fair, Marcy," Brandon said. "She was a lonely old woman. I felt sorry for her."

Was showing some empathy for Delia an attempt to sway my opinion? That's what it felt like. I was tempted to ask if he still considered me "scum."

"We don't get everything we want, do we?" Marcy countered. "But we don't take it out on others. Delia did, though. She could be vindictive."

They argued back and forth for a while before I interrupted them with a question about what they thought of Bethany's relationship with Delia.

"She didn't have a *relationship* with her. No one did," Marcy said.

"But you knew she took Clara to see Delia on a fairly regular basis."

"We all assumed she was currying favor to see if she could get special treatment in Delia's will."

"And that didn't bother you?"

"More power to her—she would have earned it."

I turned to Brandon. "Is that why you insisted that Luis and Gabe do maintenance work for her? To curry favor?"

Brandon rubbed his chin as though considering my question. "I suppose that was part of it. I kept hoping she'd soften toward them."

He sounded like he was being sincerely thoughtful, unlike the emotional and volatile person I'd encountered previously. Which was the "real" Brandon? I suppose he could be both. At that point, they'd believed I had cheated them out of their inheritance. Now they were hoping to appease and manipulate me.

I then asked whether there were other people Delia might have alienated, other than family. Like Amanda and Travis, they mentioned the neighbor, agreeing that he was probably her worst enemy. Although they also thought there were likely quite a few other neighbors who were also mad at her for not agreeing to sell.

When I brought up Climate Synchronicity, they shook their heads and admitted they knew nothing about her relationship with them. In fact, they said they were surprised that she might have made donations to *any* charity or organization. "She didn't even give our kids gifts at Christmas," Marcy said. "Not even when they were young."

It was still another dead end.

I had just enough time to grab a cup of coffee before Luis and Gabe arrived with their wives, Louise and Gabriel. I was tempted to comment on their names—Luis and Louise, Gabe and Gabriel—but the cold atmosphere in the room didn't seem to welcome any small talk. Besides, if they were like me, they'd already had enough kidding about their names.

All four were wearing jeans. The men had on long-sleeved polo shirts with straight vertical wrinkles that made me wonder if they had been recently removed from a store bag and were being worn for the first time. I couldn't blame them for not washing their shirts before wearing, like the tags always advised; I didn't usually do that either. And so far, no dye had rubbed off on my skin, although once I did get an itchy rash from a new wool-blend shirt.

Their wives were both wearing sweatshirts. Gabriel's had a row of flowers across her ample chest. Louise's plain blue sweatshirt was long and baggy, like she was trying to hide a bulky torso. It crossed my mind that she might be pregnant. Neither woman exactly looked "put together." Gabriel's haircut had no identifiable style and looked like she cut it herself. Louise had her hair pulled back in a ponytail, held in place by a scrunchy that resembled a cat toy. Neither woman wore any makeup except lipstick. I had the feeling they'd been dragged away from doing chores around the house, hastily applying a touch of lipstick because they were going downtown.

I knew from Delia's comments on Gabe and Luis that she would not consider any children either couple had as Flowers' descendants any more than she considered them as such. It didn't matter what their last names were. She'd also made it clear on the thumb drive that she had informed Brandon and Marcy of her views. She knew they were hoping for grandchildren, and she had apparently made it clear that she would not consider their grandchildren to be part of the Flowers lineage. To her, the flow of "blood" through the generations was like a river; tributaries were an extension of but not a part of the mainstream.

The four lined up across the table from me. It made me uncomfortable to be outnumbered, even though I knew I had all the power. They knew it too, as evidenced by restless movements and the fact that no one seemed to want to look directly at me. Perhaps not only did they hold me responsible for getting the two men arrested, but they saw me as aligned with Delia against stepsons Gabe and Luis.

I began with what was now becoming my standard opening question: "Why do you think Delia assigned me the task of deciding what to do with her estate and term life insurance benefits?"

"She wanted to make us all sweat," Gabe said.

"Not that we thought we were going to be remembered in her will," Luis quickly added.

"She never gave us a chance," Gabe said.

"Did you spend much time with her?"

"The usual, family get-togethers and holidays when we were kids," Gabe said. "Not that much lately."

"It was never pleasant, not even when we were kids," Luis said.

Louise jumped in: "I can attest to our visits not being pleasant. I was just thankful we didn't have to see her very often."

"How *often* did you visit with her?"

They all looked guiltily at each other. "Not often," Gabe said.

"Did your other cousins see more of her?"

"Possibly," Gabe said. "I know Bethany did. She's always been a toady. And Hal and Heather, maybe occasionally. Once Aunt Delia made it clear how she felt about us, my parents didn't make duty calls as often. Although Dad made some effort. When we got older, they didn't force us to go see her, but Dad still made us do small jobs for her."

"Like...?"

"Mowing her lawn, trimming bushes, fixing faucets—that sort of thing."

"Did she pay you?" I was trying to get a better handle on their relationship with her.

They looked at each other and laughed. "No way," Luis said. "Even when we were kids, she never gave us anything, not even candy at Halloween. She was not what you would call a giving person."

"So, you did odd jobs for her because your father asked you to?"

"Yeah."

"Was he close to her?"

"I don't think so," Gabe said. "But our grandmother was her sister—"

"Was your grandmother close to Delia?"

"Not very. But family is important to Grandma. I think she was the one who encouraged Dad to stay in touch."

I decided not to pursue the topic further; I could ask Dorothy later about her relationship with Delia. But I did wonder if the only reason anyone in the family catered to Delia's needs was to remind her of their common ancestry in the hope that she would leave them part of her estate. In the case of Gabe and Luis, it was my opinion that they shouldn't have wasted their time doing odd jobs for her. Not only was she hung up on the issue of "blood relations," but I could understand why Delia favored Bethany, Hal, and Heather over them. Bethany was the "good girl" with the cute kid. And Heather and Hal could be charming when they wanted to be. Whereas Gabe and Luis were not only "not blood," their aura was, as Delia had described, *unappealing*, two people weighed down by their lot in life. Their wives were a bit unappealing, too. But then, maybe it was just the circumstances under which I was meeting them. Maybe they were lighthearted and jovial around their friends. How much effort was I going to make to find out? And would it make a difference in how I divided up Delia's estate?

Chapter Nineteen: A Gaggle of Suspects

After Gabe, Luis, and their wives left, I managed to get in some work on one fairly simple auto accident file before calling it a day and heading to meet with Dorothy and Darby at Dorothy's home. I didn't complete the file, but I could at least honestly tell Emma that I'd spent some time that afternoon on company business. However, if she sometimes checked my desk when I was out, as I suspected Emma might, she would know how little I had actually accomplished.

Even though I was tired of meeting with members of the Flowers' family, the drive over to Dorothy's was invigorating. Hints of the summer to come were in the air. It was always pleasant living on the water when the sun was out. Maybe this year I'd finally buy that kayak I'd been thinking about purchasing. It would be fun to paddle around the lake and see everything from the water instead of when speeding past in a car. I could buy two kayaks, and Laney could go with me. We could paddle over to the Ivar's Salmon House dock and get fish and chips to go.

I was fantasizing about Ivar's fish and chips, one of my favorites, when I arrived at Dorothy's. She lived in an older Craftsman-style home with a covered porch that ran the full width of the house but ended at the edges. There were rock columns on either side of the stairs. Matching rocks reached from the foundation to just below the porch. A row of planters alongside the sidewalk leading to the house was filled with healthy-looking greenery. In keeping with the rest of the neighborhood, everything looked tidy and carefully tended.

Delia hadn't said much about Dorothy and Darby in the recording she'd made for me. She had explained that as the oldest, she always felt a responsibility to look out for them when they were children. She also mentioned that it was possible they resented her because she was their parents' favorite. Commenting on their marriages, she'd said that "Dorothy married beneath her" and that their eventual divorce had not surprised her. As for Darby, she said that neither he nor his wife seemed to appreciate the importance of carrying on the family name. By having only one son, she felt that they weren't sufficiently protecting the future of the Flowers' dynasty. Of course, she ignored the fact that she herself had been childless. And, like me, she obviously hadn't considered the possibility that Heather would keep the family name and pass it along to any offspring. That was one faux pas hole I wouldn't step in a second time.

When Dorothy answered the door, I was struck again by how much she resembled Delia, although with less panache. She didn't command the room like Delia had. Her overall demeanor was reflected in what she was wearing: sweatpants and a floral turtleneck. Not something you could accent with a mink stole.

As the younger female sibling, sandwiched between Delia and Darby, it was possible Dorothy had grown up in Delia's shadow. That might account for the difference in personality. It was also possible, given the time period, that both girls had eventually taken a back seat to their younger brother, the male heir. It made me wonder how Delia had ended up with the family home.

Darby was waiting for us in the living room. Although the youngest of the three siblings, he looked much older than his seventy-one years. His deceased wife, Celia, died of cancer when she was in her fifties, and he had not remarried. He pulled himself slowly out of the recliner he was seated in and extended a hand for a very limp handshake before collapsing back into the chair. "I have arthritis in my back," he said. I understood why he wanted to explain, but I didn't know how to respond.

"Sorry," I said. "It must be difficult to get around." Duh, I said to myself. That was obviously a stupid thing to say. Dorothy saved me from making another lame observation by pointing to a side table where there was an attractive teapot surrounded by dainty cups next to a plate of what looked like homemade cookies. She asked if I would like anything, and I said yes to both.

While she was pouring my tea, her back to Darby, she softly said, "Poor man. He's in pain much of the time."

I repeated my "sorry" and stuffed a cookie in my mouth so I could chew rather than make small talk. The tea turned out to be herbal; it smelled like the flowers you might take to someone in the hospital. But the cookies were good. Mother would have said I shouldn't eat cookies before dinner, but then, Mother wasn't there.

Dorothy poured tea for her and Darby, and we settled into our chairs. It felt like a tea party rather than an interview about their sister's death. I had a second cookie before asking my first question.

"Why do you think Delia asked me to distribute the proceeds of her estate?"

"Control from the grave," Darby said without hesitation. "Delia always liked to be in control."

"The same was true when we were kids," Dorothy said. "Granted, our parents were hard on her because she was the oldest. They expected her to work hard and excel at everything. She took that out on us. She was always bossing us around, telling us what we should and shouldn't do. Tattling on us when we did something she knew our parents wouldn't approve of." Dorothy glanced at Darby for confirmation. "Setting up the distribution of her estate the way she did was her way of getting in one last poke."

"What do you think she should have done?"

"As her siblings, and since she didn't have children, everything should have been left to us to pass on to our kids and their kids. That's the way a normal family would have handled it."

"Or she could have made Amanda, Brandon, and Bud her heirs. That would have been fine with us, too." Darby looked at Dorothy, and she nodded.

"How did she end up with the family house?" I asked.

"She convinced Mom and Dad that, as the oldest, she should have it. Like we were some royal British family where the oldest was supposed to carry on with the family name. We were lucky they didn't send me to a convent and put Darby in the military."

"Didn't it make a difference to them that Darby was the male heir?"

"We're not entirely sure how she manipulated them into turning everything over to her, but she did."

"Did you receive other assets?" The resentment seemed palpable. And they weren't making any effort to hide it.

"Our parents left us each a little nest egg, but that was it," Darby said. "I had a good job, and Dorothy was married, so financially it didn't really matter."

"Financially, it didn't matter, but I wouldn't say it *didn't matter*. It mattered to me. It wasn't fair." Dorothy pinned me with her eyes. "Do you have siblings?"

"No, I'm an only child." It's funny; no matter how old I get, I still refer to myself as an only *child*.

"Then you wouldn't understand." She dismissed me with a dainty sip of tea.

"I understand the concept of fairness. That's why I'm talking to all the family members before deciding what to do with Delia's assets."

"I meant that you can't understand how it feels to be devalued by a parent."

I didn't want to argue because it was obviously a touchy subject with the two of them. But was feeling devalued a motive for murder? If so, would they be so open about how much they resented their sister?

"I take it you weren't close, but you all lived near each other. Did you see her often?"

"Seldom these days," Dorothy said. "When the kids were young, we spent holidays together. For some crazy reason, we thought she would be pleased with the arrangement since she didn't have any children of her own."

"I think maybe she was jealous of our families," Darby said. "Holidays spent together were always stressful."

"Once our children were older, we quit pretending and went our separate ways during the holidays. After that, I kept in touch mostly by phone. Brandon's sons helped her out from time to time. And Bethany was a frequent visitor." She took another sip of tea. "It would have been nice if we could have been close, though, visited back and forth, and shared confidences, like some sisters do."

"I understand she tried to help Hal get a job with Climate Synchronicity, a nonprofit she was interested in."

Darby leaned forward. "She led Hal to believe she could help him get a job there. But she didn't have as much sway with them as she thought. Or she didn't really try. I suspect it was a little of both."

"Can you tell me about her interest in Climate Synchronicity or any other charities and nonprofits? Did she have any favorites that you know of?"

"Delia wasn't the philanthropic type. I can't remember her ever volunteering her time or talking about contributing to a worthy cause in the past."

"So, were you surprised to learn that she considered leaving some of her assets to various organizations?"

"Shocked," Dorothy said. "It would be interesting to know just how much she was actually donating to any of them over the years. Don't misunderstand me, I don't begrudge her making gifts of that nature. I have organizations that I support. But it was a side of her that I never saw."

Darby said, "It wouldn't surprise me to learn she was trying to give away as much as she could so no one in the family would inherit much."

"Darby," Dorothy said, "that's a pretty mean accusation." At first, I thought she was trying to lighten the conversation by teasing him a bit. Until she turned to me and added, "She was like Scrooge McDuck. She loved swimming in her inherited wealth but didn't want to share that pool with any of the rest of us."

"If you felt that way, Dorothy, why did you encourage your grandsons to help her out with house and yard maintenance? She could have afforded to hire it done."

"I'm not sure. Maybe because she was my sister. I always thought that perhaps someday—" She stopped talking and blinked. For a moment, I thought she was going to squeeze out a few tears. Instead, she said, "I'm not sure why any of this is relevant. Unless you are going to distribute her estate based on how much individual family members liked or disliked her."

"No, I just find family dynamics fascinating. Sorry." That was a lie. But it's something I've heard my mother say, and it seemed like a reasonable response under the circumstances. I could hardly admit I was searching for a motive for murder.

"Well, we certainly have enough 'dynamics' to go around," Darby said.

Was that a touch of dark humor? I couldn't read him at all; maybe being in pain dulled his nonverbals.

"There's another thing I've wondered about," I said. "Had she always been an avid gardener?" For some reason, that didn't fit with the emerging image of the woman. Although I realized that nurturing plants was different from nurturing people.

"It was a hobby she took up a couple years ago," Dorothy said. "But why she got fixated on carnivorous plants or ones that smell like rotting meat is beyond me."

"It was just like her to choose plants you might find in a book on witchery."

I suddenly pictured Delia stirring a soupy mix in a large black cauldron with wafts of rotten meat streaming in all directions, watched by an eye of newt. When I was a kid, I thought "eye of newt" referred to an actual eye. I was disappointed to find out it was a folk name for mustard seeds.

As I was winding up, I asked about Delia's insistence that Gabe and Luis weren't "blood."

"It was totally illogical," Dorothy said with Darby nodding in agreement.

"In spite of her attitude toward Luis and Gabe, we assumed she would leave most of her estate to her great-nieces and nephews with special bequests to regular employees, like the woman who cleaned her house, and perhaps to her only friend." Darby turned to Dorothy. "What is her name again?"

"Mildred something. How she put up with Delia, I can't imagine."

"I haven't met Mildred, but she's a friend of my mother's," I said. Somehow, I felt I should defend her. Although maybe I should have let them criticize her; she was, after all, partly responsible for laying this burden on me. "So," I concluded. "If you had to guess, who do you think was angry enough with your sister to murder her?"

"Murder," Dorothy said. "That's such an ugly word."

"Are the police quite certain she was actually murdered?" Darby asked.

"Originally, they said it was an accident."

"Quite certain," I confirmed. "Any thoughts on it?"

"Maybe that developer. Or one of her neighbors," Dorothy said. "She obviously wasn't a family favorite, but I can't imagine anyone in the family as a murderer."

"Were you in favor of her selling the family home?"

"I'm happy where I am," Dorothy said. "What about you, Darby?" He nodded. "And I'm not sure any of the kids want to take on the responsibility of such a huge house."

"Hal has expressed interest."

"Hal is still too young to know what he wants."

On that happy note, I ended the final family interview and headed for Mother's.

Laney was there when I arrived, helping Mother in the kitchen. I was glad they got along so well. Although Mother was under the impression that she wouldn't get her much-desired grandchildren from the relationship, it felt a lot like family. And not a dysfunctional one. I had definitely decided not to mention Laney's proposal for having a child together, at least not for a while. I was afraid Mother would get excited and start encouraging us to do it right away. My guess was that she would prefer I have a houseful of children with a woman I was married to, but she would most likely love any child I fathered. Or adopted. I was fairly certain "blood" would not be an issue for her. A child was a child; once in the family, they would *be* family.

After a nostalgic dinner of meatloaf and garlic mashed potatoes, we lingered over a smooth Malbec Laney had brought and talked about what I should do with my "power" and speculated about who murdered Delia.

"Now that you've had a chance to talk to all of them, if you had to pick a family member as the most likely suspect, who would it be?" Laney asked me.

"Well, Hal has the most to gain if the family agrees he should have the house if he wants it. But Amanda and Brandon, for some reason, were betting that she would die within five years and were hoping to receive the five million in benefits. Then again, maybe Dorothy and Darby's dislike reached the boiling point after simmering for so many years. Or maybe Gabe and Luis teamed up to get even for her putting them down because they weren't blood relations. Or maybe one of the spouses got greedy. Or maybe it's the least likely family member...who would be, I think, Bethany. The quiet ones are often guilty of the crime, aren't they?"

"Well, that certainly narrows it down," Mother said. "As far as family members go, I vote for Dorothy. Delia got everything, and she and Darby got next to nothing. That hurts. She could even have been in cahoots with her two kids on the term life insurance scheme. Laney?"

"My money's on Hal. He couldn't be bothered to suck up to his great aunt and wait for her to die. He thought he was the heir apparent because he felt entitled. Entitlement is a nasty trait."

"So, we agree that all of the family members had some level of motive, with the possible exception of Bethany. I can't believe she's been faking her fondness for her great aunt for this long."

"You never know what someone may be hiding from the world, though, do you?" Laney said.

"And, according to the police investigation, they all had opportunity."

"What about means?" Mother asked, clearly about to answer her own question. "It wasn't a spur-of-the-moment crime of passion. But the plan wasn't that great. They should have anticipated she might not die from a simple fall like that."

"Bruno always says that the main reason they catch as many criminals as they do is that criminals frequently make stupid mistakes."

"Anyone could have pushed her—to me, it seems like motive is the better lead to pursue," Laney said.

"Most of the family is convinced it was either a neighbor or the developer," I said. "Fairly strong motives—financial and personal."

"Well, I'm still searching for more info on Kelsey's finances. But at first blush, I think that project may be critical to his company's survival. Rumor has it that his backers are getting antsy. The question is whether he has any potential locales in mind other than Delia's neighborhood."

"Neighbors can get their tails in a knot about even small things. And this is a big thing," Mother said. "So, it wouldn't surprise me if a neighbor did it."

"Tails in a knot?" I asked. "What does that mean?"

"Just what I said."

"What animals get knots in their tails?"

"They sometimes knot the tails of show horses," Laney said. "But I don't think the horses mind."

"I agree that some neighbor might have wanted to sell badly enough that they decided to eliminate what they perceived to be the only obstacle to the sale. Tail or no tail."

"There were also a couple family members who implied that Climate Synchronicity might have wanted Delia silenced. They'd heard rumors that she had become disenchanted with them and was questioning whether they were scamming people. Then again, everyone seemed to doubt that Delia was a serious donor for *any* charity or nonprofit."

"They look legitimate online," Laney said. "And they are registered with the State and don't have any official complaints against them that I could find. But there *are* rumors. I'll keep digging."

"So many suspects," Mother said, not for the first time. "I thought you would have crossed some of them off the list by now."

"So did I. By the way, did you talk to Mildred?"

"As a matter of fact..." Mother paused for dramatic effect. "I had lunch with her today."

"And...?"

"As we knew, Mildred apparently went to boarding school with Delia. She said that even back then, Delia was argumentative and displayed a mean streak if she didn't like someone. But neither Delia nor Mildred liked boarding school, and the time spent there together created a bond of sorts. She said she wouldn't describe them as having a close relationship, but they stayed in touch over the years and met occasionally for coffee or lunch. According to Mildred, Delia was bright and well read, and their get-togethers were always pleasant. She did mention that Delia complained about family from time to time, but that she also talked about how much she enjoyed visits with her great-niece, Bethany, and her daughter.

"Unfortunately, there was no one who stood out to her as a possible murder suspect. She did, however, mention that years ago, Delia stole Dorothy's fiancé and then shortly afterwards dumped him. In her opinion, Delia did it simply to prove she could. She was apparently always a little better-looking and more impressive than Dorothy. And even though Dorothy got married the very next year, she never got over losing her first love to Delia, and she ended up getting a divorce as soon as the children left home."

"Okay, let's say Dorothy is the murderer, why now? What's changed?" Laney was thinking out loud. "All that happened almost fifty years ago."

"Maybe she really was trying to get the five million for her kids." Dorothy had convinced me that neither she nor Darby personally needed the money, but that didn't mean she had much to give to her offspring.

"I'm not sure you should call them kids—both are in their fifties," Laney said.

"Adult children, then."

"I kinda liked Dorothy...and Darby," I said. "She makes good cookies."

"Well, that definitely means we should cross her off the list of suspects," Laney said. "Seriously, maybe I should put more effort into researching Climate Synchronicity. If they're really running a scam, that would be a motive I could get next to."

"I'm suspicious of anyone named Candy Sprinkles." Although just saying her name made me want a donut.

"And I'm suspicious of any organization with a fancy name like Climate Synchronicity," Mother said. "It puts a knot in my tail." She gave me the stink eye.

"So, we all agree that the suspect pool is bigger than a breadbox," I said.

"What is this, cliché day?" Laney groaned. "Yes, I agree, we have to find a way to *prune the family tree*, determine which neighbors wanted to *bite someone's head off*, and see if the developer was ready to *spit nails*."

"You win," Mother said. "Next?"

"I'll call Bruno and see if he knows anything new. I can share what we've learned so far—which will probably be as helpful to him as it is to us."

"Depends on what he's learned," Laney said. "Sometimes one little piece of info, when viewed in conjunction with other facts, can make all the difference." I could picture her juggling and rearranging the facts we knew in her mind, searching for a pattern, like Alan Turing cracking the Enigma Code during World War II.

"Ask if he's talked to many of the neighbors," Mother said.

"I know, see if any had their tails in a knot," Laney said.

We all laughed.

"Seriously," I said. "I appreciate what you are both doing for me. And for Delia. If we can't figure out who murdered her, I don't know how I'm going to deal with her inheritance."

"The easiest thing would be to give everyone equal shares," Laney said. "That way if one of them did it, they won't be winning the whole enchilada. It's either that or give it to some charity or nonprofit that you know for sure is on the up-and-up."

"Even split ten ways, that will be a nice chunk of change," Mother said. "I'm assuming none of the spouses will be included in the distribution."

"They're all family at this point," I said. Then I chimed in with Laney to say:

"But not blood."

We sat there in silence for a few moments, thinking about next steps.

"I have an idea," Laney said, a mischievous glint in her eye. "Why don't you call the entire family together and ask them to come up with a plan for the money?"

Mother smiled. "Like one of those Nero Wolfe meetings. And even if the killer isn't revealed during the conversation, it would be great fun to watch."

"After your delicious dinner, I feel a bit like Nero Wolfe." I patted my full stomach. "Mother, does that make you Fritz, the excellent cook? And Laney, you would be Archie, my indispensable sidekick."

"And Bruno is Inspector Cramer," Mother chimed in. "We have the full cast."

* * *

171

Just before I went to bed, I checked in with the PI watching over Delia's house. She said everything was calm and that she had enough coffee to last until morning. If anything happened, she would let me know. I made sure my phone was charged and put it on the nightstand next to my bed. As if I were expecting to lie down, close my eyes, and fall asleep.

When that didn't happen, I tried an app called "The French Whisperer." In a quiet and monotonous voice, the narrator talked about things like how long the Great Wall of China would be if it reached from the equator to the North Pole and how the Vikings never wore horns on their helmets. At first, I didn't see how listening to trivia was ever going to lull me to sleep. Then he started explaining how the periodic table of elements is organized. It has to do with the order of increasing atomic numbers. The atomic number represents the number of protons in an element's nucleus, and, ergo, its respective number of electrons. The horizontal rows are called periods, and the vertical columns are called groups. Elements in the same group have similar chemical properties because..."zzzz."

Chapter Twenty: Scammers & Schemers

Before leaving for work, I heard from the PI who'd spent a quiet night watching over Delia's house. "There were no attempted break-ins, no raccoons or coyotes spooking around, no loud parties in the neighborhood, no trees fell. It was a no-event night." Relieved but somewhat disappointed, I spent Thursday focused on my "real" job—assessing the validity and worth of insurance claims. I try to be fair; that's what I think the company expects of me. But people get wrapped around the axle trying to cheat the company out of even paltry sums. That's because most clients believe that insurance companies are rolling in dough and owe them for the years they've paid for insurance protection. Kinda like family members who feel they are owed because they are on the family tree.

Laney called mid-afternoon to let me know that Climate Synchronicity looked shady as hell. At least in her eyes. As far as she could tell, there were no official lawsuits filed against them, although the organization could be under an investigation that hadn't been made public yet. She wanted to meet me after work to look around Delia's house again. She was convinced that if Delia had suspicions about them, there was evidence tucked away there somewhere. "Delia wouldn't leave it lying around in the open. She was too devious herself to trust others. But she would want to document what she found."

"You think she was devious?"

"Well, I get the impression that she was smart and domineering and a bit of a schemer who wasn't above manipulating others to get what she wanted. That's *devious*, isn't it?"

"Maybe someone from Climate Synchronicity was the intruder who trapped us in the bathroom."

"Like your mother keeps saying, there are too many suspects."

* * *

We met at Delia's. The locks had been changed, cameras strategically placed on the property, and an alarm system installed. It's surprisingly easy to get things done when you're spending someone else's money, especially a dead person's. She wasn't going to miss it.

Laney was good with alarms—I didn't probe too deeply as to why—so I had her use the code I'd been given to get inside. I could imagine myself punching in the wrong thing and setting the alarm off. And I'd read in the instructions that there was a panic code you were supposed to punch in if you were under duress. With my luck, that would be the code I would remember and end up finding myself surrounded by gun-wielding officers responding to my unintended request for help.

Once inside, we reset it so we would be alerted if there was a trespasser. We wanted to avoid getting locked in some part of the house a second time. And I definitely didn't want to be forced to depart by traversing the roof and sliding down the Wisteria again.

In spite of attempts by family members to get what they considered was owed to them by their deceased relative, we doubted anything had been stolen since Delia died. Although we had no way of knowing for certain. However, now that Laney had the pictures she'd taken the day before, we would be able to tell if something visible went missing. We wouldn't, of course, know if something was taken from a drawer, closet, container, or any place where something might have been stowed out of sight.

We started our search in the library because that's where Delia had kept her personal records. As we looked around, I saw Laney take out a picture from time to time and check to make sure everything was where it should be. Although the main purpose of our search was to find whatever Delia had dug up about Climate Synchronicity, we were keeping an eye out for anything that might give us some insight into who killed Delia.

Looking for something specific should have been easier than doing a random search, but it wasn't, perhaps because we still didn't know what form the "proof" would take. Why she would have been hiding things in her own home wasn't entirely clear either, but I didn't have a hot date waiting for me, so why not spend an evening rooting through someone else's belongings? I needed to get a hobby.

This time, we were digging a little deeper than we had before, hoping to find something tucked away somewhere, perhaps notes on her inquiries slipped in between magazine pages or in a book, or even concealed behind a piece of art. Maybe some copies of financial records. Or clippings identifying past scams by either the organization or its CEO. We might even find a box or a safe that could be unlocked by the third key we'd found. I had checked with the lawyer, but he hadn't known anything about a safety deposit box, so we were still looking for the missing keyhole.

There were too many books to flip through every one, but we did give each shelf a once-over, peering behind some books, sliding our fingers along the spines of others, checking out dust patterns. I considered taking the backs off paintings to see if she'd hidden anything inside, but it was too much work. It was easier to pick up pieces of art or vases or pots to check underneath and use a flashlight to look under sofas and chairs. At one point, I stuck my head in the fireplace and looked up the chimney to see if there was anything stashed there, retreating quickly when I got tangled in a spiderweb.

After about 45 minutes, Laney sat down at Delia's desk and closed her eyes.

"You thinking or napping?" I asked.

"Trying to catch her vibe." She kept her eyes shut.

I continued my own search, peering into pottery and opening decorative boxes to see what was inside. I even checked under the corners of a couple of throw rugs. As I searched, I thought of a book I'd been given as a kid that had stories about ancient mythological creatures. The full-page line drawing of the monster with hundreds of eyes all over his body had creeped me out. However, having a hundred eyes in this situation would have come in handy. But it would definitely be creepy.

Laney suddenly sat up straight and opened her eyes. "I wouldn't put it here. I mean, if I had some incriminating evidence, I would hide it someplace where no one would look."

"Like the attic? Or the turret?"

"Or..."

"The root cellar," we said in unison.

On the way downstairs, I said, "We still don't know if any of the family members are aware of the secret entrance to the root cellar. I didn't mention it when I talked to them."

"They *might* know that it was still accessible. *If* she talked with them after the remodel and explained how she had kept the original entrance through the pantry. But I doubt she told anyone, except possibly Bethany. And even if Bethany mentioned it to other family members, they didn't visit, so when would they have checked it out? And why bother?"

"It seems to me that it would be the Synchronicity people who would be looking for any incriminating evidence Delia had discovered about them. *If* they suspected she was looking into their organization. And it would be highly unlikely that they would know about the cellar."

"What if the Synchronicity people offered to pay a family member to search for any notes Delia might have put together on them? Someone might have considered that an opportunity to make a few bucks without much effort."

"I think you're right. But two stars would have had to collide for that to happen. I mean, they would not only have to ask the right family member, someone who not only knew about the cellar—or some other hiding place, but someone who was also willing to accept money to do some undercover work. That scenario seems unlikely to me. And if someone from Climate Synchronicity approached the wrong person, it could have been a disaster for them. In my opinion, if Delia hid something in the cellar, there's a good chance it's still there."

This time, we had real flashlights with us, and with their help, we quickly located a light switch for the stairway leading to the cellar. There were naked lightbulbs hanging from the ceiling at about six-foot intervals down to the bottom and around the corner into the main part of the cellar. The lighting wasn't as good there, so we got out our flashlights and started scanning what was on the benches along the side walls and then on the shelves lining the back wall. There wasn't much—some boxes of old canning supplies, a couple of large containers that might have been for storing fruits and vegetables, a handful of small tools, a roll of masking tape, a rusted flashlight, and a row of Mason jars with hard-to-read labels.

"These jars of jam and pickles look like they've been here for a while," Laney said. "I think this one says garlic dills."

"I can't picture Delia canning pickles. Or making jam."

We took another turn around the cellar. "This place hasn't been used for a long time," I said, looking down at the cement floor. I could see footprints and recognized my own tennis shoe tread. "Did you check for footprints before we started milling about?"

"No. My bad."

"Why would Delia safeguard a way to get down here and then leave it like this? It doesn't make sense."

Laney was studying the ancient food-filled Mason jars. "Look at this," she said as she reached over and picked up a jar of pickles and turned it around. Then she grinned at me. "Well, what do we have here?"

I went over to take a closer look at the jar she was holding out. There was a wraparound label that had a lump under it on the back side of the jar.

"You want to do the honors?" she asked.

"You found it, you go ahead."

She ripped through the label and removed a thumb drive.

"Interesting but strange," I said. "I don't remember seeing a computer anywhere."

"Maybe someone took it, hoping to find whatever is on this thumb."

"We need to ask Bethany if Delia had a computer."

"Wouldn't Bruno have told you if the police had found one?"

"I would think so. Although he might not have shared its contents."

"Did you notice a cable outlet? Or a place near her desk where she could have plugged in a charger for a laptop?"

"No, but I think we should go back up and look, don't you?"

We hurried back upstairs. It didn't take long to find the modem panel. Next to it was a convenient plug-in for a computer. "We should have noticed these before," Laney said.

"The good news is that you found *this*." I held up the thumb drive. "At least we hope it's good news."

"You think it contains photos of a naked Delia?"

"Very funny. Your place is closest. Let's go find out."

Laney had inherited a small house in a neighborhood of small houses in north Seattle. It was one story with a small front yard and an even smaller back yard. Her grandmother had painted it bright yellow, and Laney had kept it yellow for sentimental reasons, but muted the tone to a soft lemon shade. When I parked Bee in the driveway, it looked like she belonged there.

Inside, Laney had focused on comfort and functionality. A soft sofa and two recliners in the small living room, and a combination scratching post, cat tree, and condo for her beloved Dorian, a Russian Blue with a kingly demeanor and independent attitude. Her compact kitchen had a marble counter filled with appliances to make cooking for one easier and faster. One bedroom was set up for doing yoga as well as for sleeping. A second bedroom had been converted into an office where she had a desktop computer with a dual monitor alongside a laptop with screen extenders on either side.

Her house screamed her priorities. Would she add onto the house if she had a child or move to a larger place? There was no way I could imagine her fitting all of her possessions and a child into my houseboat. Maybe we would need two houseboats. Or we could move into one of the larger houseboats in the high-rent area on the other side of the lake. With our combined incomes, we might be able to swing that.

While I was daydreaming about how to accommodate a child without upending our lives completely, Laney was busy pulling up the contents of the thumb drive on her computer screen. There were more folders than we'd anticipated. Some were labeled with initials only. One was titled "Term Life Insurance." Another was my name!

"I assume CS is for Climate Synchronicity," Laney said.

"Click on my folder first, okay?"

"You shouldn't be surprised that she has information on you. After all, she entrusted you with her entire estate."

"Just click on it...please."

"Well, because you said *please.*" She clicked the folder and it opened to reveal several files: Work History, Recommendations, Legal Documents, Notes. "I'll make a copy so you can ponder your personal files later. Okay?"

"That would be nice. But for now, click on Notes...please."

The Notes file was not well organized, and some of what she'd written there was rather cryptic. She had, of course, made these notes for herself, so she didn't need details, just a reminder of considerations. Although she must have known that if I found the thumb that I would read what she had written. Basically, they contained the pros and cons of using me as her super executor.

"Rather flattering overall," Laney said as she skimmed through the file. "Her main concern seems to be how seriously you would take your role if she died under suspicious circumstances. She apparently knew you have been friends with Bruno since you were a kid. Must have been hoping you would do exactly what you're doing—dealing with her finances and investigating her murder."

"Look at this—she says here that if I took a Rorschach test that I might zero in on only a part of the inkblot instead of the whole picture. What the heck does that mean?"

"It also says that your intuitive approach should enable you to pull random clues together."

"Very strange."

At the bottom of the notes, there was a line in red: *If you are reading this, then I must be dead, and you have been clever enough to find this USB Drive.* It continued in bold black print: *Please use the information on this drive to help find my killer. I want them punished. I was not ready to die. (Is anyone ever 'ready'?) Anyway, find him or her and make certain they pay for what they've done.*

"Wow," Laney said. "I did not see that coming."

"Me neither. Well, we have our marching orders."

Next, we turned to the files on Climate Synchronicity. They were fairly damning. There probably wasn't enough evidence for a criminal conviction, but more than enough information and speculation to light a fire under investigators. If Delia had been promising them money in exchange for naming a project after her, *she* had been scamming *them*.

"I'll put the Synchronicity folder on a separate thumb so you can give it to Bruno."

"This file marked 'family' could be interesting too. And it may be something Bruno will want to see. Also the one labeled 'Kelsey.'"

"I'll make copies for us so we can view these at our leisure and put the original in a safe place, okay? We can decide later how much more we want to share with Bruno. If that's alright with you."

"He'll want to see the original."

"I agree. But I'd like a head start on this information." She began making copies.

"If he reads Delia's notes on me, he'll start calling me something annoying. Like the Inkblot Kid. Or the One Trick Pony."

"I can't swear it's the original if we delete something."

"I know. Maybe he won't ask. In any case, it's kinda exciting to think that Delia is in some ways investigating her own murder."

"She certainly dropped enough breadcrumbs for you to follow a path that could lead to her killer. A clever woman."

"We need to find out whether anyone from Climate Synchronicity knew about the greenhouse. Although having a strong motive to stop Delia from exposing them doesn't mean someone from their organization killed her."

"We won't know until we find out how serious the allegations against them are. If it's bad, well then, who knows what they were willing to do to protect themselves."

"Occam's razor suggests the simplest explanation is usually the best one. On the other hand, someone famous said, 'Things are not always what they seem.'"

"Phaedrus."

"Phaedrus? I don't know who he is."

"He was an Athenian aristocrat and poet. I believe that you're referring to is a dialogue between Phaedrus and Socrates written by Plato."

"I've heard of Socrates. And Plato."

"And now you've heard of Phaedrus. Isn't it nice to know who you're quoting?"

"It seems to me that a truth that's common sense doesn't need to be propped up by someone who's been dead for centuries." I was saved from having to argue my position further by my phone ringing. It was Bruno. "I was just about to call you," I said. "Laney is with me. I've put you on speaker."

"You already heard?"

"About what?"

"Why were you going to call me?"

"I have a question: Did you find a computer at Delia's house?"

"No. You think she had one?"

"What about a cell phone?"

"Didn't find one of those either. She had a landline, though."

"You may want to check her bills and see whether she was paying for services on either."

"Okay, John, you must have a reason for asking these questions. Spit it out."

"I have some news about Delia's murder, at least about a possible strong motive. Laney and I found a thumb drive with evidence about a charity scam she was investigating."

"That's interesting. Wouldn't be about Climate Synchronicity, would it?"

"Yeah, it would. How did you know?"

"They came up several times in our interviews with her relatives."

"I assume you want the drive?"

"Actual evidence is always nice."

"So, why did you call me?"

"To tell you about the attack on Harold Flowers. He's in the hospital."

"He was attacked?"

"Took quite a beating."

"But he's alive?"

"Barely. It's not clear if it was random, a warning, or an attempted homicide."

"Why would anyone want to kill him?" As soon as the words were out of my mouth, I thought of several possibilities.

"Maybe we should compare notes. You eaten?"

"No, Laney and I were going to get some take-out."

"Want to meet at our tavern?"

Laney nodded yes.

"We can be there in twenty."

Laney handed me a thumb drive marked with a "J" and a second thumb she said was for Bruno. Then I watched while she put the original in a wall compartment safe behind some books on the bottom shelf of a cabinet. She had to punch in a code to get into it.

"I'm impressed."

"Someone could still break into my house in spite of the precautions I've taken, but they'd have to work to find the safe and to open it." She pulled out a cabinet drawer, removed a false panel, and hid her own copy there. "If they find this one, maybe they'll stop looking. Assuming someone breaks in searching for this kind of information in my office. Which is unlikely."

"You think I should have some hidey holes like this?"

"Don't you?"

"I don't have any secrets."

She wiggled her eyebrows. "None?"

"Not that I've put in writing."

"How about on video?"

"Innocent again."

"We really have to spice up your life a little."

"I would settle for winning a couple of hands of poker."

* * *

When we joined Bruno at the tavern, we handed over his copy of the edited version of the thumb and summarized what was on it for him while waiting for our food order. Then, chewing on pepperoni pizza and motives, we came to two conclusions. First, their pepperoni pizza was pretty darn good. Second, given everything we knew about Delia's murder, the attack on Hal didn't make sense. As far as we could tell, Hal had no ongoing connection to the Climate Synchronicity group, either as a supporter or as someone looking into their legitimacy. Yes, he'd applied for a job with them. And yes, he knew Delia had some doubts about them. But there was nothing to indicate that he cared enough to bother looking further into their situation.

Nor did it seem reasonable that either the developer or the neighbors had reason to beat him up. If either was concerned about Hal wanting to keep the house, they were jumping the gun since no decisions had been made yet.

And, there was always the possibility that his beating had nothing to do with Delia's death.

"Is Hal conscious?" Laney asked.

"Yes, but he says he can't identify his attackers. It was two men wearing masks. Nothing he noticed about them that is at all helpful."

"Do you think he's lying?" Laney asked. "To protect them...or himself?"

"Could be, but I don't think so."

"Maybe he knows something he doesn't know he knows," I said.

"In that case, *you* could become a target."

"Because he doesn't know what he knows?" Laney winked at Bruno. "Or because he doesn't know anything?"

"I saw that," I said.

Bruno snatched the last piece of pizza.

"Hey, I wanted that," I said.

"Should have been quicker then." As Bruno took a bite, a slice of pepperoni fell off onto his shirt. "Damn. This will leave a grease spot."

I smiled; it was my opportunity to get back at him for taking the last piece of pizza, but I was unable to come up with a clever retort. Too often, I'm like Charlie Brown, always thinking of the right thing to say the day after the original event.

All at once, Bruno's comment about me being a possible target caught up with my brain: "You were kidding about me being in danger because I know something that I don't know I know...weren't you?"

"Actually, I *do* think that's a possibility. Not because of what you know or don't know, but because of your role as Delia's representative. I'm not saying someone is going to attack you. Threaten maybe. Try to bribe you, possibly. There's a lot of money at stake. You're the man holding all the cards."

"I wonder how much of a bribe they would offer," I mused.

Bruno made a half-suppressed laugh, close to a snicker but with only a pinch of mockery and more teasing than mean.

"Hey, don't look at me like that. I have no idea what the right thing to do is. Why not get paid a little extra to decide in someone's favor?"

"Now you're kidding, right?" Bruno asked.

Laney kicked me under the table. "You ARE kidding, aren't you?"

"Ouch. You've made your point. But if I let the right person know that I was open to a bribe and they took me up on it, at least we would know who probably killed Delia."

"Maybe we should rig you up with a body camera so we will know who attacked you, in case you're incapacitated or dead after they do."

"Okay, so that may not be such a good idea," I admitted.

"There's one other possibility that I think we should consider," Laney said. "Maybe Hal is more like his great aunt than we realize. First off, he might have been really offended when he didn't get offered a job with Climate Synchronicity. Maybe he thought Delia didn't try hard enough on his behalf. Or maybe he learned that Delia not only suspected them of some shady activities but was actively collecting information that would prove they were scamming donors. He could have killed her partly out of anger because she fell through on getting him a job, and partly to get his hands on her computer. Maybe he believed it contained evidence he could use to blackmail Synchronicity. It would have been a twofer for him—money from Synchronicity and money from Delia's estate."

"Scammers and schemers...if Hal's a little of both, he could be our killer."

Chapter Twenty-One: Theories Versus Evidence

After another sleepless night, I didn't feel in top form on Friday morning as I headed for Mercer Island to interview an older man about a car accident in which it was clear he was at fault. His wife had been in the car with him, and he admitted to me that he'd turned down his hearing aid so he didn't have to listen to her talk about their son-in-law's shortcomings. Although I commiserated, it was a good guess that his inability to hear the ambulance sirens had resulted in him starting into the intersection as the lights turned yellow for the emergency vehicle to pass through. His reflexes had been pretty good, though. He hadn't run into the ambulance but had unfortunately swerved into a car in the next lane. The driver of the new Tesla had apparently been hopping mad and had pounded on the hood of our client's car, denting the hood and frightening his wife.

His insurance was going to cover the accident, but it didn't cover the injury to his ego. He had refused to get out of the car when the driver of the Tesla yelled at him to face up like a man to what he had done. I explained that there would be a counterclaim for the damage to the hood of his car, and he could also file a complaint against the Tesla owner for attempted assault. But since neither he nor his wife had suffered any injuries, it was doubtful anything would come of it. His wife was all for filing a complaint because of the Tesla driver's verbal threats and attack on their car, but the husband just wanted it over with. It was something they would probably argue about for years. He might be turning off his hearing aid a lot in the future. And his premiums would go up.

As I drove back to the city, I thought about the work I do on a daily basis. It was a constant battle to refrain from jumping to conclusions about fault before investigating the details. Sherlock Holmes is noted for saying that "It is a capital mistake to theorize before you have all the evidence." The thing that has always bothered me about that bit of wisdom is that if you don't theorize, how do you know what evidence you should be looking for? Not that I think I'm smarter than Sherlock Holmes. But I do believe in the value of theorizing. To me, the trick is being willing to switch theories if one doesn't get you where you need to be.

Although I admit that in the past it's frequently been luck or a fluke that has provided me with the aha moment or break needed to solve a case, one of my uncles used to say that even the blind squirrel sometimes finds a nut. Although I can't say that I like being compared to a blind squirrel. And whoever heard of a blind squirrel anyway?

As I drove back to my office, I kept trying to remember the lyrics to Johnny Cash's Folsom Prison Blues. It was the only song I could remember about a murder. Well, the only song I could *almost* remember. That's why I like commercials—they're short and repetitive with just the right amount of bounce to be entertaining. I switched to bellowing out "It feels so good." I thought there was a line about no cats to chase. Or was that another song? "Good, good, good." Then, "OOoooOOOoo"

When I ran out of "ooOOoos" I switched to thinking about the idea of pretending I'd accept a bribe as a trick to catch the killer. Although, even if someone offered me money to encourage a decision in their favor, that wouldn't tell me if they were also willing to murder for money. Probably not a great plan. But I didn't reject the idea completely. Because what Bruno said about the possibility that I could be a target also kept running through my mind. The longer it took to catch Delia's killer, the more untenable my situation became. It also occurred to me that I needed to know what would happen to Delia's estate if I couldn't fulfill my duties. That might tell me who to look out for. Or simply cause me more anxiety. Either way, I needed to know.

186

When I arrived at the office, there was one other unpleasant task I felt an obligation to attend to. Emma didn't look up until I stopped in front of her desk and cleared my throat. "Ahem."

"Yes, what is it, John?" Her tone said, "Can't you see I'm busy?"

"Sorry to bother you, but there is something I think you need to know." I expected her to give me some indication that I should proceed. When she didn't, I cleared my throat again and said, "It's about Climate Synchronicity."

Emma raised one eyebrow.

"You mentioned that you give them a yearly donation, and, well, Delia Flowers was investigating them and had concluded they were a scam."

"Scam? What do you mean?"

"That they take money under false pretenses. The money isn't used to fulfill their stated mission."

Emma sat there staring at me in disbelief.

"I can show you the evidence she gathered if you would like. I have it on a thumb drive; I gave Bruno a copy last night. I just thought you should know."

"I've been giving them money for years," Emma said. "They send out annual reports."

From the look on her face, I could tell it was like learning that Santa Claus wasn't a real person or that a parent was the tooth fairy. Life can be harsh at times.

Then it occurred to me that she might want to blame the messenger—me—for what I had just told her about one of her favorite nonprofits. "I'm so sorry." I'd almost said, "Sorry for your loss," the funeral response. In some ways, that may have been accurate. When you think you're doing a good thing only to find out you've been ripped off, it's like losing someone you thought you knew.

Once back at my desk, I called Delia's lawyer and asked who took over if I couldn't fulfill my responsibilities.

"A will does not self-execute," Treemont said. "...and in this instance, it's complicated. Someone would ask the court to appoint a new executor, probably one of the relatives. Perhaps even me. It isn't unusual for a lawyer to be given that role. But to be honest, it's not something I would want to take on under the circumstances." He inhaled audibly and asked, "You aren't ill, are you?" I didn't think his concern was for my health; more likely, he was thinking about the ways in which my abdication would impact him.

"No. Just curious." I was about to hang up when it occurred to me that there was one more thing I needed to know: "Has anyone else asked you about this?"

"Well, yes. Actually, a couple of people. It is, after all, an unusual situation."

"Who?"

He paused before answering. "Technically, I represent the Flowers estate, as do you, so I see no reason why I can't tell you who made the inquiries. There were two: one from a representative from Climate Synchronicity and the other from Brandon Plover."

"It wasn't Candy Sprinkles or Eldon Cliffton from Climate Synchronicity, was it?"

"Yes, I believe her name was Ms. Sprinkles."

I was tempted to say, "And you didn't think that was strange?" Instead, I thanked him, curious what his lawyer's mind made of my inquiries. He hadn't asked "why" I was asking, except for the question about my health. Since he wasn't a criminal attorney, maybe his mind focused more on the process than wandering to thoughts of potential death threats.

I immediately called Laney and told her about what I had learned. "I don't find this at all reassuring." My voice sounded whiny even to me. "And I have theories but no evidence. I don't even know what evidence I need to prove that any of my theories are correct."

"I have a few theories, too. And I disagree that we don't have any evidence. What we don't know is how the evidence connects to our theories. We have the bones but no tissue. Sorry, that was gross. Anyway, I think we need to meet with Bruno and your mother again and go over everything in detail, no matter how seemingly insignificant. We need to review all the bits and pieces of information we've collected, throw in some speculation, and see which theories pop to the surface."

"Do we admit to Bruno that we didn't give him everything on Delia's thumb drive?"

"We can say that we didn't find anything there that we felt would be helpful. Then again, you never know how someone else might interpret data."

"I hate to have him think we lied to him."

"It was a lie of omission. But I agree."

"Both options are bad, really bad." Definitely not the *good, good, good* I'd been singing about earlier.

"I agree again. But finding a killer takes priority over the risk of ticking Bruno off. Right?"

I wanted to argue the point, but I did indeed know she was right. "Right."

"Want to repeat that and sound like you mean it?" Laney laughed. "Kidding."

Ignoring her jibe, I changed the subject. "By the way, the electrician isn't finished checking things out, but I got the appraiser's report back. We're talking a lot of money. Some of the artwork is real. And so are the netsukes."

"I thought I saw the appraiser's eyes light as she looked around. I assume Delia knew she was sitting on some pricey items. I wonder why she didn't take better security precautions."

"When I reviewed the insurance policies we found in her desk, I didn't see any fine art insurance coverage, and the personal property insurance was above average but nowhere near the appraisal valuation. Either she had no idea what some of her possessions were worth, or she didn't think she would ever be robbed or have losses from any kind of natural disaster."

"Some people are in denial like that."

"Well, I'm going to see about getting more insurance coverage on behalf of her estate."

"It won't be your problem for much longer. I think all you need to do is to turn over a copy of the appraisal to whoever you give things to."

"You're probably right, but what if something happens before I finish? I wish I understood why Delia was so meticulous in some ways and so lax in others."

"She was a real enigma."

"I guess I knew that as soon as I saw those ferrets around her neck."

* * *

Having pizza two nights in a row didn't bother me. But this time, instead of meeting at a pizza place, I picked up a couple on my way home. As a concession to healthy eating, I got one vegetarian. The other was a special called THE MEATY for Meat Lovers. Laney came with wine, Bruno a six-pack, and Mother brought a plate of homemade oatmeal cookies. If we didn't come up with any answers, we would at least be full by the end of the evening.

"I've been meaning to ask," I said to Bruno as we sat down to eat before starting on our brainstorming. "Did Delia report the vandalism to her property?"

"And I've been meaning to tell you...no, nothing."

"She probably didn't want to admit to the police that she may have deserved some retaliation from the local kids."

"Anyway, I doubt any of the pranksters murdered her. It's just a loose end."

Laney frowned. "I'm not fond of loose ends."

As we gathered around the white board I had "borrowed" from the storage room at the office, I took a deep breath and said, "Bruno, there's something we have to tell you."

"Oh, oh. Who died?"

"No more bodies, but a confession." I had given my approach some thought and decided on a strategy that would at least put part of the blame back on him. "You know how you can't share information with us?"

"As a law enforcement officer, I'm committed to following certain rules, yes."

"Well, we wanted to get the information on Climate Synchronicity from Delia's thumb drive to you as quickly as possible. Because we thought it was important."

"It was."

"We assume you will pass along the information to someone in a position to bring charges against them and prevent them from doing more harm."

"I will."

"But there was some other stuff on the drive…"

"What do you mean? What other stuff?" His hard-edged tone suggested my strategy wasn't working.

"Once we had a chance to review it, none of it seemed that relevant…" I held out a thumb drive, and he angrily snatched it up.

"Are you telling me that you didn't give me everything that was on Delia's thumb drive?"

"There are a couple of other files." Guilt pulsed through my body. My face was probably turning red, bright red, like Rudolph's nose or the maraschino cherry in a Singapore Sling.

"That wasn't for you to decide." A tiny vein suddenly pulsed at the side of his forehead. I hoped the tension didn't spread to his hemorrhoids

"We should have told you that we were holding some files back," Laney said. "And if we had found anything of interest, we would have given everything to you sooner."

Mother suddenly jumped in. "Bruno, I didn't know about any of this. But I do know that you wouldn't have shared information from the thumb drive with John and Laney after they turned it over to you. And let me point out that although you are investigating a murder, John has a lot on the line here, too. So, you might want to give him some slack." She harrumphed and ended with: "Keep in mind, *they* were the ones who found the drive, and they didn't have to tell you anything."

Bruno looked down for a moment, then asked: "Why are you giving this to me now if you don't think there's anything important on it?"

"As we thought about it, we felt like maybe you know something that we don't, and there could be something in the files that will help you connect the dots where we can't."

"Wouldn't it have been easier to simply make a copy, lie about having a copy, and give me the original?"

"We didn't want to lie to you," I said.

Laney quickly added, "We never said we gave you the original."

Bruno looked at Laney with his head cocked to one side. Then his eyes traveled to me, and I willed myself not to look away. Finally, he turned to

Mother.

"You think this is partly my fault."

"I think if you had asked either one of them a direct question, they would have told you the truth. Besides, you would know if John was lying."

Bruno nodded, "He's never been very good at it, has he?"

"Not since he was a little boy."

Bruno turned back to me. "OK. Let's move on."

I turned to the whiteboard and wrote PLAN at the top with what I hoped was the right kind of pen. I didn't have an eraser, so I tried removing the "N" with a paper towel before writing something else that might become a permanent message. After all, I had to return the board when we were through with it.

When the "N" rubbed off, I was relieved. Surely that was a good omen.

"Okay, let's start with our main suspects." I wrote "Candy, Eldon, and Brandon" on the left-hand side of the board under Main Suspects. "Anyone else?"

"I still think it could be almost any family member," Mother said. "Although I'm not sure why they would beat up Hal. And I don't think Brandon would either, even if he was tempted to do so."

"What about the developer?" Laney asked. "I still like him for it."

I added Leland to the list. "I can't help wondering if we should include one or more of Delia's neighbors. What do you think, Bruno? You've probably talked to more of them than we have. Or your officers have."

"The neighbors all have the same motive, although some may need the money from the sale more than others. Why don't you just put 'neighbors' up there? If we decide to focus there, we can get more specific."

"Let's go back to my earlier question," Mother said. "Why would any of these people want Hal out of the picture?"

"Starting at the top, Synchronicity might fear he was going to continue looking into their business dealings. After all, they rejected him when he applied for a job. Just because he acted as though he didn't really care about the rejection, he might hold a grudge. And if he managed to prove they were scamming people, they would not only be cut from Delia's inheritance but could end up with criminal charges against them. That's definitely motive for murder."

"But he's still alive," Mother said. "And that also assumes that they knew that he knew about the scam."

"What about the developer? Why would he want Hal out of the picture?" I asked. "Do you think he knew Hal wanted to keep the house and live in it?"

Everyone seemed to think it was a possibility.

"And the neighbors? Same reason?"

"But…" Bruno said, "…just because they wanted Hal out of the way doesn't mean they killed Delia. Her death could be the catalyst for the attack, though."

"There seems to be a lot of circular connections," Laney said.

"That's because John's theory is a bit high- level." Mother turned to me. "That's not criticism, John. We need to do some fine-tuning, though."

"Based on the evidence at hand," Bruno said.

"Thinking outside the box never hurts," Laney argued.

"But if you get too wild-eyed, you can end up chasing ghosts."

"Is there anyone we can eliminate?" Mother asked. "Maybe that would help."

Laney looked at Bruno. "What about the ones with perfect alibis? Not that I think there is such a thing."

"As I said before, Delia was attacked when people claimed to be at home asleep. So far we haven't been able to prove otherwise."

"Have you checked the Climate Synchronicity people?"

"Yes. And the developer. Of course, anyone could have hired it done."

"So…nothing but conjecture, wild guesses, and suppositions so far," I said, in spite of being the one arguing for theories over facts.

"How about a gut check?" Mother said. "At this point, my gut puts Brandon at the top of the list. He thought he was in line to get half of five million dollars, and he hated Delia for the way she treated his children."

"I'm leaning toward the scammers," Bruno says. "I don't like people who take advantage of others like that."

"Laney?" I prompted.

"Still thinking."

"Bruno, have you followed up with anyone about whether they knew about the alarm system?" I'd been meaning to ask him that.

"That's something we're not talking about at this point."

"Ah, one of those," Mother said.

"Do you think someone monkeyed with it to lure her to the greenhouse?" I persisted. That was what Laney and I decided was the most logical explanation.

Bruno frowned. "I'm not supposed to be talking about that."

"But we've checked it out, so you might as well be up front with us," Laney said.

"You make the rules up as you go along, don't you?" Bruno asked.

"Sorry if it seems that way." Laney didn't look or sound contrite.

"Okay, I admit that we can't tell whether the alarm went off or not the night of her death. But it seems like a strong possibility."

"Do you know yet whether she had a cell phone?"

"She did. And it's missing. Just like her computer. And before you ask, yes, one or both could have been connected to her greenhouse alarm system. The only thing we know for sure is that her landline wasn't."

We talked on, jumping from one theory to the next, poking at possibilities, bending ideas back and forth, flirting with options, probing clues—all to no avail.

"This discussion isn't getting us anywhere," Mother said. "We need something to push this investigation forward. What about getting all of the suspects into one room to try to trip up the killer?" It was clear Mother wasn't letting go of the idea of a Nero Wolfe-style gathering. She was a real fan.

"I think when Nero Wolfe did that, he had an idea about who did it and why. If we don't know where to cast down our net, we are unlikely to catch any fish." My explanation was lame, but I wasn't sure I was up to moderating a session like that. I could probably close my eyes and fake the lips in and out thing that Nero Wolfe did when he was thinking deeply, but if none of the suspects had read any Rex Stout mysteries, they might just think I had indigestion.

Ignoring my objection to Mother's suggestion, Laney said, "Let's say we bring everyone together—there are a number of questions we could pursue that might either identify the murderer or narrow the list of suspects. For example, *how many of our suspects knew Delia was investigating Climate Synchronicity? Did any family members besides Hal want to keep Delia's house in the family? Are there any neighbors who are desperate to sell their houses?*"

"We could also ask the developer if he really has an alternative site, which I question that he does," I said. "There aren't that many prime spots for a development that large close to the city." Oops, I was arguing *against* my position on the gathering.

"We could also play the dysfunctional family card," Mother said. "List the grievances we know about and see what kind of responses we get." As I said before, Mother always finds relationships fascinating.

"Bruno," I said. "You're quiet. What do you think?"

"I don't think you will get a confession in a group meeting, if that's what you're asking. And I can't sanction you doing this. But if you do decide to give it a try, I want to be sitting in the back of the room."

Against my better judgment, I decided to put it to a vote. "All in favor?" There were some murmured responses that I couldn't make sense of, but no one raised their hands, so I was forced to say, "Raise your hand if you think we should get everyone together."

Mother raised her hand, and both Bruno and Laney said "Aye."

"The, ah, ayes have it."

"Let's ask the lawyer to set up a conference room for us," Mother said. "That will make it seem more official."

An unofficial, official meeting where I would be winging it, increasing my chance of becoming a target, and with poor odds for success. What a great plan.

Chapter Twenty-Two: Car Wash

I was starting to wonder how long someone could go without getting a good night's sleep before falling completely apart. I was beginning to envy Rip Van Winkle. Although I would prefer twenty hours of sleep to twenty years. I remember my mother reassuring me that good old Rip had sufficient nourishment during his long sleep and was physically fine when he woke up. Even as a very young child, that story wasn't believable.

If my sleeplessness continued and I kept giving Wild Thing two breakfasts, he was going to have to be put on a diet. To make matters worse, it was beginning to feel like I was walking through molasses just to get to my car. This Saturday morning in particular, I needed something to get my juices flowing, so I decided to take Bee through a car wash. The crows were no longer harassing me, but there were a lot of other birds in the area. Some people apparently find it intriguing to listen to their chirpy birdsongs and to spy on them with binoculars, but I think of them primarily as poop making machines. Bee was covered in white splotches. If my landlord wasn't going to trim the limbs that hung over my parking space, then I would have to remove the bird launch pads myself.

I wasn't feeling too chipper as I drove to the car wash. I tried singing a couple of commercials, but it didn't help. Even after all the time spent looking for clues, studying the evidence, interviewing people, and mulling over possibilities with Bruno, Mother, and Laney, I was no closer to figuring out whodunit than I had been at the start. And unfortunately, I could imagine our grand plan for bringing everyone together in order to reveal the murderer not only fizzling out but becoming a total disaster. With me at the eye of the storm.

My thoughts about the case spun around in my brain, like an out-of-control dreidel. Dysfunctional family members, a greedy developer, and scam artists. I not only didn't know who was the most likely murderer, I wasn't even sure who I wanted it to be. My inclination to point the finger at a particular person wavered like a flag flapping in a breeze.

In spite of how unappealing some of the potential suspects were, I could also, at least in part, understand how they got to where they were. Some family members felt justifiably slighted, others unjustifiably entitled. Although feeling slighted and entitled went together in some ways. The developer, on the other hand, had a business to maintain, with employees who depended on him for their livelihood. And people living in huge houses that had outlived their functionality were also individuals I could empathize with. I could even imagine a scenario in which I had some sympathy for the scammers. Maybe the CEO had a loved one who needed expensive medical treatment. Or maybe they owed dangerous people money and what started out small morphed into something huge. Unless you knew the whole story, it was difficult to pass judgment. Of course, they could all just be dirtbags.

Even if I didn't reveal a murderer at the meeting tomorrow, I needed to make some decisions about Delia's estate. I couldn't drag my feet forever. Coming up with a solution wasn't rocket science. It wasn't like I was being ordered to climb Mt Everest or swim the English Channel. All I had to do was decide the financial futures of about twenty or more people, perhaps crushing their dreams. And no matter how I divvied up the money, someone or many someones were going to be unhappy. I hated making people unhappy, even those who deserved a kick in the derriere for the way they treated others.

As I arrived at my destination, it occurred to me that a car wash was the perfect place to shake up my thinking about who killed Delia. All alone in my car, with no distractions and nothing to do but *think*, perhaps I could stop the spin of thoughts and sharpen my focus. Sherlock Holmes played his violin, Miss Marple had her knitting, Poirot sipped his glass of tisane, and I would enter the equivalent of an isolation tank to revitalize my mental acuity. But first I had to get inside.

It may seem strange, but I'm always nervous when I run Bee through a car wash. Although I tell myself that it's no more difficult than pumping your own gas, or choosing a pastry from all the options in a bakery window, or changing your clocks for daylight saving time, I still worry that something will go wrong. Perhaps my biggest fear is that I'll be a little off when trying to drive onto the tracks and will get hung up at the entrance, car askew, the tracks continuing to churn without my car in them. If I get past that hurdle, then there is the issue of putting the car in the right gear for the pull-through. Maybe cars with automatic transmissions are easier to handle in a car wash, but I like my stick shift; it makes me feel more connected to Bee.

Another fear is accidentally leaving a window open partway and ending up with a sopping wet interior. Worst of all, what if something malfunctions when I'm halfway through—was there someone keeping track of what was going on inside where all the whishing and swishing was happening? And what if I got all the way through and my car wouldn't start? There were just so many things that could go wrong.

Then there were all of the options. Touchless or friction. Basic wash or extras, including such things as premium waxing, undercarriage wash, undercoating spray, wheel and tire cleaning, and hand-drying. Bee deserves the best, but it gets so complicated. And expensive.

I knew that it would be better for my psychological well-being if I washed Bee in one of those concrete places where you do it yourself using their equipment, but somehow I never feel up to it. And today I definitely didn't.

This time at the car wash, things started smoothly, well, relatively smoothly. I tried to put my credit card in the wrong slot and ended up dropping it. There was a car right behind me, so I couldn't back up, and I was too close to the pay station to open my door. I had to crawl across to the passenger side and go around to retrieve it. Of course, it was too far under my car for me to reach it from the narrow space I had to bend over in. Eventually, I managed to use a long-handled windshield cleaner tool to pull it over to the other side so I could pick it up. After that, things got easier. If you discount the fact that the guy in the car behind me gave me the finger and was shouting something at me from inside his car that I couldn't quite make out. But I think my mother would have washed his mouth out with soap if he'd been a child.

Once I was settled in the tracks and was being pulled into the car wash, I started to relax. First came the heavy downpour. Then the suds and the cloth ribbons swishing back and forth. *Swish. Swish. Swish.* Beating against my beloved Bee with their soft fingers. *Swish. Swish. Swish.* Bee was rocking gently back and forth in time with the water jet symphony. *Swish. Swish. Swish.*

My mind began swirling in time with the beat. Ideas jogged by the persistent rhythm, moving around like square dancers locking arms as they changed partners. Why did Delia consider the idea that I might only see part of the picture instead of the whole as a good thing? *Swing your partner.* What random clues was she hoping I would latch onto? Swish. Swish. Swish. Why didn't she just tell me what she wanted me to do? *Ladies In, Men Sashay.*

And why was she both afraid that I wouldn't take my assignment seriously, while at the same time telling me how much she wanted me to find her killer? *Swish. Swish. Swish.* Did she think if she made the clues too obvious that I wouldn't follow up on them because there was no challenge? *Swish. Swish. Swish.* The only thing that I could think of that might have kept me from investigating was if I considered my role as her estate executor a slam dunk, a mere go-between ensuring a smooth transition of her estate to her family. *Swing Your Partner.*

Looking back to our original conversation, I could now see that she had been testing and manipulating me even then. It seemed likely that she only *pretended* to be confused by the nature of a short-term life insurance policy, and let me think that she didn't either understand or accept what I was hinting about. At the same time, she was leaving bread crumbs behind to trick me into investigating her death in the event that she died before the term life insurance policy was moot. *Dosey doe.*

Suddenly, I understood where some of those breadcrumbs were leading. The starting point was Delia's belief that my mother was right when she said that I could be relied upon to do the ethical thing. Leaving me a note with her lawyer emphasizing my mother's opinion and linking my role to our discussion about term life insurance was her way of letting me know that she counted on my sense of right and wrong to guide my actions.

Swish. Swish. Swish.

Next came her psychoanalysis of me: based on my profile, she assumed that I would follow up on facts that seemed out of place, like the receipts we'd found in the library. Laney and I had wondered at the time about the randomness of what she'd kept in her desk. And then there were the keys in her scarf drawer. What if she had deliberately hidden them there to pique my curiosity? She'd used that subterfuge to point me to the locked drawer with the receipts and then to the cellar with the thumb attached to the jar of pickles.

Swish. Swish. Swish.

She had also let me know indirectly through comments about her relatives that she didn't really care whether I gave them anything or not. Except for Bethany. Having her picture there, along with the framed picture of Clara, was probably another breadcrumb.

Delia's references to the nonprofits of her choice might not only have been sincere suggestions for distribution of her estate, but also an attempt to alert me to her concerns about Climate Synchronicity. She had been gathering evidence against them but hadn't quite completed her investigation. My guess was that she was hoping I would make sure that if she died before she could bury their organization, that I would see to it that they got what they deserved. Especially if they'd had something to do with her death.

As for the developer, his fate was tied to the fate of the family members rather than directly to Delia's estate distribution. He wasn't in line to get anything unless whoever inherited the house decided to sell it to him.

Swish. Swish. Swish. OMG—my car wasn't moving. There were too many swishes. Too much water.

How long had I been in there? I looked at my watch, but that didn't help. I didn't know what time I had started in.

Swish. Swish.

I waited another ten minutes of swishing, my mind stuck on hold, as blank as a fresh piece of computer paper. Then I officially panicked.

I was stuck in the car wash!

Should I roll down the window a crack and scream for help? Should I get out and run the gauntlet of the beaters and spurts of water? Or should I remain where I was and hope that someone noticed Bee had gone in and had not come out? And what would happen if they started another car through—was that a possibility?

I looked at my watch again. It was still morning. Did they shut off the system at lunchtime, or did it run until the end of the day? Was it possible that no one else was going to want their car washed before quitting time? What had happened to the car behind me in line? Had the guy who had given me the finger simply turned around and left when he realized what was happening, leaving me stranded, laughing at my predicament?

No, you are NOT claustrophobic, I told myself. The fact that you can't see beyond the parameters of your car interior doesn't mean you are trapped in a tiny space. You can get out if you're willing to get wet and take a beating. Stay calm. You can do this. I said it out loud: "You can do this. Me, John Smith, I can remain calm and wait for someone to find me." All I have to do is stay calm, I told myself while an inner voice screamed: "No, you need to escape."

I could feel sweat forming on my forehead. My mouth was dry, and it was difficult to swallow. My breathing was becoming labored. If I stayed in the car, I could die!

My hand was on the door handle, and I was about to fling the door open and take my chances in the alien world of water spouts and battering shammy strips when suddenly everything stopped. Water ceased beating against my windows. The dread columns of cloth went slack. The only thing still in motion was the water on my windshield streaming toward the drains at the bottom of the glass. It was like someone had pushed a pause button so I could return to a state of calmness. But didn't that also make it easier to get out and run to safety?

I was once again about to make a break for it when a megaphone voice announced: "Please do not be alarmed. We will have the car wash running again shortly. Please remain in your car and accept our apologies for the delay. And, to show our appreciation for your ongoing patronage, you will be given a coupon for a free car wash as you leave."

A free car wash? Ongoing patronage? Another ticket to hell? Not a chance.

As I struggled to regain my composure, I realized that during all of the car wash drama, not only had my car been thrashed with cleanliness, but my brain's analytic abilities had been stimulated, stoked to a level of thought I never knew was possible. The car wash was a version of Sherlock's use of cocaine. I'd had a moment of clarity, so crystal, incandescent, so that with laser-like focus I was able to determine what questions to ask and in what order to ask them to provoke a confession during my Nero Wolfe fantasy session.

Now all I had to do was get everyone together and test my hypothesis. Perhaps when I got to the point when I was certain that I knew the murderer's identity, I would close my eyes and push my lips in and out, just like Wolfe. Mother would love it.

When I finally drove off, I had to admit that Bee's surface was sparkling clean, totally free of bird poo. Nevertheless, I made a promise to myself to learn to live with less shine.

Instead of going home, I headed to Delia's. On the way, I called Laney and told her I had a new theory and was going to check out the receipts we had seen in the library. That had been one of the thoughts that emerged from my car wash high. She said what I hoped she would say: "I can be there in twenty minutes."

I was already in the library when she arrived and had the receipts laid out. "Remember when we noted she took a trip to Vancouver?"

"Yes."

"Here's a receipt from a clinic where she saw a doctor about something."

"It isn't for much."

"And there's no detailed invoice that we found anywhere, right?"

"Right."

"I think that's because she didn't want us to find one. She just wanted to make sure I had the name of the physician."

"Why would she want that?"

"Because she lied about her health to obtain the term life insurance policy."

"Why would she pay for a policy if she wanted you to prove it was obtained illegally? Doesn't that mean they won't pay out the benefit?"

"If I'm right, the five-million dollars was an expensive hoax. A very expensive hoax. Her way of giving the finger to her family. As well as to ensure there would be an investigation."

"That's a pretty low thing to do."

"I don't think she was a very nice person in many ways, but I have no doubt that she was clever."

"We can follow up on this."

"All I have to do is give the name of the doctor and the date of her visit to the term life insurance people. They will do the rest, believe me. If there's any chance that they can avoid a five-million-dollar payout, they will be very thorough."

"Well, you will have less to distribute, but how does this help find her murderer?"

"While I was trapped in the car wash earlier..."

Laney interrupted: "While you were what?"

"Something went wrong with the car wash this morning. It wouldn't stop. It just kept whishing and spurting water at Bee. Whish. Spurt. Whist Spurt. It was awful."

"How long were you stuck in there?"

"I don't know exactly, but long enough to figure out a few things. And if I'm right, well, at least I think I know which buttons to push now to point the finger of justice in the right direction."

"The *finger of justice*? I thought Lady Justice was blindfolded and impartial; I didn't realize she pointed a finger at the guilty."

"Sometimes she peeks under the blindfold." I envisioned the statue of Lady Justice melded with an "I Want You" Uncle Sam poster.

"Are you going to share your insights with me?"

"I would, but what if I'm wrong?"

"Then we'll have to try something else."

"There's one little problem that keeps niggling at me."

"You need another trip through the car wash?"

"Not funny."

"What's the 'one little problem'?"

"I'm not sure the questions I have in mind will help determine who beat up Hal."

"Hmmm. The link between Delia's murder and Hal's beating could be a causal fallacy, assuming two things are related when they aren't. Like if the price of chocolate goes up at the same time a killer whale attacks a boat, one didn't cause the other."

"I don't get it. What does chocolate have to do with killer whales?"

"Ah…"

"Okay, hold on. You're saying the murderer is chocolate and the person who beat up Hal is a killer whale."

"You don't have to get that specific, but that's the idea."

"So, even if you manage to expose the murderer, we won't necessarily know who beat up Hal."

"I do think his beating had something to do with him declaring that he wants to keep the house. But holding onto the house may or may not be one of the reasons Delia was killed."

"Maybe a neighbor or someone associated with the developer wanted to make a point. Or, it could have been a family member who wants to sell and considers Hal a roadblock."

"As we've considered before, another possibility is that Climate Synchronicity assumes his aunt told him about what she had learned about their organization being a potential scam. They may not know that Hal and his aunt weren't on the best of terms. Maybe they really were worried that he would continue the investigation she'd started. Particularly because they chose not to hire him. We don't know whether Delia sincerely tried to help him get a job with them for his own good…or maybe she was hoping to use him as an undercover spy."

"So, are you going to share your plan with me or not?"

"Wolfe never tells Archie anything in advance."

Laney saluted me. "Well, Nero, tomorrow is your big day."

Chapter Twenty-Three: Setting the Stage

I t wasn't much notice, but everyone I invited agreed to come. No one wanted to miss out on the chance to get a piece of the pie, the financial pie, that is. Hal was still in the hospital, but he asked to call in.

I had three goals for the meeting. Number one and most important: trap a murderer into a confession. At the very least, I was hoping to get the guilty party to visibly squirm enough for Bruno to have a reason to follow up. Number two: decide who gets how much from what remained of Delia's estate after I exposed her health issues to the insurance company. I didn't actually have any criteria for making this decision; it would most likely be based on how I felt about the behavior of the individual family members during the meeting and if I was able to eliminate any from the murder suspect list. Number three: figure out if Delia's murder and Hal's beating were connected. I had absolutely no idea how I would accomplish number three, but if the opportunity arose, I would go for it.

It was an ambitious agenda for a guy whose primary job was investigating fender benders and for someone who was playing Nero Wolfe for the first time, minus the girth, the keen analytic skills, a red leather chair for the guest of honor or prime suspect, and no prime suspect. But I would have my sidekick and police detective on hand, and Mother, in her fantasy role as chef, had asked if she could bring snacks. I'd said no.

I hadn't managed to get in touch with the doctor Delia had an appointment with in Vancouver, and he probably wouldn't have shared her diagnosis with me anyway. But I had given the term life insurance company his name and suggested they might want to look into it. I'd also checked out the doctor's website and had a few hunches about why she'd gone to see him and why she'd kept quiet about it. I'd shared those hunches with Laney, Bruno, and Mother, and we were all in agreement that Delia had been purposely secretive but had wanted me to uncover her health secrets in order to sabotage her policy and to further my investigation of her murder. A devious strategy on her part, but one I intended to honor.

The specific questions I had come up with to get the murderer to reveal him or herself, I kept to myself. I think Nero Wolfe kept his approach secret for dramatic impact, but for me, it was my way of managing expectations for the meeting.

The conference room with its long table was perfect for what I wanted to do. From the end position, you could see everyone seated around the table without having to move your head more than a few inches. I could probably accomplish the same thing with side-to-side eye movements, but that might look freaky. Like the cat eye clock Mother gave me one Christmas when I was about five. Its eyes moved with each audible tick, like it was planning an attack. I finally hid it in my closet and told Mother that the cat ran away.

As planned, my small group of accomplices arrived ahead of the rest. Bruno, Mother, and Laney seated themselves in chairs at the back of the room. I was once again going to be at the head—or the foot—of the table, depending on which way you looked at it. This time I hoped I didn't have to fight my way out of the room. With Bruno as backup, I felt safe.

As the others arrived, there was not much handshaking and a fair amount of jostling as participants vied for what they must have considered the prime seats. Although what criteria they used for determining that, I have no idea. Best view of the outside corridor to see who was coming and going? A desire to be seated next to someone in particular? The ability to keep their eyes on the three visitors at the back of the room? Fastest escape route? Or simply a display of dominance?

The developer and two Synchronicity people seated themselves at the other end of the long table from me, nearest the door. Two neighbors we'd talked to—Graham and May—sat next to the developer. The family members took seats on either side of the table, elbowing each other to get their chair of choice. The last four seats to fill were the ones nearest to me. Luis, Gabe, and their wives were the last to arrive, hence forced to take the only open chairs remaining. I noted a brief tussle between Gabe and Gabrielle before she finally acquiesced and sat in the chair closest to me. Louise had automatically let her husband take the seat furthest away. I was therefore buffered from "blood" relatives by two seats on either side. Or surrounded by them, depending on how you looked at it.

As everyone settled in, I pushed back my chair and stood up. Laney had suggested I do that. "It's a power thing," she'd explained. "Seated, you are just one of the group, an equal. Standing puts you in charge." Since this was my one chance to extract some truths and perhaps a few confessions, I was willing to use every tool in the toolkit of persuasion, so I stood.

Laney had also told me that Aristotle believed "truth will out," but argued that it needed help from persuasive strategies. She didn't remember him addressing the issue of manipulative questions per se, but she was certain that, under another label, they were part of his theory of persuasion. I haven't read Aristotle, and although based on his reputation, I am certain that he was a wise man, I was relying more on what I've learned from the prosecutors on the TV series *Law & Order*.

The large conference room felt crowded with the sixteen family members, the developer guy, two of Delia's neighbors, and two people from Climate Synchronicity. Everyone was sitting shoulder to shoulder with two people straddling the table corners at the far end. There were no outside windows to create a sense of spaciousness because the room occupied a large area in the center of a ring of offices. The one wall of glass facing a long hallway took away from the privacy, and in spite of its probable architectural intent to make the room feel wide when it wasn't, it actually had the opposite effect. The empty hallway made you even more aware of how crowded it was in the narrow space. I hoped there wasn't a fire drill, or a real fire for that matter. Evacuating quickly would be problematic, especially from where my "team" and I were seated.

As soon as everyone was settled, I asked them to each state their name so everyone would know who was present, as well as for the record, since we were recording the session. "I assume no one objects to having our conversation recorded?" I said casually, as if I had no reason to expect anyone to object. I looked slowly around the room as they all checked out how the others were reacting. I knew I needed to ask permission in case I came up with anything that could be used as evidence. My hope was that everyone would feel pressured to go along with the recording to avoid having to explain why they were uncomfortable with it. When no one spoke up, I asked the conference room speakerphone, "Hal? Are you there?"

"Yes, present."

"And you're okay with the recording?"

"Yes." Put on the spot like that, it would have been hard for him to be the only one to say no.

Since most of those seated around the table were family members, I'd considered just introducing the non-family members, but Laney had said that asking individuals to introduce themselves was a technique used by moderators to make people feel less anonymous. It was also supposed to make them feel more comfortable with one another, although I had no illusions about that happening with this group.

When introductions were over and I started to speak without first identifying Bruno, Mother, and Laney, Darby held up his hand and said, "Just a minute." He nodded toward the trio and demanded to know who they were. I was surprised by the forcefulness of his request. To this point, I had thought of him as weak, partly because of his health issues, partly because of my general impression of him as soft-spoken and reasonable. Either he was feeling better than usual, or he considered himself a spokesperson because of his place near the top of the family tree.

I explained that the three people seated behind me were "observers," not official participants. "They are here to witness and take notes on our discussion."

"They don't have names?" Darby asked with more sarcasm than necessary from my point of view.

"Yes. They have names." I turned slightly toward them and said: "On the left is Bruno McGinty, then Laney Drew and Eleanor Smith." I didn't identify them further because I didn't want to explain that Laney was "a friend" or that the older woman was my mother. Mother goes by Nora, but I'd introduced her by her legal name; I'm not sure why. I especially didn't want to call attention to the fact that Bruno was a local detective, although some of them must have recognized him from recent interactions related to the investigation into Delia's death. To my surprise, no one mentioned Bruno's role but zeroed in on my mother.

"Smith?" Amanda said, copying Darby's sarcastic tone. "She a relative of yours?"

"Smith is a common name," I said. When Amanda raised one eyebrow, I added, "Besides, she's an excellent note taker."

"But she's related to you?" Travis asked, sounding surprised yet certain he was guessing correctly.

"Yes," I reluctantly admitted to avoid further discussion, "She's my mother."

There were some giggles and eye rolls at the announcement.

Bethany asked, "Is she on your payroll?"

After the slightest of hesitations, I said, "All three of these observers have been helping me sort through this complicated situation as a favor. No one is getting paid." That wasn't exactly true for Bruno, but without pausing for further pushback, I said, "Which brings me to my first question—"

Chapter Twenty-Four: Narrowing the Field

"How many of you know that Delia was investigating Climate Synchronicity?" I asked. Candy and Eldon frowned, and Hal's telephone connection cackled, but no words came through. "Please show me your hands if you know about her investigation."

When no hands were raised, I added, "May I remind you that I have Delia's very complete notes related to this. And I've already talked with some of you about it. Hal, I assume you've raised your hand. Now, what about the rest of you?"

Hal's connection cackled again. I suspected he was rubbing something across the receiver so he wouldn't have to put any comments on record. The rest looked around at each other. Then, apparently reluctantly, most of the family members in the room put up a hand. At this point, all the family members I interviewed knew the rumors, even though they may not have talked with Delia about them. I'd started off with that question to put Candy and Eldon on notice and to make the others let down their guard a little by assuming Climate Synchronicity was at the top of my suspect list.

The two neighbors present looked puzzled, and both shook their heads "no." Kelsey also shook his head and kept his hand down. And of course, neither Candy nor Eldon raised their hands. Instead, both pinched their lips together like they had serious cases of heartburn. They would soon get their comeuppance, one way or the other.

Satisfied with my opening volley, I intended to slowly build toward more critical issues for culling the suspect list.

"Moving on. I know I've talked to most of you about whether you want to see Delia's house remain in the family. But again, I would like to have you make public where you stand on this issue currently. Hal," I said into the speaker in the middle of the table, "do you still want to live there?"

A mumbled "yes" popped up into the room, hanging there about a foot above the table. At least that's where everyone looked when he answered.

"How about the rest of you? Is anyone else opposed to selling the house to make way for the development project, whether you want to actually take up residence or not? Please raise your hand if you oppose the sale."

The two neighbors and Kelsey were frowning at the family members, with the Climate Synchronicity duo looking relieved to have others on the hot seat. They obviously had no idea what was in store for them, given Delia's due diligence.

Heather lifted her hand halfway up. "I support Hal's right to keep the house." She smiled at the speakerphone as if she saw her brother's reflection there, and he could see her face in return. I didn't bother pointing out that she had changed her position since we last spoke. Actually, supporting her brother's wish after he received a brutal beating was a positive thing in my mind, an indication of filial love and empathy.

Dorothy spoke up next, quite forcefully: "It should have been jointly owned by Delia, Darby, and me in the first place. Then it would have reverted to Darby and me at Delia's death, and, in turn, our children would automatically inherit it through us."

I didn't point out the obvious fact that there was nothing automatic about inheritances. "Does that mean you want to keep it in the family, Dorothy?"

Dorothy and Darby exchanged looks. "We'd have to talk to the rest of the family before making a decision."

"What about you, Graham, and May? You went with another neighbor to talk to her about selling her house, and were shut down rather rudely. How do you feel about Hal or someone else in the family taking possession and perhaps living there?"

"I think I can speak for both of us," Graham said, glancing briefly at May.

I assumed he'd brought her for moral support, knowing he would be greatly outnumbered by family members. "In fact, I believe I speak for everyone in the neighborhood. We would like to encourage the family to agree to sell the house to Pioneer Development Enterprises. The houses in our aging neighborhood were built for large families and visitors who had to travel long distances by rail, water, or horse and often stayed for weeks at a time. Few people have large families these days, and these huge, older houses are expensive to maintain. We've been offered fair prices by Pioneer. Selling is the best option for everyone."

A number of family members frowned while he was presenting his history lesson, and their frowns deepened when he placed more emphasis than necessary on the word "everyone."

Kelsey nodded in agreement and said, "We're offering above current market value for the houses in the neighborhood as an incentive. Given the quality of the Flowers' home and its location, it would be at the high end of the scale. We aren't trying to cheat anyone. The neighborhood is a prime location; that's one of the reasons we want to build our development there."

"Is there anyone in the neighborhood who is particularly anxious to sell?" I directed the question to the two neighbors and the developer, but Brandon answered.

"*Everyone* wants to sell. Delia was the only holdout."

The telephone cackled again, then Hal said, "That isn't true. I've said all along that I thought the house should stay in the family."

The room fell silent. I decided it was time to push the developer's buttons. "As we've been investigating this situation, one other thing has come to our attention." I used collective pronouns to emphasize that it was a team of investigators uncovering facts and not just me jumping to conclusions. Looking directly at Kelsey, I said, "We do not believe that you have an alternative site for your project."

Kelsey's face registered shock, then he flushed and shifted in his chair, his hands grasped tightly together on the table. Instead of denying my allegation, he countered with: "We have several leads."

I felt like I had him backed into a corner and decided to take advantage of it. "Given your financing for such a large project, you need to move quickly to get this started, don't you?"

"We've been in business a long time. One project that starts a little later than we'd hoped isn't going to have a big impact on our company." He sounded like he was telling the truth, but one eye twitched slightly. I'd had Laney look into his finances, including talking to a few of his employees, so I wasn't buying his story. And I had one more card to play.

"Isn't it true that you've told your employees you may have to lay many of them off?"

"Well...contract work is seasonal." He pulled at the corner of his collar as if the half-truth was choking him.

Originally, my idea had been to start with Climate Synchronicity and put them under the spotlight, then turn to Kelsey to show that he, too, was suspect. In the process, I would also be pointing the finger of justice at the neighbors and some family members, building slowly toward more specific questions to start narrowing the list of suspects.

But Kelsey was looking so guilty, I decided to go for the jugular, like an attack dog, a real attack dog, not one of those ridiculous sweater-wearing mini-monsters. Remembering my mother's comment about his expensive lifestyle and based on the facts we did know, I ad-libbed with what I hoped was a reasonable leap of faith: "And if we take a closer look at your finances, will we find that you're struggling to stay afloat?"

"As I said, contract work is seasonal. It's always either feast or famine." He looked down at his hands and then added, "I admit that a couple of my employees overreacted."

Bruno coughed, and I glanced over my shoulder at the trio behind me. Bruno raised his eyebrows, and Laney gave me a sign I didn't understand, but I knew it had something to do with the idea that this was a topic to pursue. Mother was leaning forward as if she could barely keep from leaping up and pointing an accusing finger at the man. *That tenacious finger of justice.*

I turned back to Kelsey and said, "Would you like to tell us a little more about that?"

"I don't know for sure, but I have my suspicions."

"About...?" Was I the blind squirrel about to find a nut?

"Well, I've been reluctant to talk to the police about this because I don't have any evidence, but..." He paused, his facial expression suggesting he was struggling with whether it was wise to speak up in front of everyone. He stretched his neck and once again tried to loosen his collar with a finger. "My employees know going ahead with the project in the near future depends on getting the Flowers property."

Instead of maintaining my cool and giving my strategy a chance to adjust, I blurted out a thought that flashed in my mind like an unexpected lightning strike: "You think one of your employees murdered Delia?"

"No, no, that's not what I meant," he said quickly, sounding almost horrified that I would think that. "I hadn't even mentioned the possibility of layoffs when that happened. But..." He took a deep breath. "Harold Flowers was beat up the day after I made the announcement. And—"

Some muffled sounds came from the receiver on the table. I could imagine Hal being angered by the fact that Kelsey hadn't come forward sooner. Leaving him to fret and agonize over the thought that someone he knew was responsible for the beating he'd received. It was probably a relief to know his attackers were most likely strangers, while at the same time, if Kelsey was right, they'd come after him for something that was not his fault, something outside of his control.

Kelsey obviously didn't want to finish what he'd started to say; then apparently decided he'd said too much to stop. "Two of my men looked like they had been in a fight the day after. That's when I began worrying that the two things were connected." I remembered Bruno saying that Hal had defensive wounds on his hands and arms. He might have fought back harder than they expected, perhaps causing them to do him more physical damage than intended.

I tried to assimilate what Kelsey had just revealed in order to decide if I needed to change tactics. His two employees might be guilty of attacking Hal, but it sounded as though they didn't have a lot of skin in the game until *after* Delia's death. Was Kelsey sacrificing his two employees to divert suspicion from himself? Even if that was what he was trying to do, I could think of no reason I couldn't go ahead as planned.

In any case, if Kelsey was telling the truth, then Delia's murder and Hal's beating were not connected, and I'd separately achieved goal number three. The ball was now in Bruno's court, so to speak. Although I didn't know exactly what the cliché referred to, I knew it meant that Bruno was the one to follow up with Kelsey as soon as the meeting ended by asking for the names of the two men. It was up to him to sort through that mess. At least Hal would have closure.

Still addressing Kelsey, I said, "I assume you actually looked at the Flowers' property. Walked around on the lot. Checked everything out."

"No, I never set foot on the property; Mrs. Flowers wouldn't let me. I studied official records and satellite pictures to come up with an offer to tempt her. I agree that it's a shame to destroy a lovely Victorian house, but the neighborhood will most likely be transformed into a commercial enterprise at some point because of its proximity to downtown and the fact that the majority of houses are in need of extensive repairs and updating. One way or another, they will be torn down and replaced."

"So did you tempt her?"

"You know I didn't." He sounded bitter, like he was sucking on a lemon.

"Since you evaluated her property to put together an offer, you know she had a greenhouse in her backyard."

"Yes."

"But you swear you were never there in person." Before he could answer, I added, "There are cameras in her yard, you know." There are *now*, although there weren't before. But I didn't need to tell him that."

"No, never."

He sounded so confident in his answer that I believed him. I glanced over my shoulder at Mother and Laney to see if they believed him, too. They were frowning, probably displeased at having to eliminate him from the suspect list. I was displeased, too, although he was still just part of the warm-up act.

It was time to ramp up my questions about the greenhouse.

Chapter Twenty-Five: Murder Will Out

"I need another show of hands," I said. "How many of you are familiar with her greenhouse, either through conversations about it or because you've been in the backyard?"

Everyone raised their hands, except Kelsey.

"Candy, Eldon, you're familiar with the greenhouse?" That surprised me.

"Yes, she invited us to tea and showed us around." They'd had tea with Delia; wasn't that cozy? I wondered if they now realized that Delia was playing them while they were playing her? Or had they already reached that conclusion and decided to put a stop to her investigation?

"So, all of you family members—and neighbors— are familiar with her greenhouse?" Most shook their heads in agreement. Marcy and Marigold both made a "so-so" gesture with their hands, smiling at each other when they realized they were mirroring each other's hand motion.

"How many of you have been inside?"

No spouses raised their hands. And neither neighbor. Only a few hands went up.

"I liked her greenhouse," Bethany said. "She was so proud of some of her plants."

"We peeked inside one time when we were mowing her lawn," Gabe said, and Luis nodded agreement. "But that was it."

"Your maintenance work never involved the greenhouse?"

Luis responded this time: "She didn't want us doing anything in there. And that was fine by us."

"I stopped by once to have a look at the Venus Fly Traps," Heather said.

"Bethany suggested they were worth seeing."

"Hal?" I asked. "I don't think I heard a response from you."

"Yes," he mumbled. "A couple of times."

"How about the garden shed. How many of you have seen inside it?"

Hal's immediate "yes" echoed in the room as Dorothy, Darby, Amanda, Brandon, Luis, Gabe, and Bethany raised their hands. Again, no spouses claimed to be familiar with the shed's contents. Nor did Heather raise her hand. Though there had been some concrete blocks in the shed, as well as in the greenhouse, the killer could have found them in the shed and put a few in the greenhouse to set it up as an accident. Another non-starter question. But the group was getting trained to respond by raising their hands.

"It's been a while since I was there," Dorothy said as if an afterthought.

"Same for me," Darby said.

"It has a lock on it. Anyone have keys to the lock?"

"At one point, we all had keys to the house and the shed," Dorothy said. "She kept a spare key to the shed in the pantry. At least she used to."

Hal's connection made a buzzing noise before we heard him say, "I've never had a key."

Heather spoke up and said that she never did either.

"How about a key to the greenhouse? Anyone have a key to the greenhouse or know where she kept a spare?" It wasn't a critical question; Laney had determined that the greenhouse lock wouldn't have been that difficult for even a novice to pick.

Only one hand went up—Bethany's. "I delivered supplies for her from time to time."

"Next question: How many of you are familiar with her greenhouse alarm system?"

Again, only one hand went up: Bethany's.

Bethany looked around and said, "She got it about two months ago." Then she turned to Dorothy: "Remember us talking about it, Aunt Dorothy? You thought it was foolish that she was raising temperature-sensitive plants. You made some remark about why would anyone want to grow Venus Flytraps in the first place?"

Dorothy's neck and face turned blush pink, as if she was experiencing a hot flash. She tried to recover by saying, "I remember talking about the plants but not about the alarm system."

Bethany's eyes darted from me to Dorothy and back to me. Then she turned to Heather. "Heather, didn't I mention it to you, too?"

Heather shook her head 'no.' "I only remember you talking about the Venus flytraps."

"I'm sure I told someone about it..." Bethany seemed to be trying to distance herself from her own words so she wouldn't only be accusing her grandmother of lying, but her spontaneous finger pointing had done its damage. The room was so quiet that you could have heard a feather drop.

It was as if everyone in the room was suddenly connecting the dots, a collective AHA moment. They all must have speculated about why Delia went out to the greenhouse in the middle of the night. Unless she normally wandered around in the dark in her nightclothes, she had to have had a reason to go there. Now that I had brought their attention to the fact that there was an alarm monitoring temperature changes, they had an explanation for her behavior. She went to the greenhouse to protect her precious plants from a drop in temperature. The question was, if it wasn't an accident, then who had tampered with the alarm system?

Obviously, the killer would have had to have known about the system if the plan was to set it off to get Delia's attention. Since the police hadn't included any references to the system in the information they'd made public, the fact that only two people seemed to have known about it put the spotlight clearly on the jealous sister and not on the doting great niece who had openly admitted to being aware of it.

"I have another question," I said, moving on as if the latter had not been a huge revelation. "Anyone know anything about Delia's health?" I left the question deliberately open-ended.

Again, it was Bethany who responded, sounding relieved to move on to a new topic. "I knew she had some issues."

"Can you be more specific?"

"Well, it was nothing serious for someone her age. At least she told me it was nothing. She was fatigued, had lost some weight, and occasionally suffered from breathlessness."

I looked directly at Dorothy and Darby, then asked: "What was the cause of your mother Reba's death?"

For a moment, I thought Dorothy was going to faint. Her face had been pinkish, but now all the color vanished, and she seemed to be having some breathing troubles of her own.

"I believe it was ovarian cancer," Darby said. "Not a comfortable way to go."

Dorothy nodded.

"And if discovered at a later stage, how long is life expectancy?"

"I'm not sure," Darby said. He looked at his sister for her opinion and seemed startled by her appearance. Hesitantly, he added, "Mother wasn't diagnosed in time for treatment as I remember."

Dorothy still said nothing.

Although this didn't appear to be on topic, everyone seemed fascinated by the exchange, following the back and forth as intently as if they were watching a high-stakes tennis match. And as if they sensed that this was where I had been heading all along. Which it was. Although it was going better than expected.

"It's my understanding that the symptoms in its early stages mimic common problems that are not always cause for concern," I said. "If not detected early on, it can grow quickly, in weeks or months." I paused before asking, "Bethany, did you mention the health problems your Aunt Delia was having to your mother or to your grandmother?"

Bethany was slow to see where I was going with the line of questioning, but I could tell that she sensed there was a "right" answer. She had already pointed the finger of justice at her grandmother once, and she hesitated to point it at her or anyone else a second time. Rubbing her hands together, she finally slowly admitted, "I may have."

"Did you mention it to either your mother or your grandmother before or after your mother and uncle suggested that Delia apply for term life insurance?"

I heard the scrape of a chair behind me, then, out of the corner of my eye, saw Bruno poised to get up.

"Come on," Bethany said, looking around at the other family members. "Aunt Delia had been having health problems for quite a while. All of you must have noticed." Then it suddenly seemed to register that no one else in the family visited her great aunt on a regular basis, more like seldom or never. She looked directly at me and gave it one last try: "Why does it matter?"

"There's a hereditary factor involved," I said.

All eyes were glued to Dorothy. Her brother Darby turned toward her and said, "What did you do, Dot?"

I always hate it when someone assumes I've done something stupid, so for an instant I felt sorry for Dorothy, but only for an instant. Killing her sister had not been an accident but a deliberate act that had taken careful planning. It was time for me to summarize.

"Dorothy," I began. "Correct me if I'm wrong about anything. You resented your sister for things that happened when you were children. She bullied you and Darby and positioned herself as the favorite child. When you were older, she made a play for your fiancé just to show you she could take him away from you, and immediately dropped him. Then she inherited the family house that you felt should belong to all three siblings. But that wasn't all—

"After your son Brandon married a woman with two children from a previous marriage, she refused to accept them, even though your son adopted them. She proclaimed publicly time and again that they weren't 'blood' and therefore not really family. Based on that, you assumed that she intended to leave them out of her will, which included the house that you felt was rightfully in part yours.

"Then Bethany told you about the health issues Delia was experiencing, and you recognized the symptoms. That's when you started encouraging Amanda and Brandon to ask Delia about getting term life insurance with a five-year limit. You reasoned that it would appeal to Delia because it wouldn't cost as much as a longer time period. Although I'm surprised that you thought she would be at all interested in a policy to benefit anyone in the family. And even after all those years of being mistreated by her, you underestimated the lengths she would go to in order to exact revenge from the grave.

"Unfortunately, she hung on longer than anticipated. My guess is that you decided to hurry things along. Perhaps you rationalized by telling yourself that she didn't have long to live anyway, and the symptoms would just get worse and worse. The question was how to remove her without getting caught. When Bethany told you about the new alarm system in the greenhouse, your plan started to come together.

"Stop me if I'm missing anything."

Dorothy remained absolutely still, shoulders hunched, eyes closed as if in silent prayer. Bethany had tears in her eyes. So did Amanda. The other family members were expressionless, as if trying to reconcile the Dorothy they knew with what they were hearing. She had been the matriarch, the glue that held the family together. Delia, on the other hand, had been negative and divisive despite inheriting the generational wealth that perhaps *should* have been shared with the rest of the family.

Bruno stood up and moved over to where Dorothy was sitting. "Mrs. Plover," he said to get her attention. "I'm Sergeant Bruno McGinty. Would you mind stepping out into the hall with me?"

"He's a police officer," someone said. "I knew it."

"I recognized him right off," Brandon said. "I wondered why he was here."

For a minute, nothing happened, then Dorothy slowly got up without saying anything, assiduously not looking at anyone, and preceded Bruno out of the room. As I watched, I felt another pang of sympathy for Dorothy. Delia's feud with her siblings had been going on for a long time, resentment expanding like moss on a rotting log. If Delia hadn't been such a selfish and mean-spirited person, none of this would have happened. Nor would Delia have needed to set up a scheme to capture her own killer. And I wouldn't have had a chance to play Nero Wolfe.

I glanced back at Mother and Laney. Mother was beaming as if her son had just won a decathlon. Laney, too, looked happy for me. As for the family members, they were still sitting there, staring at the door that Bruno had failed to close. Except for Darby. He was bent over the table with his head almost touching it, like a tube man slowly deflating.

Unlike the stunned family members, the two neighbors, Kelsey, and the Climate Synchronicity duo were sitting up straight, bright-eyed, looking around for cues as to what they should do now. They were probably relieved; they'd appeared to have had much stronger motives than Dorothy for murdering Delia, and now they were off the hook. Although things weren't all rosy for either the developer or the non-profit group.

Climate Synchronicity would likely be facing some criminal charges in the near future. I wasn't sure if it would result in prison time for Candy as well as for Eldon Cliffton, but I was confident Climate Synchronicity was history. There wouldn't be any project named for Delia. But I imagined them cursing her from time to time, a legacy of sorts.

As for Kelsey, even if his project went forward, he was still in deep financial difficulty. It would be a struggle to hold onto that fancy car and expensive home. But people like him often land on their feet. Until they don't.

Kelsey's shaky future would, in turn, impact Delia's neighbors. If Pioneer Development Enterprises couldn't act quickly, another neighborhood might be chosen for the development, and the above-market offers on their houses would evaporate like dew on a leaf in the morning sun. Whether whoever ended up owning Delia's house wanted to sell or not could be a moot issue.

After Bruno left with Dorothy, I had collapsed in my chair, utterly exhausted by my role in identifying Dorothy as a murderer. Suddenly, I realized that everyone was looking at me, waiting for me to tell them what was happening next. I said, "I want to thank you all for coming," but before I could finish my sentence, Hal's voice suddenly blasted from the speakerphone: "What about Delia's estate?"

I was surprised he was asking about the estate instead of showing concern for his soon-to-be-indicted-for-murder grandmother. No, on second thought, I wasn't surprised. Delia was right: Hal only cared about Hal.

Perhaps everyone in the room should have been embarrassed about wanting to know the answer to Hal's question so soon after learning about Dorothy murdering her sister Delia, but since, for the most part, they were a greedy, self-interested lot, they pushed embarrassment aside, waiting anxiously for me to respond to his question. Bethany was crying more openly now, but Amanda managed to dry her tears so she could focus on what I was about to say.

"I'll get in touch with my decision about Delia's assets within a week." I named an arbitrary timeline off the top of my head. I needed to get this over with and move on. Also, I wanted the meeting to end before any of the family members figured out that Delia's lies about her health would invalidate her term life insurance policy. Eventually it would occur to them that she had deliberately lied to spite the family, and that would make them even more angry at her. There was still the house and its contents, however, as well as the money she'd had in the bank. Altogether, it was enough to justify at least some self-interest.

"What's going to happen to Dorothy?" Heather asked. I thought I detected a hint of regret in her voice. Or maybe I just wanted to believe that she had a heart.

"I'm afraid I don't know. I've already outlined the facts; now it's up to the police to decide her fate." The police and perhaps a jury of her peers. After a brief pause, I added: "You are free to go." As if I had the authority to keep them there or to free them to leave.

To emphasize that I was through talking, I turned my chair around to face Laney and Mother. Mother leaned toward me and whispered, "We should give them a head start before we leave." She put her hand on my knee and added, "I'm proud of you."

Laney winked at me. An actual wink. No one winks at anyone anymore. Except Laney, that is. Then she put her hand on my other knee and said, "Me too."

Together, we waited until they all filed out. "Let's give it a few more minutes, okay?" Laney said. "And maybe we should slip out the back."

"Why?" I asked. "No one should be mad at me; Dorothy was the one who killed her own sister."

"Let's see," Mother said, holding up her hand and then the first finger. "You let that Candy woman and the boss, who I'm sure she's sleeping with, know that you have evidence that can result in criminal charges against their organization and perhaps them personally." A second finger when up to join the first. "You exposed a big-time developer's financial problems and sicced the police on two of his employees." Finger number three appeared, like a Girl Scout salute. "You pointed the finger of justice at the remaining family matriarch in a room full of emotional family members." She put up a fourth finger. "You still hold power over their financial futures. And fifth..." All five fingers were now splayed in the air. "Laney, can you think of anything else?"

Laney gave both of us her full-dimpled grin. "The only thing you didn't do was share Delia's descriptions of individual family members—they would have loved that."

Mother put her hand down and smiled. She and Laney were still gloating, like satisfied cats about to lick their paws after a good meal.

"And I'm sure that under the circumstances, Bruno won't be upset about you revealing the bit about the alarm." Mother added, "And if he says anything, you tell him to talk to me."

"I *was* good, wasn't I?" It was starting to hit me that I'd achieved two of my three goals and hadn't made a fool of myself while doing it. All that was left was to divvy up the estate.

Laney playfully hit me alongside my head. "Even a blind squirrel finds a nut now and then." I wished I'd never told her that story.

* * *

The next day I decided it was time to install the deadbolts on my houseboat. Of course, I would have to give a key to Valerie so she could visit Wild Thing. And I could hardly give her a key and not give one to my mother. Although it was tempting. Having a mother with a key to your home wasn't such a great thing for a bachelor son, even one with a lackluster social life.

After the deadbolts were in place, I decided it was also time to take steps to protect Bee from those pesky bird droppings. Using a cordless saw borrowed from a neighbor, I managed to cut off the limbs that hung out over my parking spot without falling off the ladder or cutting off one of my own limbs. I also checked for cameras but didn't find any.

It was no surprise that my landlord heard the buzzing sound—it was as loud as three jackhammers or a swarm of Cicadas. At one point, I'd seen him waving his arms at me from below the parking area, but I didn't stop until I was finished. By then, it was too late; no amount of Gorilla Glue would hold those limbs back in place.

Afterwards, I poured myself a beer, plopped myself in a chair facing the lake, and thought long and hard about the last unpleasant task remaining as Delia's executor. I'd promised the family answers within a week. But even knowing who the murderer was hadn't helped me make my decision. I still had no idea what Delia would want me to do. It was all so morally and logistically complicated. Maybe I needed to consult a Magic 8 Ball.

Epilogue

TWO WEEKS LATER

Two weeks later, Mother fixed Bruno, Laney, and me a celebratory dinner. She went all out. She made one of my childhood favorites, a special macaroni and cheese casserole with three kinds of cheese including the nostalgic Velveeta of my youth. She made a huge salad to satisfy Laney's palate. And we concluded our meal with Bruno's favorite dessert, a red velvet cake with chocolate fudge frosting. Afterwards, we toasted "the finger of justice, dysfunctional families, and ourselves." After all, tracking down clues had been a team effort. Each of us had played an important role.

"To tell the truth, John, I didn't think you could pull it off," Bruno said.

"I wasn't sure I could either," I admitted.

"Maybe you ought to wash your car more often," Laney said.

When Bruno and Mother looked puzzled, I explained about being stuck in a car wash and how the persistent swishing of those ribbon cloth strips and the water pummeling the car as well as the uncertainty of an escape had all worked together to shake up my thinking, enabling me to connect the dots and come up with the right questions to ask.

"Also, I think you were right about needing theories in order to know what evidence to pursue," Laney said. "Asking the right questions in the order you did was truly brilliant."

Mother added, "I think *brilliant* is only halfway up Einstein's five ascending levels of intellect, isn't it?"

Laney laughed. "Okay, *almost* genius. Is that better?"

"Enjoy your fifteen minutes of fame," Bruno said. "But I want you to know it didn't escape me that you made public some of the information I shared with the understanding that you wouldn't leak it."

Oh, oh. If things hadn't worked out, he would have been angry with me instead of giving me a soft slap on the hand.

"Also," he continued in an official-sounding voice, "I'm not unaware that you withheld some critical facts."

Oh, he *was* angry with me. About more than one thing.

Coming to my rescue, Mother looked at Bruno and asked, "What I don't understand is how you know what evidence to withhold from the public. And how you manage to keep anything at all out of the press."

"In this instance, it wasn't really deliberate because we couldn't prove that someone had access to the shed or that they had picked up the concrete block somewhere else. Nor could we prove that someone set off the alarm to lure her down there. If the neighbors had heard it, that might have been different. But it was a silent alarm that only went off in two rooms in the house—Delia's bedroom and the kitchen. As to keeping things away from the press, it's an ongoing challenge. What can I say?"

"Did Dorothy admit to taking Delia's cell and laptop?" I asked. "They haven't turned up at the house."

"No, she lawyered up right away. Hasn't admitted anything. We searched her house and didn't find the cell, laptop, or anything incriminating, for that matter. It won't be an easy case to prove to a jury. My guess is it will end in a plea deal."

"And we didn't find what the third key was for," Laney said. "I envision some kid digging up a chest filled with jewelry in her back yard."

"Nor do we know who was searching the house that first day." I almost said that we didn't know "who trapped us in the bathroom." That was another "fact" that we'd withheld from Bruno, although Laney and my mother had quite a good laugh about my descent into the bushes the night we told her about it.

"It could have been any of the family members, even one or more of the spouses," Bruno said. "They were all so eager to get their hands on anything they thought was worth a few bucks."

"The person I feel sorry for is Bethany," I said. "The lawyer told me she feels like she betrayed the family. She not only had feelings for Delia but for her grandmother too."

"I can't decide if the family tree was poisoned from the top down or the bottom up," Laney said. "Delia's treatment of Luis and Gabe apparently made Brandon bitter, even though he remained the dutiful nephew and insisted his sons help Delia with maintenance work. He obviously passed along his bitterness to his mother, who already hated her sister for the years of what she felt were putdowns and unfair treatment. And her anger was fueled by similar complaints about Delia from her brother Darby."

"Bud seemed to me to be the most neutral of the nieces and nephews, but his kids appear to have inherited the 'it's all about me' gene. Although to be fair to them, there was no family cohesiveness, even around holidays, so I'm not sure anyone could expect them to have feelings for someone they seldom saw."

"And everyone except Bethany felt like they wouldn't get much from Delia's estate," I said. "Not that Bethany expected to inherit anything, but everyone else thought she might get something, maybe even the house."

"So, who wins the lottery?" Bruno asked me.

Even knowing who killed Delia hadn't helped a lot with my decision. But not having to deal with the five million dollars made it easier. I made the lawyer tell them about that—I couldn't face their in-person hostility another time. I just hoped the whole family didn't decide to storm my houseboat to complain.

"Well, the one thing I agree with the family about is that I'm fairly certain Delia intended that I give something substantial to Bethany. They were obviously fond of each other, no matter how warped Delia's relationships were with the rest of the family. However, in my opinion, giving a disproportional amount of Delia's estate directly to Bethany would have caused Bethany more grief than she deserves. I had the lawyer set up a hefty trust fund for Clara to be used for her education. Whatever remains after her graduation becomes hers at age twenty-five.

"That still left quite a bit of cash. When I went back over Delia's list of nonprofits, I saw three I particularly thought appropriate. One offers family counseling for low-income families. Another is an advocacy group for organizations trying to protect the planet from the consequences of climate change. And the third was for cancer research. No one thought she was serious about giving money away to support causes, but the fact that she left a list told me that she would rather have at least part of her estate go to a nonprofit than to her family. And I felt good about that. So, I gave them each a modest but significant chunk of Delia's cash assets in her name."

"What about the house?" Bruno asked. "That's worth a bundle."

"And its contents," Laney added.

"I don't really understand how Delia came to be so at odds with her family or why she decided to play games with her inheritance, but it seemed to me that she wanted me to poke her family one last time on her behalf. Although I'm not as certain that she wanted to completely disinherit them. She could have done that on her own. But since I found them unsympathetic as a group, that's what I'm doing, poking them one last time. Although it's up to them if they will have the kind of fight I'm sure Delia anticipated they might have if they had to work things out on their own. They could choose to negotiate like normal people and resolve the situation equitably."

"What did you do?" Bruno prompted.

"I gave the adult family members, not including spouses, ownership of the house and its contents 'in common.' That means they all have to agree, or no one gets anything. It's up to them to figure out what to do with the house. If I were in charge, I think I'd turn the house itself over to the fourth generation— Bethany, Luis, Gabe, Heather, and Hal. If only some of them want to live there, they could buy the others out. Apparently, Bethany and Heather have indicated they wouldn't mind living there with Hal.

"The advisor I originally asked to identify the value of the house's contents is going to provide the list to the family. As for the third key, it has crossed my mind that maybe Delia did that just to annoy everyone. I bet it will drive family members crazy." That made us all smile. "Anyway, they could divvy up the valuables or sell everything and decide what to do with the proceeds. I have, however, offered to let Mildred choose a few things she would like for herself before the family gets access to everything. She was, after all, Delia's only real friend."

"It's a team-building exercise," Laney said with a grin.

Mother smiled. "I'd be willing to bet it's not a successful one."

"It depends on what you believe the outcome *should* be. I can't help but think that Delia would be pleased with my decision. I only wish I could be the proverbial fly on the wall."

Bruno said. "In my opinion, that family deserves each other."

"If you had to guess, do you think they'll sell the house?" Mother asked.

"Hard to say. If they get picky about making it equal for everyone, that may be the only answer that works. Kelsey is probably lobbying them like crazy to save his own butt. If they agree to sell, his company may survive. And think how happy it would make the neighbors."

"If they keep the house, I doubt that hosting the occasional neighborhood party in the back yard will help them make friends." Laney grinned. "Maybe they could organize a community book club."

Ignoring her, I said, "If they do decide to live there, what I wonder is whether they will keep the Voodoo Lilly and the other carnivorous plants. Personally, I still find it hard to understand Delia's obsession with them."

"In some ways, those plants were responsible for her death," Mother said. "At least they provided the means. And the Voodoo Lilly is, after all, known as the corpse flower."

"Perhaps there should be one engraved on her tombstone," I said.

Everyone moaned.

"Think about it," Bruno said. "One plant attracts flies, the other eats them. It's the perfect symbiotic partnership."

"More compatible than the Flowers' family descendants, for sure," I said.

"It's ironic, isn't it?" Laney said. "The Climate Synchronicity people had such a strong motive to want her dead, but they either had *some* principles or didn't act in time. The developer and her neighbors also had a lot at stake, and without lifting a criminal finger, it looks as though they could benefit from her death. But in the end, it wasn't greed or financial gain but petty bickering over time that ended in Delia's demise.

"Perhaps her epitaph should read: *I wish I'd taken time to smell the roses instead of the Voodoo Lilly.*"

"You just can't give up on the Voodoo Lilly thing, can you?" Mother said.

"A more apt epitaph might be: *Loved by few, cursed by many,*" Laney said.

"How about: *She died surrounded by flies.*" Bruno grinned.

Mother shuttered. "I hate the image of flies swarming a corpse of any kind."

"What would you like on your tombstone, Mother?"

"I've always liked *I was hoping for a pyramid.*"

"Bruno?"

"I want to be cremated. Ashes scattered on the water in the San Juan Islands."

"Laney?"

"I want a green burial with a tree as a marker. You can carve your initials on my tree if you outlive me, John."

"What about you, John?" Bruno asked. What inscription do you want on your tombstone?"

"Maybe something like *I'd rather be in Acapulco.*" Or, I said to myself: *missed by his beloved children and forever friend.* Laney and I would need to talk more about becoming parents, but I was definitely leaning toward "yes."

"I have a suggestion," Bruno said: *"Here lies John Smith, not related to Jane Doe, never met Pocahontas, and no more insomnia."*

Laney straightened her shoulders and said: "How about *My name was Smith, John Smith.*" When reciting the James Bond line, her voice had just the right degree of swagger. "It could be next to an engraving of you in a tux with a bow tie."

Bruno said, "I thought you'd want your company's name next to a tiny heart on your tombstone."

They all had a good laugh at my expense. But I didn't care. I had fulfilled my responsibility to Delia's memory. And I had solved her murder. I'd even made a tidy amount of money in the process. I could buy those kayaks, take a trip to Acapulco, and have enough left over to take some curvaceous woman to a fancy restaurant. Life was good.

That night, when I was greeted at the door by my rambunctious cat, who was always mad at me for some reason, no matter how hard I tried, I asked, "Wild Thing, what epitaph would you like on *your* tombstone?"

Maybe it was my imagination, but I thought he said, *I made your heart sing.*

* * *

Writing epitaphs for tombstones is like singing the blues—a touch of joy immersed in sadness and melancholy. Honoring life while accepting death. In some ways, term life insurance is a blues metaphor for an epitaph. It's supposedly about someone's life, but the catalyst is death. In Delia's case, her "life" insurance started a chain of events, like the chord progressions in blues songs, and ended with In$urance Blues.

Acknowledgments

Most families have one or more dysfunctional family members. Or, at the very least, they experience the occasional dysfunctional moment brought on by disagreements, hurt feelings, jealousy, misunderstandings, and all of the serious and the trivial things that stress relationships.

None of the family members in this book are based on real people, although they may have recognizable flaws. Learning to laugh at ourselves, let go, and move on is a life-long challenge for most of us. I'm thankful for the people in my life who have put up with my idiosyncrasies and for the warmth and joy of friendship.

John Smith stumbles through life in a good-natured attempt to do the right thing. In writing his stories, I find myself smiling—and I sincerely hope readers have the same response. We all need the occasional chuckle or chortle to brighten our day.

With special thanks to Shawn Reilly Simmons for her editing and cover design. And to my readers—without you, I wouldn't be an author.

About the Author

Charlotte Stuart PhD left a tenured faculty position to go commercial fishing in Alaska, spent a year sailing "around the world" in the Washington and Canadian San Juans, became a partner in a management consulting group and later a VP of HR and Training.

Her current passion is for writing character-driven mysteries with twisty plots. Most include at least a dollop of humor, but she describes her "In$urance" series as "Murder with a Laugh Track."

In$ured to the Hilt, the first in this series, won a Global Book Award Gold, A Reader Views Silver, and was a Killer Nashville Silver Falchion Top Pick in Comedy. *In$urance to Die For* was a finalist in the Global Book Awards and the Chanticleer International Mystery & Mayhem competition. It also took 3rd place in the Book Fest Awards.

Charlotte lives on Vashon Island in the Pacific Northwest and is the past president of the Puget Sound Sisters in Crime and a member of the Mystery Writers of America and the International Thriller Writers.

AUTHOR WEBSITE:

https://www.charlottestuart.com

SOCIAL MEDIA HANDLES:
 Website: www.charlottestuart.com
 Twitter X: https://twitter.com/quirkymysteries
 Facebook: https://www.facebook.com/charlotte.stuart.mysterywriter
 Goodreads: https://www.goodreads.com/author/show/19305587.Char lotte_Stuart
 Instagram: https://www.instagram.com/cstuartauthor/
 LinkedIn: https://www.linkedin.com/in/charlotte-stuart-ph-d-967403 /
 BookBub: https://www.bookbub.com/authors/charlotte-stuart

Also by Charlotte Stuart

In$ured to the Hilt (A John Smith Mystery) – 2023

In$urance to Die for (A John Smith Mystery) – 2024

Raven's Grave - 2023

Raven's Legacy – 2025

Moonlight Can Be Deadly (A Discount Detective Mystery) - 2023

Shopping Can Be Deadly (A Discount Detective Mystery) - 2021

Campaigning Can Be Deadly (A Discount Detective Mystery) - 2020

Survival Can Be Deadly (A Discount Detective Mystery) - 2019

Not Me! Speluncaphobia, Secrets and Hidden Treasure - 2022

Who, Me? Fog Bows, Fraud and Aphrodite (A Macavity & Me Mystery) - 2021

Why Me? Chimeras, Conundrums and Dead Goldfish(A Macavity & Me Mystery) - 2019

Bogged Down (A Vashon Island Mystery) - 2020

Disastrous Interviews: The Comic, Tragic and Just Plain Ugly - 2013

Midnight for Justice, with Don Stuart – 2025